NO ONE CAN
HEAR YOU
SCREAM

Bestselling psychological thriller author, A.B. Whelan is returning with another ruthlessly addicting and terrifyingly twisted story for fans of true crime and domestic thrillers.

ADVANCED REVIEWS

"I definitely had chills with this one!! I absolutely loved the ending!!"

Debbie Brogan, NetGalley

"I loved this one. Very fast paced, had me turning pages as I tore through it – I had to see how it would end. The characters were well rounded and the narrative felt believable. Gave me chills. Solid five."

Morgan Schulman, NetGalley

"What a read, this book absolutely kept me spellbound. A timely story about social media and influencers, I would highly recommend this."

Lynn Beck, NetGalley

"I wasn't sure what to expect with his book but I absolutely loved it. It's a scary thriller that reads fast and is full of twist and turns. I absolutely would recommend this book."

Beck Williams, NetGalley

"Talk about a page turner.... this suspense novel written by A.B. Whelan is seriously a book I could not put down until I finished.

"It's a quick paced book that holds you hostage. Exceeded any expectations I may have for it before."

Rubie Clark, NetGalley

"Have extra time when you read this because you won't be able to put it down."

Liza Wetzel, NetGalley

"Okay, so what can I say. AB Whelan has done it again. I think this is her best book yet. But be warned - and warn your family too, when you start reading this book be prepared to not be available until you have finished it."

Mary, Goodreads

NO ONE CAN
HEAR YOU
SCREAM

A.B. WHELAN

BURBANK BOOKS

No One Can Hear You Scream: a novel / A.B. Whelan
1. Psychological thriller
2. Suspense, Thriller & Mystery
3. Domestic suspense
4. Atmospheric thriller
5. Kidnapping
6. Sexual abuse

"Life is a walk through the forest.
Don't fear the trees,
fear what lurks behind them."

—Richelle E. Goodrich

JENNIFER

The flashing lights of a police vehicle are the first thing I see as Tyler steers the car around the corner. The distinguishable zebra SUV and the two officers form stark silhouettes in the purple mist of the blending red and blue lights.

My fingers tighten over my stomach as reality sets in, as does a sense of panic.

Tyler leans closer to the windshield to look outside. His breath fogs up the window. "I can't believe this is happening."

Today was supposed to be a special day—a happy day. My boyfriend, Tyler, has moved in with me. We had a candlelit dinner at home, celebrating a new chapter in our lives. The divorce was hard on my kids, but welcoming a new member to our family seemed to be more than they could endure. After grimacing through the three-course meal, they retired to their bedrooms without saying goodnight. I ended the day with a twenty-minute heated phone call with my ex. He was telling me that I was making a big mistake. I went to bed believing that my life was a big mess and that everybody close to me hated me. And now this…

I roll down my window to get some fresh air. "What kind of monster would do such a thing?" I don't recognize my voice. I sound sleepy, weak, and discombobulated, and that's exactly how I feel.

For over a decade, the animal sanctuary has been operating in Woodland Hills, an affluent Southern Californian suburb where I live with my family. I've been a volunteer for nearly four years. The recently renovated building and the enclosed small lot provide a home for dogs in all shapes and sizes and cats in all colors. But the crowd's favorite was our long-haired Highland cow, George. He was our internet star that brought in the most revenue and helped to keep the place afloat. We, the humans, were responsible for the operations. The residents were supposed to be safe behind these walls.

Jayden, my oldest, leans forward in the car and puts a hand on my seat. He looks mature, almost a man, and a lot like his father before age and hard work took their toll on him. "Do you think someone did this because today is Friday the thirteenth?" Even his voice reminds me of my ex in his youth before cigarettes and drinking had made him sound like a pirate. Jayden resents Tyler the most out of my three children—not aggressively, only passively, but I do notice it. I'm sure Tyler does too.

"I'm so shocked I can't even think," I say, wiping my right eye with my knuckle.

Tyler pulls to the curb and lets the engine idle. He puts a hand on my knee. "Don't worry, babe. Whoever did this, I'm sure the police will find him." Tyler can be annoyingly optimistic sometimes. I blame his overbearing helicopter mother for that trait. For his entire life, she has sheltered her only child from the world. Tyler is a grown man, but his mother still treats him like a baby. But it was his childish optimism and easy-going attitude that drew me to him. It was a pleasant change after a lifetime of marriage to a man who had long stopped trying to be happy.

I look at Tyler appreciatively. "Let's talk to the cops and see what they know."

Tyler removes his glasses and pinches the bridge of his nose. The indentation from the crease of the pillowcase still sits deep on his face. From this angle, it appears to me that he has more gray hair than black in his sideburn. It may have been the dim light that tricked my eyes.

I turn to Jayden in the back seat. "I want you to stay in the car."

"Mom, I'm not a kid, all right? I'm seventeen." He opens the door and gets out.

Tyler's eyes follow my son as he walks away from the car. "You want me to handle it?"

"What, Jayden's attitude?"

"No. The police."

Jayden was fifteen when his father moved out of the house. The ink hadn't even dried on my divorce papers yet when Tyler reached out to me on social media and asked me out for dinner. According to my mother, a year wasn't nearly enough time to build trust with a stranger, let alone allow him to move in with my family. Most of my friends and family agreed with my mother. They all warned me that I was moving too fast with this new man, and their constant whispering in my ear made me alert to Tyler's interactions with my children. I started watching Tyler's every move like a hawk. I'd left Connor because his constant negativity rubbed off on me, and he kept pulling me down with him into an emotional abyss. Now it was me who was becoming paranoid in a relationship.

"I'm coming with you," I tell Tyler and step out of the car onto the wet concrete, glossy from dew.

The relentlessly flashing blue and red lights draw my eyes. In the halo of the pre-dawn haze, I spot an officer pinning a cell phone to his ear and talking while his free arm is tucked across his belly and underneath his vest. The other cop is a woman, holding up a flashlight and peeking through the bars of the gate at the front yard of the animal sanctuary.

I activate my phone to glance at the latest Instagram photo of George that glares up on the screen one last time. It's a picture of utter cuteness and happiness, taken only a few days ago. The fluffy little bundle of adorable cow is standing on the pasture in bright sunlight and munching on a mouthful of alfalfa, his long, messy butterscotch hair in front of his eyes, his tiny horns pointing out of his round head. All my self-control isn't enough to stop the tears from welling up in my eyes.

"Are you Jennifer Parker?" The officer with the handlebar mustache approaches me. It's my married name. I haven't had the time to change my documents after the divorce.

I offer him my hand. "Yes. I called 911."

He slides his fingers over mine. His grasp is firm and confident. We are in good hands. "So, what do we know so far?"

"Just what I said on the phone." I start unlocking the gate as I talk. "I had an alert on my phone from the night vision security camera at 4:17 this morning. When I opened the app, I saw a man wearing a hooded sweater and face-covering, beating George with a baseball bat—"

I need to pause for a second before I can continue.

The gate flings open, slams against the stopper, and bounces back. Then it rattles for a few seconds to add a sinister touch to the escalating horror of the night.

"All right. I need to ask you to step aside and remain here until we clear the premises."

Weapons drawn, the two officers enter the lot. Tyler puts his arm around my shoulders. I reach out to Jayden, but he's standing a few feet away from us and shakes his head, which is more like a dismissive side-nod. I open the security system app on my phone and watch the officers descending on the area, checking every door and crevice of the lot. I no longer see George. While I was still in bed at home, talking to 911, I'd watched the attacker drag his body out of the camera's sight.

A phone beeps into the eerie night.

Jayden checks his messages. "The twins are on their way," he tells us.

Jayden often comes with me to help out at the sanctuary after he's finished with school. He is as fond of George as I am. Countless times he's brushed his hair and fed him and played with him. Over the months, the two of them developed a special bond. It was Jayden who started the Instagram account for George. It was he who took all the pictures and posted them online. I worry that what we may encounter inside the sanctuary will scar my son's soul for life. In no measure is he a little boy. With his six-foot frame, deep, resonating voice, and chiseled jaw, he looks so grown up. But he will always be *my little boy*, and I can't help but feel protective of him.

The squealing of brakes and the screeching of tires break through the tense silence of the night. I recognize the owner's old 3-series red BMW come into view. The driver steers the car toward the sidewalk, tight enough to rub the front tire against the curb. A hubcap pops loose and rolls down the street. I pick it up and walk toward the headlights.

Both passenger doors squeak open, and the twins exit the run-down vehicle.

"Fucking hell, Jen! Un-fucking real!" Veronika roars as she slams the door behind her.

"What a nightmare!" adds Monika as she takes the hubcap from my hand, walks back to her car, and tosses it into the back seat.

The owners of the animal sanctuary are immigrants from Hungary, a small Eastern Bloc country. They dedicate their lives to saving discarded family pets. Neither of them is married. No kids. No life outside of their work. Their desire to help innocent animals is their sole passion in life. They are a little eccentric compared to what I had grown up with here in Southern California. They say what's in their hearts and on their minds without a filter, whether a compliment or criticism. But they are both hardworking and honest people who live their lives with honor and integrity. And for that, I trust them more than I trust most people I know.

Veronika nods at Tyler, then turns to me. "Did the police find out who did it?"

I shrug off Tyler's arm. "Not yet. We just got here ten minutes ago. Two officers are inside, searching the place." I show my boss the video footage on my phone.

A chorus of angry barking erupts from the BMW's back seat and alerts us to the returning police officers. "It's all clear. You may enter the premises, but fair warning, you'll need a strong stomach for this one," Handlebar Mustache says.

We all move toward the kennels—even Jayden, who ignores my repeated request to stay outside.

The motion sensor lights turn on and illuminate our path as we move into the bowels of the property. Jayden is the first one who notices the blood splatters on the ground and alerts us. I see them, too, the asymmetrical round dark red drops on the concrete and the drag marks that lead to the kennels.

I can smell the heavy metallic scent of blood as I enter the kennel with Tyler, Monika, Veronika, and Jayden following me closely. The female cop shines a light onto the furry body of George nestled in the hay. Blood still oozes from the stump that once held a cute little head. Everybody gasps at the sight of butchery. Monika lets out a weak scream next to me, making me shudder.

Her twin sister, Veronika, punches the wall of the stall. "Fucking hell! What the hell is wrong with people in this world?"

Tyler crouches down and looks around to inspect the bloody mess in the cold room. "Where is the head?" he asks.

The officer sweeps her light over the area, illuminating all parts of the floor. "We didn't find it," she says. "The perpetrator may have taken it with him."

I stagger back from the bloody scene. A hand over my mouth is the only thing that keeps me from emptying the contents of my stomach on the crime scene. I watch the others stand in a semi-circle around the carcass that steams in the cold air, and my head starts buzzing with horror and sadness.

The officer with the mustache pulls out a notebook and a pen. "Do you know anybody who would have a reason to do this?"

Veronika looks at him with contempt. "Who on earth could have a reason to do something like this?"

"What my partner meant was, do you know anyone who might hold a grudge against you or your business? An upset former pet owner? A disgruntled employee? An angry neighbor who complained about the noise, perhaps? Anybody who may have a vendetta against you guys?"

Veronika shrugs and slips her hands into the pocket of her hooded sweatshirt with the logo of the University of North Carolina, which she attended at least twenty years ago, and looks at her sister.

"We do get hate mail sometimes from puppy mill owners we helped the police bust over the years, but we never took the threats seriously." Monika looks at me. "What do you think, Jen? Do you have any idea who might have done this?"

I take a deep, relaxing breath before I answer. "I can't think of anybody," I say, rubbing my forehead. "But I find it extremely troubling that a seriously sick, mentally disturbed person is roaming the streets of our city right now. If someone is capable of doing such a horrible thing like beheading an innocent, beautiful creature, then I can only imagine what else he is capable of."

Jayden steps closer to the mutilated body of George, his phone in his hand. "Don't worry, Mom. We'll catch the bastard. And the internet will help."

He takes pictures. The flashes of white light turn the crime scene into an even more sinister sight, as if I were watching an amateur black-and-white horror movie. A chill touches my spine and makes me shiver.

The twins, finishing each other's sentences, answer questions from the police about security and business operations. The cops annotate the details with the seriousness of a double homicide investigation.

The female officer flips her notepad cover closed. "All right, I think we're good for now, but we may need more information later. If you remember anything, any little details that might seem insignificant to you, don't hesitate to contact us." She looks at a message on her phone. "The forensic team should be here in a couple of hours. Can someone turn on some lights here?"

Monika volunteers to walk back to the main building to turn on the light for the area, and her twin sister accompanies her. I stay near the barn, taking in the complete damage that brutal *animal* had done, the smell of blood still strong in the air.

My first husband, Connor, and I moved from downtown Los Angeles to Woodland Hills when I was pregnant with Jayden. We settled down in a family-oriented and quiet neighborhood within the San Fernando Valley because we wanted to provide a safe home for our growing family. But violence had followed us here, too. The mere memory of it all fills me with dread and panic.

The sun crawls over the horizon at a painfully slow pace. I stay at the shelter to help distribute breakfast among the impatiently complaining residents. The twins are calling the volunteer students who were supposed to come in today to cancel their shifts. We don't need a bunch of kids poking around the crime scene. The word will still get out about what happened to George, and some parents may not let their teens come back to work at the sanctuary. Connor often says that today's parents shelter their kids too much from real life. We bring them up soft. He accuses me of babying our boys, too. Lately, he even compares me to Tyler's mom. I know he exaggerates to hurt me.

I ask Tyler to take Jayden home and check on my other kids. He's been walking around me all morning, pale-faced and fidgety, talking to his mother on the phone. He annoys me more than comforts me, so I think it's better if he leaves.

Emily, who turned fourteen last July, and Noah, who will be nine in a month, stayed at home. My phone is on fire from their texting. I've been dodging their questions, but the truth will be out eventually. If I don't tell them, they will read about it online or hear it from Jayden. Kids should be allowed to grow up innocent.

As I busy myself with responsibilities around the sanctuary, I watch the team of investigators as they collect footprints and fingerprints at the crime scene. A forensics investigator tells me that he will collect several blood samples because the person who cut off George's head might have injured himself during the process. If he left some of his blood behind and the lab can isolate it, then they can run a DNA analysis. I hear the words that come out of the man's mouth, but I have difficulty grasping their meaning. George is gone, brutally murdered, but my brain hasn't fully processed this information yet.

It's two o'clock in the afternoon when we are allowed to reenter George's shelter and clean up the bloody mess. Veronika, Monika, two other regular adult volunteers named Toby and Andrew, and I take George's body to the corner of the property with a wheelbarrow. We bury him in the hard, cold soil and plant a small oak tree over his grave. Andrew says a few words of prayer, and the rest of us stand around with fingers intertwined and heads hanging. The fresh mound of dirt is making it all too real. But scrubbing off the dried pool of blood in the stall is the part that helps me to accept the truth finally.

As I hose down the concrete, I struggle to block out the images of the beating my mind conjures up relentlessly. I can't even imagine the pain and fear that little cow must have felt. Was he hoping for help to arrive? Was he wondering why that man was hurting him? Did he think he might have done something wrong to earn such brutal treatment? I used to feed George with a bottle when he was only a calf. He was always in my lap and followed me around the yard. He trusted me. He trusted all of us…I can't even go there. I need to shut down my brain before I lose it.

I ask Toby to finish up the cleaning. I'm drained mentally and physically, and I can't stay here any longer. Veronika gives me a ride home. She is beside herself too. If she had the murderer within her grasp right now, she'd be capable of skinning him alive. I think I'd help her.

Tyler is waiting for me at home with a freshly baked chicken pot pie he picked up from Costco earlier.

While Noah is oblivious to what's going on, for which I'm grateful, Emily cries through dinner. Jayden holds his fork with one hand and answers Instagram comments with the other. I don't allow phones at the dinner table usually, but he is helping us find the person responsible for this unspeakable crime. His followers are stunned with shock from the news of George's violent and brutal execution. They unleash their hatred on the unknown person who beheaded their beloved internet star in uncensored comments. Jayden reads a few out loud:

It makes me feel desperate to think that such sick people live among us. I am very sorry for poor Georgie. My sincere condolences to the caregivers. What kind of soul can such a man have? I can't imagine.

The things I would do to the perpetrator would make Hannibal Lecter's actions seem like fairy tales! Rest in peace, dear George!

I am ashamed of being human. My tears are flowing.

How can we live in such a repulsive world among so many evil "people"? My God, poor George. He never hurt anyone. I'm so sorry.

After the fourth comment, I ask Jayden to stop reading what people are writing because it's making us all upset.

I push away from the table. "I think I need a drink. I feel light-headed."

Tyler glances at the mess left behind after dinner.

"We'll clean up," Emily says to Tyler. "You go with Mom."

As I pass the living room, I look at the yoga mat unrolled on the carpet in front of the TV. I didn't record any material today. I already know that my followers will flood my inbox with inquiries. Since I started my lifestyle vlog five years ago, I haven't stayed dark longer than ten days. We need the money. Views bring sponsors and royalties. Content brings views. People have a short attention span nowadays. If I don't post for a day or two, they forget about me. They move on to other influencers. I can't afford to let my two hundred and sixty-seven thousand subscribers find new vlogs to follow.

Tyler catches my eye. He seems to read my face. "Are you going to post about what happened to George?"

I shrug as I take the can of hard seltzer from his hand. "I think I have to."

The doorbell rings.

"It's Dad," yells Emily as she runs to answer it.

I still feel awkward watching Connor being allowed inside the house like a guest, as if he hadn't lived here for years. He looks skinnier since the last time I saw him. The washed-out jeans hang on him in a grubby and stretched-out way. His hair is long, almost brushing against his shoulders. He started smoking and drinking again during the months that led up to our divorce. The effects are now showing on his face. His dimples are deeper. His pores are more prominent. He has been letting his beard grow, and now I can see that his dirty blond hair has some gray and turned lackluster. At least the patterned bright-color button-down shirt he's wearing helps give him a bit of a youthful appearance. I like this new style. I wish he'd dressed like this when we were married.

"Can I get you a drink?" Tyler greets my ex with the offer, not wasting a second to establish the roles of the host and the guest.

Connor calls Tyler a "mama's boy" behind his back, and it annoys me because he's right, and also because after a divorce, you want to do better, not worse. I can't give Connor the satisfaction of validating that I would never find a man like him—a phrase he frequently recited to me during our married life.

Connor and Tyler have had a few arguments in the past year, but they behave in front of the kids.

"I'll take an 805. Thanks, pal." He slaps Tyler on the back.

I join Tyler in the kitchen while Connor talks to the kids.

"Why is he here?" Tyler grumbles as he pops open the beer.

I dismiss him with a flap of my hand. "Don't start, please. Probably the kids called him."

"And he ran over here as fast as he could? Now he wants to be their father?" He slams the bottle down hard on the counter.

"I'm not going to fight about this right now. Okay?"

I go back to the living room and ask Connor to follow me. We walk outside to the patio. He lights a cigar and sits down on a chair underneath the grapevines he planted years ago. I take a sip from the black cherry–flavored White Claw hard seltzer.

"The yard looks nice," he says, puffing smoke.

"Yeah, Jayden really stepped up his game since you left. He's helping me a lot."

"How about the Fruitcake? Is he helping you, too, or does he just enjoy the oasis I built?"

I roll my eyes. Here we go again—the same old record playing. People who divorce may remain civil toward one another, but they can never be friends. It's against some code of nature.

"I'm so tired, Connor. Not physically but mentally. These past five years have been tough. And now with what happened at the shelter." I look away and sigh. "I need a break. I need to get away from it all."

"Why don't you dig up some old content and schedule a few upcoming posts. Then just unplug for the rest of the week."

I let my shoulders droop and look down at my hands. My eyes land on a line of dry blood underneath my fingernail. I frantically begin to scrape out the dark red residue with a stick. When I'd got home from the sanctuary, I'd taken a long bath. This blood shouldn't be here. My whole body starts shaking.

Tyler appears, cloaked in hostility and annoyance, and hands a bottle of beer to Connor. I smile at him appreciatively.

"I don't need a break from my vlog, but from this house, this town, this whole place," I continue. "We've been talking with Tyler about taking a trip somewhere."

Connor takes a long draw of his cigar. The smoke he exhales is thick and white. I like the scent of it. "You need me to watch the kids or something?" he asks, looking at me with his honest puppy eyes.

I catch Tyler pushing his glasses higher up on his nose. His eyes never leave my ex. That chair might have been Connor's favorite place in the yard, but now it's Tyler's, and he is boiling from being pushed out of it. I wish Connor had taken it with him when he moved out. Then it would be one less reason for confrontation between the boys.

"You know, I read this post on Facebook the other day about an old college friend of mine who rented a yurt in the mountains of Montana," Tyler says, reclaiming the attention. "He said it was the best thing they have ever done as a family. He said they were completely refreshed mentally and physically when they returned. It's on a peaceful mountainside with breathtaking views, but the yurt has no power or running water. It's an off-the-grid place. Maybe we could take the kids there too? Go off the grid for a few days. Reconnect with nature."

Connor lets out a burst of mocking laughter. "Good luck with taking city princess here to the wilderness. I've tried it many times, pal."

When we were still happily married, Connor was adamant about planning a family camping trip. He wanted to drag us all out of our comfort zone, but the idea rarely passed with the kids. The mere thought of spending days without their cell phones meant the end of the world to them. I was never too eager to give up the comfort our home offered either, even if it was only for a few days. Connor is right. I am a city girl. I always have been.

I take a sip of my drink. My eyes glimpse a silent shadow glide across the star-ridden dark skies above me. Something rattles the fronds of the tall palm tree next to us that stands tall by the fence, followed by a blood-curdling shriek.

"The owl must have gotten a rat or a mouse," Connor says.

"Oh, god." I sigh and rub my face. "I'm sorry, honey, but I don't think I can stay in the middle of a forest with no indoor plumbing, no light, and surrounded by wild animals. We won't have any protection."

"What protection will you need in the middle of nowhere?" Tyler shows me his friend's post on Facebook. "And look, there is an outhouse. It looks okay. Got a real toilet seat cover and everything."

"So, what if I have to pee in the middle of the night?"

"Then you take the flashlight and go do your business."

"That sounds insane! What if a bear shows up, or a mountain lion, and rips me off the pot?"

Tyler starts to sweat. He needs me to agree to this trip in front of my ex. "Humans have done their business in the wilderness for centuries. I'm pretty sure a bear won't go near a stinkpot."

"I wouldn't wanna go near it, either."

Connor crosses his legs and leans his head back on the chair. "I don't know. I think it would be great to get away from civilization for a few days. Chop wood for a fire. Sleep outside and stare at the sky all night. I bet the stars are so bright there—like you've never seen them before."

I remember the only camping trip we ever took, in Big Bear a few years back. The hike was nice, but the tent was uncomfortable. The toilet at the common area was infested with flies and spiders and was splattered with an assortment of brown colors of human waste. We had some noisy neighbors who tried to bring their entire kitchen to the campsite for *glamping*. I was jealous of their setup. But the guy turned out to be an amateur wilderness expert, only acting as if he were Indiana Jones. He was cutting down fresh trees and chopping them up for firewood. The moist logs wouldn't catch on fire, only emitting thick clouds of smoke. Their kid was hungry and crying. The mom was complaining. It was deep into the night when they finally settled down, but not before the whole campsite had lost their patience. The night rang with "Shut the hell up!" and "Put out the fire, you moron!" for hours.

That was our first and last camping trip.

"I don't know, Connor. This is not the same world you grew up in. "

"Says who? My parents took me fishing and camping all the time. I feel like I'm failing as a father if I don't teach my kids the old ways. They need to be survivors, but they have no skills. Without Google Maps, they would get lost in their own neighborhood. I think it's our duty as parents to prepare them better for real life."

Tyler crosses his arms. "I didn't invite you on the trip, Connor."

"No, of course not. I was only speaking figuratively. You could step into my shoes as a father." I recognize Connor's smirk. He knows Tyler isn't cut out for a wilderness adventure. That's why he supports the idea. I could tell Connor was relishing the thought of Tyler failing.

The patio door slides open, putting a pause to our conversation.

"Look, already eight thousand people liked the post," Jayden says, holding up his phone. "Over six hundred comments. And hundreds more have shared it."

I glance at the post that is brutal but tasteful. "Any information that may help?"

"No, but look at how many people are angry and upset."

"And will their anger and upset catch who did it?" There is an unnecessary amount of disdain in Connor's voice. He's never understood people's fascination with social media. He deems it a tremendous waste of time. He still resents me for "frolicking" around in front of thousands of strangers in our home.

I catch Tyler sighing. "I think we should go on this trip," he says. "It would be good for all of us."

"What trip?" Emily asks as she pulls out the AirPods from her ears and joins us outside.

"I'm taking you guys to Montana. We will spend a few days away from civilization. Just the five of us."

Emily makes a face. "What are we going to do there?"

"Play games, go on hikes, and work all day to survive. There won't be electricity. We need to come up with a food plan, too, because there won't be a refrigerator there either."

Jayden puts his phone away with obvious disappointment that we didn't adore him longer for his post's success. "Oh, it's one of those trips? I'm not doing it. What if something happens in the world and we won't even know about it?"

Connor tosses a tiny pebble at Jayden. "You will be fine without the internet for a few days, son."

I watch the boys discuss the possibility of this trip, and it is like watching a power struggle between an old lion and a young one. One so desperate to hold onto the old ways and

19

share his wisdom. The other in such a hurry to start his own life and have his opinion heard. Jayden is a fine young man. So eager to make an impression on the world and make his dad proud. Yet he is so naïve. It will take years for him to understand how the adult world truly works. His knowledge will come from a path of disappointment and success and sadness and joy. Maybe creating an opportunity for our kids to prepare for the real world isn't such a bad idea. Life can be harsh and brutal. George's violent end has reminded us all of that fact today.

A trip to the wilderness where we can only rely on each other could also bring my kids closer to Tyler. However, it won't be easy to convince them why that would be necessary. They treat Tyler like an uncle.

"You could livestream from the road and record the rest of the trip once we are off-grid," Tyler presses on, eagerly waiting for a yes from me in front of Connor. "Leaving your subscribers with a cliffhanger would pique their interest. They would have to wait for days until you checked back in again. This is the kind of material that keeps people coming back to a vlog."

I ask Emily to bring my phone to me that I left in the kitchen. She complains about the trip with the same vigor as Jayden does. She doesn't want to miss talking to her friends. Her best friend, Tina, has a birthday coming up too. We will have to schedule the trip around the party.

"You know what, guys? Let's do this. Why not? What's the worst thing that can happen?"

Connor leans forward in his chair. "Are you being serious?"

I shrug. "Yeah, why not? You always say I'm making our boys soft. It's time for them to learn to be a man."

Connor points at his chest. "You couldn't come to this conclusion when we were a family?"

I bite my lip.

Tyler's eyes are shining underneath his glasses.

Connor pops up from his chair and ushers the kids inside the house, leaving Tyler and me alone outside.

Tyler nods toward my ex. "He'll make you pay for this decision."

"I know. But it doesn't matter which option I choose. One of you two was bound to get upset with me."

Tyler smiles. "I'm glad it wasn't me."

I kiss my boyfriend on his lips, take a swig of my drink, and then record a short video for my followers, letting them know about our upcoming adventure to which they are all virtually invited to join.

JENNIFER

My hair is flat and greasy. I don't feel like dealing with it, so I put the entire tangled mess up in a lazy bun and secure it with a blue scrunchie I stole from my daughter's bathroom drawer. Technically it's my scrunchie because I paid for it, but Emily tends to be overly possessive of *her things*. She freaks out if Jayden eats the last yogurt from the fridge or if Noah plays with her toys. God, I hope I'll never have to rely on her for help when I'm old.

On that note, I remind myself that I didn't take my vitamins today. I shuffle through the sea of bottles in the kitchen cabinet and gather a handful of pills—iron to keep my anemia at bay, garlic with GABA and B1, B6, and B12 vitamins to manage my stress and overcome my fatigue that seems to be my constant `111companion these days. Who knew that trying to meet a younger partner's expectations would put so much pressure on me.

I take a high dose of vitamin D and a gummy vitamin with elderberry, echinacea, zinc, and vitamin C for immune system health, especially as we are coming out of the winter gloom. Glucosamine for my joints so my followers can't hear my knee and ankles pop every time I exercise.

"God, I'm old," I groan and swallow the handful of pills. The labels of the recently purchased bottle face me on the shelf, taunting me: eye health, collagen, multivitamins by Life Extension, to name a few. I'll leave those for this afternoon.

As I stand in front of the kitchen sink in my bathrobe, I feel someone's eyes on me. I look out the kitchen window at the neighbor's yard. The father is standing on his patio, a steaming mug against his lips, staring at me. As much as I love our house, the lack of privacy will drive me away from suburbia one day.

That was always my ex's dream—living on a ranch off the grid somewhere. If I weren't such a coward, I'd have gone along with Connor's plan to buy a farm on a green meadow and raise my kids surrounded by cute barn animals. Teaching our children to love and respect nature should have been more important than telling them to be wealthy and successful. But what can I say? I am a coward—I'm a sheep.

My neighbor is a strange man who keeps his family locked up in their house all day. Connor used to tell me that we should report them to child services, but I'm not convinced of the idea. What if the investigation came back with nothing? Then we would be stuck with a vengeful, angry man to annoy and torture us every day. Tyler thinks we should mind our own business and leave the neighbors alone. Lately, it seems that every decision I'm faced with forces me to choose between my ex and my boyfriend.

Suddenly feeling irritated, I toss the remaining water from my cup into the sink and jerk the blinds closed.

My livestream yoga starts in thirty minutes, but I'm not up for it today. I already scheduled a post with a pre-recorded clip last night.

I sit in silence on a barstool by the island, staring with little enthusiasm at the state of war in the kitchen left behind after the morning school rush. I'm still gazing ahead of me, at nothing in particular, when my phone rings and vibrates on the polished concrete counter. Judging by the ringtone, I know it's my dad calling.

"Hey, beautiful!" My father is my rock. He cheers me on in everything I do. He still makes me believe that I can do anything I set my mind to. I answer his call because I could use a few words of encouragement right now.

"Morning, Dad. What's going on?"

"I loved your breakfast burrito this morning. Your mother and I followed every step. I even ate the avocado, if you can believe it." The cooking bit was pre-recorded too. The kids had cereal, and I only had a cup of coffee for breakfast.

I pour myself more coffee as I talk. I've never gotten used to the idea of my parents watching me online. I'm okay with strangers, but I always feel awkward when people I know talk about my videos.

"Dad, it's a lifestyle vlog for stay-at-home moms. It's weird that you guys are watching me." I try to remember my performance in the clip. It wasn't my best; it seemed acted and weird. That's why I didn't release it in the first place.

"How else are we supposed to see you?"

"You could always visit us."

"We will be there for Jayden's graduation."

My parents always liked and respected Connor, and they didn't support our divorce. My dad still keeps in touch with him as if nothing has changed. It was a big challenge for Tyler to step into Connor's shoes and earn my parents' respect, especially my dad's. Tyler doesn't know that my father considers him a snowflake and a big mouth, all talk but little action. There is civility between the two men, but it will never be more than that, certainly not for lack of trying on Tyler's part.

"What?" Dad's voice fades. "Well, come here, then." I hear shuffling in the background. "Your mother wants to talk to you, too," he says into the phone, loud and clear.

"I'm so proud of you, chipmunk," Mom says.

"For what?"

"For what? For everything you do. I noticed that over twenty thousand people joined you this morning. What an accomplishment, Jenny!"

"It's not a big deal, Mom."

"Of course it's a big deal! You've created a network of friends. You're helping women all around the world feel less isolated."

I think I've gained more from my YouTube channel than I've given. Now I regularly exercise because people expect me to show up every day and inspire them. I eat healthier now because I do my research about nutrition. The camera also records every meal I make, and my viewers hold me accountable, not just toward them but also to myself. In the past five years, I've lost over twenty-two pounds, and I've been keeping my new figure on point. My mood is also better. With so many people depending on me to inspire them, I've found a new purpose. Not like being a wife and mother of three didn't give me a purpose, but this vlog is for me and me alone. Besides, our integrity truly shines when people scrutinize our every move.

But I won't tell any of this to my parents, because it feels good to hear their praise.

"Just please don't tell my sister that you guys have been watching me, okay? I don't want to listen to her complain again that I'm your favorite child."

"But you are our favorite child."

"Stop it, Dad. It's not funny."

Footsteps descend the stairs. Tyler is making his way downstairs, dressed in khaki shorts and a zip-up sweatshirt. His face looks tired. His eyelids sag. He teaches middle school English and spends most of his days in front of a computer screen. His glasses are getting thicker. His posture is getting worse. But I can't tell him any of that because he becomes very defensive.

"Are you going for a walk?"

He pulls a tissue out of his pocket and blows his nose. "Yeah, why?"

"Can I come with you?" It's cold outside. Forty-two degrees Fahrenheit. Enduring a crisp, chilly morning isn't as tempting to me as staying indoors, but I need to air out my head. I grab my hoodie with Jayden's high school logo on the front from the back of the couch to show Tyler I'm serious.

"If you want." He is short and snappy with me. He takes his morning walks alone to think and for peace of mind. But now he's living with me, and I'm ruining his mojo.

"We could talk about the trip to Montana," I say for encouragement as I change into a pair of sweatpants and pull the hoodie over my head.

"Aren't you doing yoga this morning? I was going to talk to my mom on the phone. She's expecting my call." He makes one final attempt to get rid of me, but I've already resolved myself to this plan.

"Can't you talk to her later?" Here we go again. It's me against his mother, and I usually lose.

He scratches his head, eyeing me with worry. "You know how she gets when I cancel our plans."

If I didn't know better, I'd think Tyler has a secret lover on the side. But I do know better. It's his mother who has a hold on him, not another woman.

I open the patio door to allow my goofy and overweight German shepherd, Milo, to storm into the house. "Blame it all on me. She hates me anyway."

Tyler grabs the dog's leash off the hook. "She doesn't hate you. Don't start that again. But you know how she is. Nobody will ever be good enough for me in her eyes."

"Especially not an internet influencer."

I close the back door behind us, and we start down the narrow path around the house to get to the side gate. "She is a little conservative, that's all. She doesn't think it's a good idea for you to tease strange men online."

"And how am I doing that, exactly?"

Tyler sighs as he locks the latch on the gate behind us. "Well, you do create this perfect wife image online. Some men might believe the act."

I stop and do a hard spin to face Tyler. "Act? Everything I do, I do it with honesty."

He runs his fingers along the side of my face and smiles. "Yeah, you are amazing, honey. Forget what I said. I don't want to instigate a fight. You know how my mom is."

"Yes, I do. And it would be nice if you'd defend me just once."

"Look, she's old. She's survived breast cancer recently. Who knows how long she has left? Can we just make her happy for whatever time she has left on this earth?"

"She could live another thirty years. I won't walk on eggshells simply to please her."

"And nobody asked you to." Tyler takes my hand, and we start walking. "I'll call her later, okay?"

No, it's not okay. I shouldn't have to compete with my future mother-in-law. I make her son happy. What more does she want from me?

Milo acts overly excited this morning. Tyler grabs the leash from my hand.

"Were you planning on taking Milo with us to the yurt?"

Tyler jerks on the leash to pull Milo back. "It's a seventeen-hour drive. He'd hate it."

"He'd love the yurt and the mountains."

"Until he meets a big black bear."

I click my tongue. "See, you keep saying things like that, and then you act surprised I don't want to go."

"Jeez, Jen, I was kidding." Tyler steps on Milo's paw, and he whimpers as he jumps away. "You need to teach this dog how to walk. I see other dogs sit at every street crossing, while this one walks in front of me, zigzagging like an idiot."

I yank out the leash from his hand. "Stop hating on the dog."

"Maybe we should take him. I mean, he may get lost or eaten." Tyler says this with a somber face, but I know he is joking. He would prefer to pick a new dog for our new family instead of catering to a pet I shared with my ex, but I know he likes Milo.

Tyler waves at the neighbor across the street as we make our way along the sidewalk. He knows most of the people who live in our neighborhood. When he was spending time with us on weekends, he would be out in front of our house, racing remote-controlled cars. That's enough excitement for married men around the block to be lured out of their homes. I'm not as social in person, but I feel comfortable with creating online content. Maybe I was more social at some point, but wives tend to bring up the comments I get on social media about my tight yoga pants, and it gets old after a while.

Even Jayden's friends tease him for having a mom who does yoga and aerobics online. I can no longer crawl back under a rock, but I try to make less of a spectacle of myself if I can help it.

"Joe got back from a hunting trip in Colorado this week." Tyler nods toward our neighbor. "We are the only ones who never take cool vacations."

"Fine! Book the damn yurt, then."

"What?"

"I said you've won. Let's take the kids behind God's back to sleep in a hut on a floor. I'm sure we're all going to learn something from being so uncomfortable." I yank on Milo's leash to get him away from a pile of dog poop on a neighbor's lawn.

"Stop being so dramatic. You know what your problem is? You're spoiled."

I scoff. "A couple of days ago, I was the perfect wife and mother. Now I'm a spoiled brat?"

"I didn't call you a brat. And you are not my wife, yet." He waves again at a couple pushing a stroller. I want to elbow him in his ribs for pretending to be a gentleman in front of strangers. "You yourself said that you needed a break. Look around you. Where can you find any peace and quiet here? It's constant noise and action. Cars going, helicopters flying, police sirens blaring, ambulance, the phone rings, the phone beeps, neighbors having parties, kids are screaming. If you want to find peace, you need to do something drastic. Something unconventional."

"Stop making this trip about me. You want to go so you can stomp on Connor's dream."

"And is that such a bad thing, that I want to feel you guys are on my side?"

"What are you talking about? We are on your side."

Tyler offers me a dubious look.

"What?"

He stops me on my walk. "I just want us to be a family. And yes, we could go to Hawaii or the Bahamas, but everybody would do their own thing there and be on their phones. In the mountains, we need to rely on each other. It could bring the whole family closer." He clamps my face with his hands. "You need to trust me on this. You always say no to everything. I understand. You're a mother. You like to take the safe, beaten path. But we all could use a little excitement, and we can only get that with a change of scenery."

I take a moment to catalog our most beautiful memories together as a couple this one short year, but my memories with Connor keep invading the images in my head.

"You need to trust me on this. Have I ever let you down before?" Tyler says this as if we've been together for decades.

For Tyler, a year-long relationship means the longest commitment of his life to another person who isn't his mother. He frequently says things like, "You know me, I wouldn't do that," or "I'm an open book for you." I was married to Connor for sixteen years, and we dated for three years previous to that, yet he still had a side of him I barely knew. I'm sure I had one too. If Tyler thinks that our life is mundane because we haven't gone on a vacation in a year, then how will he manage the years to come with my "boring" family life? Sometimes I think it takes more effort to make our relationship work than it's worth, but I also hate to admit failure, and one ruined relationship for this decade was enough for me. I must at least try to save this current one. Not just for me, but for the kids. They need a stable home environment and not a lonely, emotional wreck of a mother who brings home a new guy every month.

"All right," I say with a sigh. "But we are getting a hotel halfway there. No way I'll drive seventeen hours straight."

He smiles mischievously. "Already done. I booked us a room in Mona in Utah. It's a small town south of Salt Lake City. There is a giant lavender farm there we can visit. The online pictures look amazing. You could create some quality content there for your vlog. There are a few cheap restaurants where we could grab something to eat. You'll love it," he explains with vigor as he takes his glasses off and cleans the lenses.

I watch him semi-enthusiastically. A fresh idea for content sounds tempting, but the drive and the isolation and the discomfort...ugh. The mere thought of it makes me depressed. Why did I agree to his plan?

"Connor will go nuts that I'm taking you there," Tyler adds, an accidental spilling of his most inner thoughts. He isn't any more of a mountain dweller than I am. He planned this trip to rub it into my ex's face.

"Wow! Cheap fast food. You know how to make a woman happy." I purposely avoid his comment on my ex.

He kisses my lips. "Nothing but the best for my baby."

I shake my head as we resume our walk. "What are we going to do with Milo?"

"Can you ask your sister to look after him?"

My sister is ten years my senior and lives in Encino in our former home I shared with Connor. It's a good ten-minute drive from Woodland Hills if there is no traffic. My sister owes us eighteen months' back rent, which she blames on the financial hardship she fell into two years ago. In reality, she has money for Disneyland, dozens of pairs of shoes, getting her hair done, manicures, and eating out all the time, but not for paying her debt to us. Connor has been chewing my ear about kicking her out of the house and get a real tenant that pays, but I don't have the heart to put my nephew on the street. My sister knows that I'm soft, and she uses it against me. Most of these days, I try to avoid talking to her, tiptoeing my way through the problem, driven by my shame for being my parents' favorite child. The mere thought of asking her a favor makes my skin crawl. But Milo hates people. He would eat strangers for breakfast if we let him. My twelve-year-old nephew, Jordan, is the only person who can enter our property without getting his pants ripped off of him by our dog when we aren't home.

"She owes you," Tyler adds for good measure.

* * * * *

For the next three days, I feel depressed. I've been putting off the task of planning for the mountain trip. But this morning, I pull out a sheet of paper from the printer, grab a pen, and start making lists of items we need.

My hand leaves a sweat mark on the paper as I put together our meal plan for our time in the yurt. It's all canned chicken meat, oat milk, almond milk, cereal, Slim Jims, peanut butter, and jam without refrigeration. Monika at the shelter emailed me a list of Hungarian meals I could cook with simple, nonperishable ingredients. Something called potato stew with sausage, bean soup with smoked bacon, and chicken noodle soup using boxed broth, canned chicken meat, and peas.

After my morning videos, I head to the grocery store and load up my cart with protein bars just in case we get stuck on the mountain for some reason. The weather forecast promised 75 Fahrenheit and sunshine. Still, Connor is one of those doomsday prep guys who like to prepare for every possible calamity, and he has been bugging me on the phone every day, giving me his advice that sounds more like instructions. "They are my kids, too, you know," he always says when I don't comply with his requests.

The night before the trip, my phone rings around eight o'clock. Tyler and I usually don't go to bed before ten, but tomorrow is the big day, so I've already tucked myself in bed with the book *The Road* by Cormac McCarthy. I don't know why I choose to read this particular title about a father and his son surviving in a post-apocalyptic no-man's-land, because it only fills me with more anxiety, but now that I started it, I can't put it down.

"Is something wrong?" I answer the call once I see Veronika's name on the screen.

"I forgot to tell you earlier that I got a call from Topanga Police Department today," she says in a rushed, urgent manner. "I guess they have a suspect. They followed up on a tip that came from Jayden's Instagram post, and it led them to some guy."

I sit up in the bed and tap at Tyler to get his attention. I put the phone on speaker.

"Did they release his name?"

"No, not officially, but I heard the guy is a twenty-six-year-old homeless man from Algeria who was annoyed by the noise the animals were making at the shelter and he couldn't sleep."

The electrified way Veronika talks always quickens my pulse, but I am over-the-top agitated now. "You are telling me that George was brutally killed because a homeless guy decided to set up camp behind the shelter but he didn't like the dogs barking?" I have a hard time comprehending the words that come out of my mouth. Tyler is equally shocked and appalled.

"Well, the cops couldn't prove anything yet, but yeah, pretty much. That happens when you put all kinds of people in the same box, shake it up, and pour them out, saying there you go, go and make something of yourselves. Not everybody can prevail with odds like that."

"You and your sister did."

"Yeah, through hard work and persistence. They don't teach you that at school. Oh, whatever. Let's not get riled up on politics. The police better not release his name, though, because if I find out who he is, I'll hunt down that sheep-shagging cave-dwelling fuck and skin him alive."

"Don't hype yourself up, Veronika. Now the police know who he is. Justice will be served."

"What justice? He gets to spend a few years in a three-star hotel-like prison cell with three free meals a day, conjugal visits, and earning his college education on the taxpayers' dime?"

"I don't agree with the system either, but what can you do?"

A long sigh, a clicking sound, as if she had used the microwave while we talked. "Anyway, are you still going in the morning?"

"Yep, we're all packed up."

"Make sure you watch your back. It's apparent that this guy has been stalking us. If he hates George for his Instagram account, who says he doesn't hate you for your YouTube channel."

"I do lifestyle videos for middle-aged women. I doubt an unemployed illegal alien with anger issues would be following me."

"All I'm saying is to read the comments on your recent posts. He may have expressed some anger online. Ask Jayden to check George's posts too. The guy is still at large.

The police have no information on his current whereabouts. He can be anywhere."

"I'll do that. And hey, make sure you watch your back too."

"Yeah, the guys are coming tomorrow to install a new security system. It's more advanced and professional. It'll set me back a freaking fortune to get it installed. Then I'll have to pay a monthly fee for the company, and without George's posts, the money will be tight. Well, I don't want to trouble you with my problems. Enjoy yourselves. Call me."

"We won't have service in the mountains."

"That's right. Well, call me when you can. I won't send a search and rescue after you, I promise."

I disconnect the call but hold the device in my hand a few moments longer.

"See, and you thought being on a remote mountain range is dangerous? Getting out of town might be the best thing we can do now."

I purse my lips and nod without a word. It's not that easy for me to admit that Tyler turned out to be right again.

I turn off my light and put my head on the pillow. Sleep will make the time go by faster. We'll be gone for only a week, but all I can think about is when the trip will be over. I already know how the next few days will unfold. The kids will do their best to make their father proud but to irritate Tyler. They will complain so we can return home before planned.

Tyler fixes himself against me and slips his hand under the blanket. He already had his victory today, but that wasn't enough. He is going for a home run. All this thinking about

George, Connor, and the homeless man who was suspected of killing George dwindled my desire, so I push his hand away. But Tyler isn't the kind of man who gets easily discouraged once he sets his mind on what he wants.

ALEX

"You're a fat, worthless piece of shit!" Hoffman's eyes bore into mine, two cold marbles void of emotion, as he blurts the words into my face with so much bile and resentment that his reenactment sends a chill down my spine.

I lift the pen from the paper, then tap the tip against the tabletop a few times, trying to find a balance in my soul and in my head to allow me to keep my cool and appear unbiased and professional. "Is that what your mother used to call you?"

"Usually, but she also had a laundry list of other nasty things to say to me."

I catch the eyes of the corrections officer who stands in the corner with his back against the wall, providing me with security. The small size of the meeting room confines us together in close proximity, and he will hear every word of this interview unless I start whispering.

I don't know why I look at the guard. Maybe, subconsciously, I hope to catch a glimpse of empathy for this prisoner in his facial expression, but his face is a blank canvas. So, he either stopped giving a crap about the inmates' sob stories or learned to swallow his emotion over the years.

I refocus my attention on the subject of my inquiries. "Can you tell me how an average day passed in your house?"

"When I was a kid or when I was on my own?"

"When you were a kid."

Hoffman unfolds his arms, leans back in his chair, and scratches his stubble with his thick fingers. I can hear the coarse sound his nails make rubbing against his rough facial hair.

"My childhood wasn't all bad," he starts with a sudden change of tone. "We had good days and bad days. But as I got older, especially after my father left us, things got worse."

"Let's start with your childhood, then. What do you remember? Where did you live? With whom? Describe your days to me." I ready my pen to take notes. I could have used a voice recorder to capture every word of Paul Hoffman, the infamous murderer, but then I couldn't use my note-taking as a distraction to look away from this monster. I've read every article about his case. I've absorbed every detail the newspapers shared about his crime, and I am holding the information inside my chest cavity like a thoroughly soaked sponge, making my heart feel heavy.

My mother disapproves of my obsession with writing books about crimes from the criminal's point of view. Since she was the one who introduced me to crime shows and thriller novels when I was still living at home, I suspect what bothers her the most are the royalties these men receive from the book sales and not the act of writing itself. But there is more to every story, and the families on both sides deserve answers. I believe that there is an insatiable hunger in most of us to know why someone did something or why things happen to us. In our order of the universe, most people have some control over their lives. When something unexplainable happens to us, we can't move on with our lives until we learn why it happened. We are desperate for answers. And that's the reason I'm here. I want to hear this man's side of the story so that I can have answers. I want to dissect his brain to find that turning point where this man turned evil so that I can provide the families with some explanation—even if it won't be satisfactory. A cruel, mindless death can never be explained rationally, but I can certainly try to do my best to paint a more detailed picture.

The minds of criminals have always fascinated me, but Hoffman was the first inmate I corresponded with over the years who agreed to let me write his biography. I can't mess this up and miss my chance. But most importantly, I can't let my readers down, especially the families of the victims.

I feel Hoffman's eyes on me. He's trying to read what I write, but my chicken scratch lies upside down on the paper for him, and I doubt he can make out any words.

This story is important to him. His lengthy and detailed letters to me suggested as much. He wants people to understand what motivated him. I suspect he yearns for approval that would prove he isn't insane—the world is. But I could be wrong. Maybe he is in it solely for the money.

As my mind wanders, my stomach contracts painfully.

I look up at my interviewee again to encourage him to begin with his childhood life story. He shrugs and looks away as if recalling his past requires some cataloging in his brain.

"My mother was an overly emotional woman," Hoffman starts his story. "Her mood depended on many things, like how much money she made a month. Or if she was on good terms with her crazy family or not. But ultimately, her relationship with my father was the biggest trigger in her mood. If they were good together. If he was nice to her. If he came home on time and ate dinner with us. Then my mother was happy. Then she would bake us brownies or make pancakes after dinner. If she was angry with my dad, then shoes were flying, things were breaking. I spent most of my days in my room, doing what I always did, doing my homework and playing video games. And most days she was okay with that. But when she was pissed at my father, oh man, she would come into my room and yell at me for no reason. She would call me a slob for not cleaning my room. She would pick up my clothes from the floor and throw them in a trash bag. 'If you don't appreciate the things I buy you, then I'll give it to someone who does,' she would yell. And I would cry and beg her not to take my stuff away." His imitation of his mother's voice crawls under my skin. Though I never met the woman, I saw her pictures during my research, and she seemed like a nice person—an average middle-class woman in her late sixties, with a trustable round face and sweet smile. The devil has many faces.

"Did she take your stuff often?"

"She would take the bag, but she never gave it away. When she calmed down, she would bring it back to me and even help me put everything away."

"That must have been tough, being subjected to her mood swings."

"What was hard about this is that I lived in this constant fear and insecurity. I never knew if I was waking up to a happy morning and allowed to eat breakfast with my family and go about my day. Or if I'd be dragged out of bed and yelled at because I forgot to take the trash cans out to the street the night before, or because I left the milk out and it spoiled by morning."

"But you were a kid. Kids make mistakes."

"Hmmm." Hoffman allows his smirk to respond to my somewhat naïve statement.

I decide to lead him to different waters. "Did you do good at school?"

"I only went to school up to middle school. I was homeschooled for high school. Well, nobody was helping me with my school. It was more like do-it-yourself school, but my mother needed someone to look after my younger sister when she was at work, and with my father gone, I was the only option for a free babysitter."

"Did you graduate from high school?"

"Nope." His answer is short and definite. He must be ashamed of his lack of education.

"Did you try to get your GED once you moved out of your mother's house?"

"I did when I was twenty or twenty-one, I don't remember, but I couldn't see it through."

He uses the word *couldn't* instead of *wouldn't*, which means he is a type of man who always finds excuses for his shortcomings. He never apologized publicly to the families of his victims. He showed no remorse during the trial. I can't wait to get to that point where I've earned his trust enough to ask him the question: Do you regret what you did? I could cut to the chase and ask him right here and right now, but he'd lie. He would say what he thought I wanted to hear. But what I want to hear is the truth, even if I have to wait and play him to get to it.

"What stopped you from finishing school?"

"You know. This and that. Life. I had no money. I had to work for a living. I didn't have enough time to do school, too." Excuses, excuses. The recognizable trait of every loser. I already learned from the police reports that he was hanging with the wrong crowd and used drugs frequently during his teenage years.

"Where did you live at that point in your life?"

"My older brother took me in. They live in Woodland Hills. He owns a bunch of haircutting places. They do pretty well financially."

"How long were you living with your brother and his family?"

"Not long. Eight weeks, maybe? Ten?"

"You sound as if it's not a pleasant memory."

He tilts his head and licks his lips as if deliberating between telling the truth or lying. "It started out good. My mother threw me out of the house for the third time. I was living with a friend of mine, but his parents told me that I couldn't stay any longer. I had no place to go. I was going to sleep in my truck when I got a phone call from my brother.

He heard from someone—I think it was his wife—that I was homeless and he offered me his help."

"You were not in touch with your brother at the time?"

"No. Neither was my mom. They had a huge falling-out a few years earlier. My brother is twenty years older than me. We don't have much in common. We never lived together when I was growing up. We don't even have the same father. Don't even share the same last name. He is a McKeehan. My mom and his dad, Keith, were never married, and when Keith left my mom, my brother, Josh, decided to move in with him. My mom could never forgive him for choosing his father over her, but I guess he'd had enough of her theatrics and needed a safe and quiet place to exist. Even if that meant breaking all ties with our mother."

"Was she heartbroken when your brother left?"

"I don't know. I wasn't born yet, but knowing my mother, I think she was more worried about what people would say than she was about losing her son."

I need to steer the conversation back to Paul's life to find the critical points in his development from an innocent baby to a heartless killing machine.

"So, your mother was an emotionally unstable, narcissistic woman who had a hard time holding onto a relationship with men," I say to earn a few good points with Paul. "It's not your fault that she had created an unstable environment for her children. Did your brother suffer the same hardships growing up as you did?" If I can pinpoint the differences in the kids' upbringing, I may find the reasons why Josh had become a successful businessman while Paul had lost his way.

Paul raises his brow and looks at me as if offended. "I don't know. I wasn't there." I detect a hint of envy and hatred against his brother—a touch of rivalry, perhaps. I'll scrape at that scab to make the wound bleed.

"Do you look up to your brother? Were you two ever tight?"

Paul licks his lips again, then wipes them off with the back of his hand with two aggressive side-swiping movements. "Dunno. I guess I was closer to his kids, especially to his oldest son, Mark. He is only five years younger than me. We got along, but man, it was tough to compete against a perfect dude like Mark." He spits on the floor.

"Watch it, Hoffman!" the guard yells at him.

Paul turns his head a little but doesn't look back at the uniformed man who stands between him and his freedom. "I loved that little shit, you know," he continues. "Mark was the only one in the family who accepted me for who I was. He never judged me. Never expected anything from me. He was always a scholar-athlete, but he never looked down on me for not playing sports and being dumb. He was cool."

"Are you guys still tight?"

He purses his lips. He looks more innocent now, like a child in a man's body. "Nope. Haven't talked to Mark in years." He leans forward in his chair, and I reflexively put more distance between us by pushing back on my chair. I immediately worry that he noticed my reaction, but he doesn't show it.

"I'm hungry. Can you get a sandwich or a burger in here?"

He is stalling. Talking about Mark is his kryptonite. Or at least one of his weaknesses. I'm glad I found something that can make Paul drop the act and show me something real. These emotional backstories will put the meat on the frame of my story. I make a note to keep coming back to the topic of Mark until I manage to peel back Paul's layers of facades and get down to his naked, raw emotions. But first, I'll cater to his needs to make him believe that I'm here for him. But what he doesn't know is that this time, I'm the hunter and he is the prey.

JENNIFER

When I was a little girl, my favorite magazine was *National Geographic World*. The afternoons would often find me sitting on my sofa bed and reading about majestic landscapes and exotic animals. Gawking at pictures of dense forests and snow-covered mountains was how I spent my free time. In my child's mind, it seemed to me such places existed only in magazines. To bring those images to life, I decorated my bedroom walls with posters and handmade collages with pictures of natural life. It was my only escape from the landlocked desert city of Henderson in Nevada, where I spent most of my childhood. During World War Two, Henderson was a significant magnesium supplier to the army. Now people live here because it lies a short drive from the bustling city of Las Vegas—a fascinating city that was so close yet so far out of my reach, as if I lived on the other side of the globe. In our home, the Gambling Capital of the World was considered a city of sin and waste. Yet as a young woman, I craved to taste the forbidden fruit.

My first chance to visit Las Vegas came during my teen years, and I was enamored by the casinos' blinding lights like so many of my friends. If I hadn't gone to college in Los Angeles, where I met Connor, I might still be lost in those lights.

My parents were hardworking, respectable people, and they raised my sister and me to be respectful and diligent and a productive part of society. My father was a carpenter, and my mother worked as an elementary school teacher. Their tendency to choose a life of routine glued them together well in marriage. The farthest we went from our home were the beaches of California that we visited every summer for a short two weeks. Not until the internet had become a commonplace, and sites like YouTube started to grow, did it occur to me that those places I saw in books and magazines as a kid did exist indeed.

But then life happened, and I never became a world traveler.

* * * * *

On our second day of driving to the yurt, we reach Montana, where the highway splits between endless flatlands so vast and majestic that I feel equally intimidated and amazed. Beyond the sea of land, an endless wall of tall mountains stretches along the horizon, their jagged edges and steep sides concealed ominously in the shadows where the sunlight can't reach. Our home for the next few days is on one of those mountaintops.

I look at the screenshot of the yurt nestled in the silent forest and realize that soon we'd be entering the magical world of my childhood dreams.

I had managed to livestream most of our journey to my followers all across California, Nevada, Utah, and some parts of Montana, but our cell reception had cut off miles ago. I pull out my cell phone to record the moment when I take the first inhale of the pristine air. I'll save these videos on my phone and upload them when we return to civilization.

Jayden puts his hand up and shoves my phone away from his face. Good thing it's a recording and not a live feed.

"What the hell, Jay!" I snap at him.

"Mom, enough of the videos. The whole world doesn't have to see every moment of our lives."

Jayden appreciates my work the least of my three children, so I quickly redirect my attention to Emily. "Are you okay with answering a few questions for me?"

She won't even look at me and only shakes her head. I find her indifference upsetting. The money I earn from social media pays for a lot of things they own.

"Let them be," Tyler says. "We're all tired and look like shit. Not the best content material."

He doesn't look that bad, but this is the first time I've seen him unshaven and disheveled. His beard and mustache grow in patches, like a pubescent teen's. The skin on his neck and face looks saggy and wrinkled from dehydration. He couldn't sleep in the hotel last night, and it shows. He has a hard time sleeping anywhere else but in his childhood bed.

I put the phone back into my purse. Not because I submit to my family, but because my mood for fun has suddenly evaporated.

"So, do you still care if I'm excited, or was that question only for your video?" Jay says as he's fixing his jacket he uses as a pillow against his window.

I smile as I rotate my body toward the back. "Of course I care!"

"Don't be a dick, Jay," Emily reprimands.

I snap my eyes at Noah, who is blissfully watching a downloaded cartoon on his iPad, oblivious to our conversation. "Watch the language, sister," I warn my daughter regardless.

"Why don't you tell Jayden to watch his tone? Dad does."

"Well, Dad isn't here."

"Speaking of Dad, I texted him earlier, before the service cut off. He sent me a few pictures of that survival camping trip we took together years ago. He asked me to take a bunch of pictures of this trip for him, too. I think he's pretty upset he couldn't come."

I make a face to warn Jayden that this isn't the right moment to talk about Connor with nostalgia. Maybe we should have gone on a trip like this when we were still a family, but by the time the kids were old enough to do it, my relationship with my ex was irreparable. Connor buried himself in work. I was always lonely—busy with the kids and the house, but lonely emotionally. Then I started to vlog, and he resented me for it. He was sick to his stomach from all the guys who tried to connect with me online. All that resentment led to the spreading rot in our marriage. Without strong roots, our love and respect for one another had become damaged beyond repair. There was a time when I believed that I should have fought harder for our family. But now I understand that the past is fixed. What's been done can't be undone. There is only one way from this moment, and it's forward.

I look at Jayden with pride. My marriage, however it ended, was not a waste. "I'm eager to see you put those survival skills to use this week, aren't you, Tyler?" I call out to my boyfriend to make him feel included.

Tyler locks eyes with Jayden in the rearview mirror. "Of course, buddy. I'll certainly need your help to take care of these ladies."

Jay took a three-day-long Survival in the Wilderness course with his dad a few years back. I remember being mortified by their stories of building a shelter with logs and leaves and starting a fire with wood friction. I knew the longest I could survive in the forest alone with limited supplies would be three minutes, not three days. Yet as I was absorbing the beauty of nature around us, I found a long-buried childish enthusiasm for adventure in the deepest recesses of my brain. I do feel the pull of the wild.

After endless stretches of deserted lands, we come upon a small gas station that sits stark against the darkening pale sky, like a forgotten edifice from another era. Tyler pulls next to one of the four gas pumps and gets out of the car.

"Anybody need to pee?" I ask, thinking that this might be our last chance to use a decent bathroom.

Emily grimaces. "No, thanks. I choose not to get kidnapped."

"I can hold it," says Jay, and Noah also turns me down to impress his siblings.

"Let's go pee." I talk specifically to my youngest. "There's no need to hold it. It's another forty minutes' drive, at least."

"I don't want to get kidnapped either," he says, grabbing his blanket and leaning against Emily.

"See what you did?" I have a few more words for my daughter, but Tyler's voice catches my ears. His door is open and the alarm is beeping. I pull out the key to stop the noise so that I can hear better.

The man Tyler is talking to appears to be the gas station attendant in dark gray overalls and a baseball cap displaying the gas station's logo.

"Are you here from California?" the attendant asks.

Tyler folds his arms over his chest. "Is it that obvious?"

The guy nods at the license plate, resulting in Tyler making an effort to downplay his lack of observation.

"Yeah, from Woodland Hills. It's in Southern California. We drove up here to stay for a few days in a yurt," Tyler says.

"Which one? There are a few scattered in the woods."

"The Bell Lake Yurt."

"Beautiful place. Very peaceful. You won't have any cell phone service there, though."

"That's the point. We're here for an off-the-grid vacation."

The guy cranes his neck to look inside the car. Suspicion, like an electric current, runs through my body.

"Got any dogs there with you?"

"No, we left him at home. We didn't want him to get lost in the woods."

"Smart. Dogs get lost all the time up in the mountains. They chase after a rabbit or a squirrel. And whoosh. They're gone. Never find their way back. Sometimes they get snatched up by a predator. It's not unheard of."

They exchange a few more words and share a laugh, but I miss most of them because my head is fuming.

Tyler finishes pumping the gas and offers his hand to the attendant. "Thanks, man. Appreciate the help. See you when we get back."

"Have fun! And take care."

Tyler gets into his seat with a new sense of excitement growing around him like a bubble. "Nice dude."

"Why did you tell him where we're going?" I snap, bursting his bubble before the door slams shut.

"What are you talking about?"

I wait until we are on the road before continuing. "We don't know these people, and you just told him that we would be in a yurt, unprotected, with no way of calling for help. What if he comes after us with his buddies in the middle of the night, and they break into the yurt?"

"Why would they do that?" Tyler looks at me as if I'd lost my mind. I am the only reasonable adult here, it seems.

"I don't know, to take our money, or whatever reason people do bad stuff. Why did that guy attack George? You can't answer these questions with logic."

"I think you're overreacting. People in Montana are more friendly than in California, and they just like to talk to visitors without having an elaborate plan to get over on them."

"I think you're very naïve," I conclude, not because I have nothing more to say, but because I sense my kids are picking up on my worry. I don't want to freak them out, but that doesn't mean I don't feel the tension in my chest from Tyler foolishly giving away our personal information to a stranger.

The final thirty minutes of the drive takes us along dirt roads that climb deep into the mountain. The woods are getting thicker with each minute, and the temperature continues to drop. I catch myself holding my breath a few times—either from the anticipation or my concern about the gas station incident. I'm not sure.

The carpet of green at the feet of majestic pine trees is thick, and the vines and shrubs connecting them create an illusion as if we are entering the world of Narnia. The kids are still annoyed about the long drive and the prospect of our next few days without electronics, while Tyler keeps reminding them to look out the window and enjoy the view.

"I booked us two hours at the hot springs in Norris on Wednesday," Tyler says with a reassuring smile. "It's a small town about a forty-minute drive from our yurt."

I know he says this to make our vacation plan seem more civil and conventional. This trip is his first outdoor adventure, and the weight of being responsible for the rest of us has been sitting heavily on his shoulders, though he's been trying his best to hide it from me. His mom opposed this trip and used every weapon in her arsenal to talk Tyler out of it. Now Tyler wears his need to prove himself like an armor. I'm not sure which desire is stronger in him—to prove himself to his mother or to us.

"Sounds great!" I say, because even though we haven't even experienced any discomfort yet, I'm already yearning to soak in hot water. As an afterthought, I loop my arm around his and lean against his shoulder. He is trying his best to step into Connor's shoes, and I don't give him enough credit for that. He also needs to know that we are good. We must be if we want to survive the next few days.

"I know you're worried about our safety, but I think you're a little paranoid," Tyler says carefully, and I wish he didn't keep chewing on this bone. "That's what living near LA for years does to you. We learn to look for the angle in everyone who approaches us. We hide when the doorbell rings. We watch the mailman on the Ring app to catch him doing something wrong. We install cameras around our houses to be alerted to intruders or mailbox robbers."

"I'm paranoid? You still live with your mother because she's scared to be alone." The moment the words leave my mouth, I know I shouldn't have said them. I look away from Tyler and bite my lip.

"I live with you now," he says, somewhat downcast.

I don't want to fight with Tyler. He is trying so hard to fit the image he thinks I need, and it feels wrong to keep bringing him down just because he isn't perfect. I'm not just older than him, I'm also more independent and experienced in relationships. My parents didn't hold my hand after I left the house. I relied on Connor, and he leaned on me. The two of us against the world. Until we weren't.

I push earbuds in my ears and look out the window to realize that the thick forest has swallowed us completely. The charming woodland has slowly turned into an ominous, impenetrable forest. I think I see a deer standing frozen in the thickets. I alert the kids to it, but when I look back, it's gone.

I may have imagined it.

We come upon a crescent-shaped dirt path, like an appendix next to the road that continues to curve higher up the mountainside. Tyler navigates the car into the spot in the cradle of giant pine trees and kills the engine. "I recognize this place from the pictures. We're supposed to park here."

"Where is the yurt?" asks Emily. Her face is against the window as she scans the land around us.

"According to the instructions, it's a bit of a walk from here," says Tyler, examining a sheet of paper.

Jay points at the tower of bags and boxes behind him in the trunk. "How are we going to carry all this stuff?"

"There is a wheelbarrow at the yurt. We can use it to haul everything we need back and forth."

I jump out of the car to get going. The soil is moist underneath my feet. The air feels thin and chilly and surprisingly quiet. I put on my parka as I watch Jay and Noah running into the woods. It takes discipline to subdue my worries and let them out of my sight. To distract myself, I pop the trunk open and start taking out the luggage. Joyful screams echo through the land, giving me a shiver.

"Can you go check on them?" I ask Tyler.

He drops a suitcase on the ground. "They're fine. They're happy."

I give a closed-mouthed smile. I don't know why I am on edge, but I am.

"Will you give us a hand?" I ask Emily. She is taking pictures with her phone while chewing her gum like a maniac. She pretends she doesn't hear me.

"Give that to me." Tyler takes the food bag from my hand, sets it on the ground, and pulls me to him. He kisses me on the lips—small peppering little pecks. I do my best to embrace the moment because this is supposed to be a fun vacation and I'm ruining it with my worrying.

Emily's chewing becomes louder in my ears when I realize that the boys' voices went silent. The first thought that pops into my mind is Tyler exposing us to that stranger at the gas station. As if there weren't enough danger lurking in these woods, he had to add the human element.

I separate us, not with hostility but with enough force for him to let me go.

"Let's get moving. It'll be dark soon," I say and slip the pepper spray into my pocket.

ALEX

"How about your father? How was your relationship with him?" I ask Paul because he seems weary talking about his much older brother's successful life, and the last thing I want is to force the first convicted felon who decided to sit down with me to quit on me before my book is finished.

Paul scoffs as he scratches the back of his head. As he moves his hand away, subtle white flakes fall to his shoulder.

"He was okay, I guess. A lazy bastard, really. I mean, I never saw him doing the things around the house he demanded of me. He only watched TV in his free time." He purposefully avoids looking into my eyes. Some say the unmistakable sign of someone lying is when they look to the left as they talk. Paul holds his gaze to the left as much as he does to his right. I can't read him, so I write everything he says down in my notes. I'll fact-check his statements later.

"Did he have a steady job?" I don't know why I ask this irrelevant question. I could search the internet for this trivial information to fill my book with details, but perhaps the reporter in me wants to keep the ball rolling.

"He did for a while. He was a manager at a feed-and-seed store in town. Not exactly a brain surgeon profession, but he made decent money, I guess." Paul says this with a smirk, as if he thought less of his old man for earning his money with a nine-to-five job. It's an unwarranted criticism from a high school dropout.

"But after his third heart surgery, he went on disability, and that was the end of his career." He puts "career" in air quotes.

"I read about your father's heart transplant. It couldn't have been easy to support a family while battling a serious health condition."

Paul puts both his hands on the edge of the table and leans toward me. "Maybe you should interview my mother about that," he says with force. "She never thought my dad deserved a heart transplant. You know how much our insurance was billed for the surgery? It was a million bucks. For a fucking heart, for Christ's sake!"

"Would you rather have had him die?"

"That's not what I'm saying, but he certainly didn't do anything to prevent his heart failure. Even after the transplant, he was drinking and smoking weed. As long as he had a bag of M&M's or Pringles in his hands, he was happy to sit on the couch all day and watch TV. There were years when I was scared to show my face in our living room because he always found something to yell about as soon as he saw me. He called me a disgusting zit face. A loser. All I heard was I'd never amount to anything. Because when he was my age, blah, blah, blah…as if I ever wanted to be like him. Having my father around was like listening to my mother's clone, singing the same old song."

"Do you think he was projecting his own failure onto you?"

Paul shrugs. His face relaxes. "Dunno. He was a piece of shit, if you ask me."

"Did he ever abuse you physically?"

He tenses up again as if the mere suggestion of this would make him less of a man.

"I'd have broken his hand if he dared." He is short and firm. I can't tell if he is lying or telling the truth. Based on various studies, men are less likely than women to admit prolonged abuse committed against them by the hands of others. If someone exploited me, I suppose I'd feel angry with myself for not being strong enough to prevent it. I'd consider myself weak—less of a man—if I let bad things happen to me. But I'm not a psychologist, and I could be wrong about Paul's reasons. Besides, my ability to understand abuse is impaired. It's difficult for me to fathom how someone can hate their parents. I grew up in a loving home where basic chores and responsibilities were in equality with praise and rewards. I've always believed that people stand up against injustice, driven by their moral conscience, but they can only understand someone's suffering to the furthest extent if they walk in their shoes. We can pretend compassion, especially if that's what society is demanding of us. But what will become of us if we lose our moral compass? Paul seems to have never found it. His parents didn't draw clear lines between right and wrong. It's only my first day of meeting with this murderer, but I'm starting to feel sorry for him.

I shake my head and rub my face with both hands to get my head back in the game.

"All right. I think I get the picture of how it was for you growing up with your parents. A few solid examples, with details from your childhood, would certainly help move readers to your side. But let's leave that for another day. How about we fast-forward a bit? How did you get to know Jennifer Parker?"

Paul's entire complexion lights up with anticipation. This is the story he's been waiting to tell.

He rubs his chin. "Well, that's a long and interesting story. You should order us something to eat first. Chick-fil-A?" He smacks his lips. "Or a good juicy burger?"

JENNIFER

The grass is a different type of green on the mountain than what we see in the city. Compared to the uniform green carpets we have back home, the ground vegetation here grows more organically and parades in brilliant shades of jade. I find beauty in the random flow of nature that gives me a sense of peace.

I inhale deeply as I walk on the path toward the yurt. The forest is alive around us as the colors shine brightly from the sunlight or fade into gray from the migrating clouds in the pale blue sky. I spot random little birds that follow our activities as if they haven't decided if we are friends or foes.

Jay is leading the way, pushing the wheelbarrow with Noah sitting inside, cradling the sleeping bags. I watch them treating each other nicely as they race along the narrow dirt path. Jay is making the ride an exciting one for his little brother, and my heart swells with pride. I can't remember the last time he did anything with his little brother voluntarily. "What am I supposed to do with him? He's a little kid," he'd say to me whenever I call him out for ignoring his brother. To be honest, I can't blame him for not finding much in common with Noah. The age difference between my boys is nine years. One more year and Jay will be off to college. Noah is still in elementary school.

Loaded with two coolers and a massive backpack, Tyler shuffles in front of me. His shoulders slope from the weight, but he doesn't complain. He can never let go of his competition with Connor, even when he's not here to taunt him.

I take up the rear. The food cans rattle against each other in the bags I carry. So much for blending in with nature.

As our path curves to the right, the forest opens ahead of me as if someone pulled aside a stage curtain. There is a bench built on the edge of a small overlook, and I stop there to take in the breathtaking view of the sentinel snowcapped mountains and the untouched valley below. The reality of how alone we truly are on this mountaintop hits me. There are no quaint little villages in the valley with gift shops. No oversized million-dollar second homes built in the mountainsides. This place is nothing but unspoiled, raw wilderness.

"Mom! Come on!" I hear Emily's voice echo.

With a better sense of how vast and majestic this place is, I tighten my grip on the bags and get back on the path.

I'm the last to reach the clearing that houses the yurt and the campfire area. This valley looks much bigger in life than in the pictures Tyler showed me online.

I consider setting down my bags to spend a moment recording a video for my followers, but I'm too tired to bother.

"Isn't this fantastic?" Tyler exclaims.

I have to admit that his positive attitude never wavers.

"Let's settle inside before it gets dark."

I make it to the wooden patio that wraps around the circular base of the heavy-duty tent. Thick wood panels and metal hardware create the frame and the cone-shaped roof over our heads.

"Look, we have windows," Tyler says as he rolls up the plastic cover and ties it with a rope.

There is a single door with a padlock, which, considering how easy it would be for someone to cut their way in with a knife, seems pointless.

I pat the plastic-sheet-covered yurt to feel its thickness. It seems sturdy enough to keep out predators but not humans intending to break in. I think of the man at the gas station again, but I don't bring it up.

"Do you like it?" Tyler asks as he relieves me of my bags and sets them on the bench. He turns me around and wraps his arms around my chest from behind. "Look at that view!"

I allow myself to relax in my boyfriend's embrace and enjoy the spectacular view that reminds me of the images in my childhood magazines. When I hold my breath, I can hear a distant creek gurgling and the whispering wind between the forest crowns. Majestic pine trees surround us as they stand erect on sloped hillsides in dense clusters, bracing themselves against the wind. Trees in all shapes and sizes face the valley like spectators in an arena. I wonder how many wildlife battles they have witnessed over the years.

The tranquility of it all makes me feel at peace.

"Look at all this firewood!" Jay yells up to us from the clearing.

I lean over the sturdy railing to look at the layers of logs stacked neatly underneath the patio. Jay jerks out a thick limb of wood and starts chopping it with an ax with so much energy, it's as if he's been waiting for this moment his entire life. Noah is right behind him, running in circles on a patch of grass and playing airplane in the wind. His game leads him to an assembly of a table, two wooden benches, and a firepit by the forest line. "Can we do s'mores?" he shouts back up the hill.

"Of course we can, honey," I yell back.

"See? This was a great idea. C'mon, you have to admit it." Tyler is so cute when he is proud of himself. The same fuzzy sensation fills me that I used to feel when we first started dating.

Spending time with a new man after being married to the same person for almost two decades wasn't easy for me. I didn't think I was worthy of a new relationship. Who would want to date a mother of three in her forties? Why would anyone take on the responsibility of a family to be with me? But my early worries were in vain. Somehow Tyler never seemed to mind carrying the package that came with being in a relationship with me. He stayed against the odds, against his mother's warnings.

I press my face against his cheek and pull in my shoulders. I'm like a little bird now under his protection. He likes it when I make him feel like a man, a provider. Sometimes I think he needs me to help him through the painful and emotional task of detaching himself from his overbearing mother. If we had met fifteen years earlier, I might have encouraged his efforts more vigorously, but the older my boys get, the more I think of the day when they will fly out of *my* nest and start their own families. How would I feel if Jay only called me once a month and no longer asked my opinion on anything? Maybe I'll latch onto my adult kids in the same overbearing way Tyler's mother does. I push the negative thoughts from my head because it's not the time to think about a troubling future. This is the time to celebrate life and our family.

"Oh, yuck." Emily rounds the yurt to intrude on my special moment with Tyler. "The shitter is disgusting."

Tyler releases me. "It can't be. I saw the pictures online. The toilet looked pretty decent."

"Yeah, right." Emily taps on the AirPod in her ear, rolling her eyes. "You can't put a fancy toilet seat over a hole of shit and call it a toilet. It's still a hole of stinking shit."

"Emily, language, please!!" I say without the tone of reprimand. "What did you expect? You knew we wouldn't have indoor plumbing and running water here," I point out. "People in rural India have to use toilets like this every day," I add for good measure.

When my mother used the example of starving children in Africa and China as a way to get me to eat my dinner, I had sworn I'd never do the same to my kids. Yet here I go.

She rewards me with her special eye-roll she's developed by living her privileged life. "Good thing we don't live in India."

"There is no door," yells Jayden, who has dropped the ax and run to the outhouse to verify his sister's claim. He seems more amused by this development than upset.

"At least you won't need to use a ton of air freshener to mask the smell," I shout back to him, amused.

I catch Tyler gazing at me lovingly. "What?" I say.

"I knew you'd come around." He takes a deep breath, picks me up, and spins me around. "Isn't this amazing!"

I always feel awkward when he shows affection to me in front of the kids. It's not guilt, but I don't know, discomfort, maybe.

I clap my hands. "Okay, let's unpack, then eat something, and what do you say we discover the neighborhood before we call it a night."

Tyler pulls out a tactical flashlight and points it at the kids. "Who's up for a night hike with flashlights?"

Only Jayden raises his hand.

* * * * *

After we carry our stuff inside, we each choose a bed. I take the bottom bunk underneath Emily, and Tyler picks the one below Jay. Noah is happy to sleep on the futon by himself. It's the closest bed to the door, so I expect him to crawl into my sleeping bag when the lights go out, but for now, I let him feel like a big boy.

The yurt has a small dresser-like cabinet with two shelves retrofitted to hold cups and plates, an aluminum-sheet-covered counter to prepare food, and a double-door pantry to store pots and pans. A two-burner propane stove sits on a small table next to the cabinet, also protected by an aluminum sheet to prevent fires.

While Jay and Tyler bring in stacks of wood and commence lighting a fire in the cast iron fireplace, I make everybody a peanut butter sandwich with strawberry jam, cut up a few apples, and set a box of nonperishable milk on the table for everyone.

I'm already done with putting everything away and cleaning up the crumbs to make our yurt less inviting for mice, but the logs are still lying dormant and smoking in the chamber. The failure to get the fire going gives the boys another reason to bicker.

"Seriously, Ty, you suck at this," Jay grumbles, nudging my boyfriend out of the way. "Let me do it."

At moments like this, I wonder if my children would be more respectful to a man I chose as my partner if he were my senior, not someone younger than me. My father always says that it's our actions that earn us respect and not our age.

I decide not to intervene and let the boys work out their differences. But if there's something Tyler hates, it's being shown up by a teenager.

When after a few minutes, hungry flames lash up from the neatly stacked wood inside the fireplace and the smoke leaves through the chimney instead of choking us out in the yurt, Tyler doesn't view Jay with the pride of a father, but he sulks instead. I should have eased the tension with a few lighthearted jokes and comments. But I didn't, and it's too late now.

While we eat dinner, Tyler sits at the table with a tense posture, avoiding everyone's eyes. He is a great teacher, fun company, and a fantastic lover. He is not good at outdoorsy stuff, so what? Nobody is perfect. Maybe this trip wasn't a good idea.

After dinner, the tension is still vivid, and the yurt is too small to contain it. I urge the family to take a leisurely walk outside to air out our heads. As we don our windbreakers and coats and arm ourselves with flashlights, I pull Jay aside and ask him to dial it back a little. The only thing I achieve with my request is to make Jay upset with me. I can't win.

When we step outside the yurt and onto the balcony, a drastic change in the weather confronts us. The sun has ducked behind the ridge of the mountains and the valley turned still.

Tyler hands a canister of bear spray to Emily.

Emily points at the dirt trail disappearing into a dark, dense forest. "There is no way I'm walking into that."

Jayden is happy to take the hunting knife, and Noah proudly carries the spear Jay carved for him during dinner. "Don't be a sissy, sis," Jay teases her.

"If you want to stay here, I understand. But I need to move after sitting in the car for two days," I say.

Emily needs the exercise too, but she'll accuse me of calling her fat if I dare mention it. I don't know when society started believing that the suggestion of fresh air and exercise equated to an insult of calling someone out on their body type, but that's where we stand. It's easier for me to trick her into thinking she has a choice than use force and face pushback.

"I'm not staying here alone," she says, looking behind herself as if she had seen someone in the shadows. My paranoia is rubbing off on the kids.

I only bring an umbrella on the walk. I have this idea that I can deter predators by opening and closing it at them.

I insist we lock the door, and even though Tyler thinks it's silly since nobody else is on this mountain besides us, he humors me.

We stroll down the hillside and cross the meadow. The air is chilly and heavy with moisture. The ground is soft and spongy underneath our feet.

Noah is running ahead, holding up his spear like a Viking warrior going into battle. Emily plugs her ears with her AirPods, pulls the hood over her head, and slips her hands into her pockets. She wasn't always a moody teenager. She's only begun blessing us with her attitude these past couple of years.

Connor told me more than once that I didn't have the right to break up our family when the kids were at a vulnerable age, but he was the one who became a stranger in our house, not me. From my standpoint, Connor is a better father now since he's realized what he lost and wants to get it back.

Once we reach the forest line, I count three different paths that lead into the dense woods from the clearing—each would take us into the land of the wild, territory of bears, wolves, and mountain lions, so in the sense of caution, it doesn't matter which one we take.

"Bella's family is going to Hawaii this spring break while I'm crapping in the woods and eating canned food," Emily grumbles as she walks beside me.

At this point, it's best to ignore her and let her come around on her own terms. Nature has its way of crawling into your heart and making you a fan.

I never traveled much with my family growing up. Then all too fast I became an adult with responsibilities and forgot the promises I made myself as a kid. Being here feels like I'm honoring my childhood dreams.

I shoot an appreciative smile at Tyler. He must have thought it was a signal because he offers to record me walking in the woods for my followers.

"Not now. Let me enjoy this moment with you guys," I tell him, and he looks confused. Amused, but confused.

The soil is muddy here, with occasional puddles along the way, telling of a recent rainstorm. We stay on the main fire road because the woods are dense and eerie in the dying light of the day.

We don't venture far due to an abundance of fresh animal footprints preserved in the mud. It gives us a good idea of the number of apex predators in these parts of the wilderness, and it's better not to disturb them during their hunting time.

After a thirty-minute walk to get our blood flowing and stretch our limbs, we return to the yurt, where it's nice and warm thanks to the wood-burning fireplace.

As we relieve ourselves of the extra layers, I remember that we don't have a bathroom with indoor plumbing. I ask Jay and Emily to bring water in from the reservoir tank outside to heat up on the stove. Tyler hangs the outdoor shower with a bag full of water by the fire, hoping it will be warm by the morning for us to take a shower, but we still need warm water to wash our faces and brush our teeth before bed.

While the kids do the dishes in the plastic bin, I make some tea. Then I walk Emily and Noah to the outhouse. Once they're finished with their business, they run back to the yurt, leaving me alone in the dark. I open the umbrella and set it on the ground next to the flashlight by the outhouse's doorframe. Squatting over the pot, I stare at the hillside in front of me that climbs steep and is overgrown with bushes and tangled plants. If a mountain lion decides to say hi while I'm in this vulnerable state, there is no way I could protect myself.

I use the racket of two little blackbirds engaging in a dance that could be either a display of aggression or love to steer my mind to calmer water.

When I hear the sound of branches snapping in the distance, I speed-walk back to the yurt as a chill dances up my spine. I've never been surrounded by so much darkness. There is always light in the city and the suburbs.

On the balcony, I run into Tyler's arms with an urgency, as if someone were chasing me.

"There you are. I thought you'd been eaten."

I rub my face. "Stop talking like that. You're really freaking me out."

"How can you be freaked out in a peaceful place like this. Look at that sky! Have you ever seen so many bright stars?"

The sky is a vast black sea, and the stars look like billions of flickering candles. "It doesn't look real," I say, putting a hand on my racing heart.

"See the big dipper there?" Tyler takes my hand and points it at the most recognizable constellation. "Look, the top left corner points toward the road and the town. If we are lost, we only have to follow the stars."

"If I get lost in these woods at night, I'll die."

"Come on, guys, enough *cringiness*. Let's play a game!" Emily calls out to us.

The solar lights inside the yurt illuminate over the dining table. The kids are settled in their chairs with a set of UNO cards spread out in front of them.

"Stay," Tyler teases. I know he is eager to preserve our romantic moment, but we haven't played a family game for ages. Romance can wait.

"Come," I tease back, holding out an inviting hand.

He complies, and we join the kids.

We sip hot fruit tea and snack on peanuts while playing cards. Without music, passing cars, and sirens, it's deadly silent in our shelter, save the crackling of the wood in the fireplace. For a moment, I forget that we are in the middle of nowhere in a defenseless tent. For a moment, I allow myself to cherish the sounds of my children's laughter.

Family games have a way of building bridges between people. I watch Jay and Tyler reversing each other back and forth like competing college buddies. Their former bickering is long forgotten, at least for right now.

"Mom, Noah keeps cheating," Emily cries.

"How can you cheat in UNO?" I ask, ruffling my youngest's hair.

"He sits on his cards." Emily points at her brother's lap.

"Shut up, Em! You cheat! Not me!" Noah retorts with a flaming-red face.

"It's just a game, Emily. Don't take it so seriously," I say soothingly.

"Can you be any more obvious about who is your favorite child?" Emily groans, folding her arms over her chest and leaning back in her chair.

"Don't be ridiculous. Jay is my favorite," I joke to ease the tension, but it backfires.

JENNIFER

"Great. That makes me feel a lot better."

Jay laughs into his sister's face. "Ha!"

Emily pushes him away.

"Relax, I'm teasing you. I love you all the same. No favorites."

Emily is the first to throw in the towel as she drops her cards and leaves the table.

Tyler smashes his soda can and throws it into the trash bin. "Come on, guys. We'll be here for four days. Let's not kill each other the first day."

Jay pushes up from his chair. "I'm going to bed too. I've had enough of this day."

I turn to Tyler. "Why are kids so sensitive?"

"They aren't sensitive. They're spoiled."

My eyes enlarge. "What are you saying? I'm a bad mother?"

"No, but these kids have never experienced hardship. Too much comfort makes people sensitive."

"Oh, you're an expert on raising kids now?"

"Okay, I think it's better if we all go to bed. It has been a long day. Everyone's tired." Tyler nods at me and leaves the table, too, leaving me wondering how a fun family night could turn into a disaster so fast.

Tyler calls for volunteers to go with him to the outhouse for a final visit, but no one's interested.

"Last chance," he says as he grabs his jacket off the hanger by the door. "You won't want to go outside in the middle of the night alone if you need to pee, trust me," he warns, but it does little to convince the rest of us.

When he walks out the door, a terrible feeling of dread descends on me. I keep glancing at the utter darkness through the glass panel on the door as I assist Noah in brushing his teeth. I've been trying hard all day not to think of the fact that we are alone in the wilderness, at the mercy of the elements, with no means to call for help, but the thought keeps wiggling itself into my mind. Maybe it's the mother in me that worries too much. Maybe it's because I'm a soft, comfort-loving, spoiled city woman.

The bunk bed creaks from Emily settling into her sleeping bag. "Can we get carbon monoxide poisoning from the fireplace?" she asks, her head hanging over the edge.

"No, we can't. The smoke goes out through the chimney," I explain as I pull a pajama top over Noah's head.

"But a spider can crawl into your bed and bite your face," Jay says in a sinister voice.

"Stop it, you idiot! I hate you," Emily screams, throwing her socks at her brother. "Mom, tell him to stop saying things like that."

"Okay, settle down. There are no spiders here. Look how clean this place is."

"Clean, my ass," remarks Jayden.

"Jayden Scott Parker!" I snap at him. "Watch your mouth!"

"It's true." He gives me the puppy eyes.

"All right. Let's not talk like this in front of Tyler. He's desperate to impress you guys."

"Then he should have taken us to Hawaii," sneers Emily.

I frown at her. "Everybody goes to Hawaii. What's so special about it?"

"I don't know, luxury hotels, room service, hot baths, sandy beaches, warm water, massage, facials."

I lift the blanket on the futon for Noah to slip underneath. "Okay, princess," I say to Emily.

"Why? We can afford it."

I kiss Noah good-night. "This vacation isn't about money."

"Clearly," she groans and zips herself into her sleeping bag.

I sit down on my bed and clamp my hands between my thighs. It's been two long days of driving and intermittent stress to get here. The weight of it all is beginning to settle on my shoulders. I want a hot bath, a glass of wine, and a good movie. Instead, I sip at my tea and put on a pair of thermal socks.

My heart almost leaps out of my chest when a blood-curdling scream rips into the night.

"What is it?" I call out to Noah in panic, who is sitting up in his bed with a look of terror on his face.

I follow his gaze to the door, where a hooded figure appears like a horror movie poster pressed against the glass. Out of instinct, I jump to my son and pull him to me. Then the door opens, and I snatch the hunting knife from the table.

"It's just me." Tyler barges inside the yurt, hunched, hands up defensively in front of him. "Easy. I just wanted to scare you."

My grip loosens, and the knife drops back onto the table. "Well, you've succeeded."

"Sorry, Noah. I didn't mean to freak you out. I thought it would be a good joke."

"A terrible joke." As I hold Noah in my arms, I'm hyperventilating. "I've got this terrible feeling now. What if those guys from the gas station come up while we're sleeping tonight?"

Tyler kneels in front of me and takes my hand. "Nobody will come here. You've been reading too many thrillers. It was a stupid joke. I'm sorry, Noah, if I scared you."

"Le douche," Jay murmurs from the top bunk. We all heard it, but none of us address it.

Noah starts crying. "I don't want to sleep here anymore."

I hold him with my shaking hands.

"It's okay," I say. "Nobody is here to hurt us. It was a bad joke."

Tyler closes the curtain on the door and pulls in the latch. "See, nobody could get in here even if they wanted to."

"Do you want to sleep with me?" I ask Noah.

He nods and slips his legs out from underneath his blanket.

We lie in the sleeping bag together as I watch the stars through the circular skylight at the top of the yurt roof, thinking that Tyler is right. I've been gripped by fear because the civilized world tells me that we are not safe anywhere. I need to let go of the fear. I need to free myself and be one with nature. I need to be a cool and collected mom. And a cool girlfriend. Otherwise, I'll become one of those influencers who talk the talk but don't walk the walk.

ALEX

The California State Prison in Lancaster squats on 260 acres of desert land, surrounded by a few swathes of single-family home developments. Driving north on Highway 14, before I took my exit onto W Avenue, I remember passing a Wendy's and a Jack in the Box, but I don't recall seeing a Chick-fil-A.

Paul must know that the visitation ends at 4:30 p.m., and sending me on a fool's errand to find him a chicken sandwich would end our session for today. He is playing games with me, trying to stretch our time together by stalling and withholding key information. He sees himself as a cunning, calculating schemer who can manipulate people. In his letters, I've noticed that Paul is quick to make empty promises and admit responsibility for his actions, but his words are meaningless because they aren't followed up with actions. It's a defense mechanism—saying things he thinks people in charge around him want to hear. But he doesn't mean a word of it.

My disappointment is rising. My previous feelings of sympathy for Paul go up in smoke, and once again, I see this murderer for who he is: a simple-minded criminal with ideas of grandeur about himself. I'm surprised Paul didn't ask me for steak and lobster. I'm sure he thinks he deserves it.

With less than half an hour remaining in our meeting and no Chick-fil-A nearby, I promise to bring Paul a burger to our next meeting, hoping to finish our interview without talking about food.

I've driven almost two hours in traffic to meet him today, and I want to get the most out of my time here. But Paul dismisses me by saying he doesn't want to miss his outdoor break and gets out of his chair with a scornful look.

Despite his efforts, I don't feel guilty for failing his request, but I am annoyed.

I wait until the guard ushers Paul out of the meeting room, then I head down to the visitor center and schedule a new appointment in three days' time.

The lack of accomplishment keeps me in a state of restlessness as I drive home to my studio apartment in Santa Monica to face its miserable emptiness. When I signed the lease two years ago, I didn't consider how difficult it would be to keep this overpriced bachelor pad on my own. Back then, I was driven by my ideas and drowning in ambition. I spent every waking moment researching shocking crimes and corresponding with inmates. Back then, I browsed expensive furniture online to make my first place look cool.

The pictures in my head included hip furniture, voice-controlled gadgets installed in every room, remote-controlled blinds, a talking fridge stocked with organic food. Now, after the childish dream is long gone and reality has set in, not having to ask my relatives for financial support when rent is late is the only thing that excites me. Also my focus has shifted in the past year, and money and fame no longer motivate me. I've found a higher calling. Or it found me, I should say.

I open the fridge to be confronted with its gaping emptiness. Then I go through the cabinets in search of a forgotten can of soup, but no such luck. A walk on the sunny streets to the grocery store would clear my head and bring me out of my vampire-like state, but it's hell-like heat outside—dry and hot, and I'm too irritated to deal with that kind of weather right now. I drink a glass of tap water to quench my hunger. Then I sit down at the IKEA desk, which is kind of hip but undoubtedly cheap, and open my laptop. I start typing up my notes. When I'm finished, I realize how little content I collected today. I need more—much more.

A pinned note on the wall with the name and phone number of Paul's brother flaps from the air conditioning, catching my eye. I've been putting off calling him, but it's time to pick up the phone.

Josh McKeehan doesn't share the same last name as Paul. They don't have the same father. But thanks to an old, inactive Facebook account Paul used to have in his early twenties, I found Josh listed as his brother, among a few other relatives. Only Josh wrote back to me when I messaged various family members of Paul's, mentioning the book I was writing about his brother's life and infamous crime.

Since then, we've talked on the phone a few times, but never in person. My initial observation of Josh was that he is a decent man and a person of reason. He understands that some stories need to be told. He always sounded heartbroken over his brother's actions and seemed to be bearing some of the blame. With a bit of persuading, he agreed to share his side of the story, but I've been so fixated on my first meeting with Paul that I never followed up on his offer. No better time than the present, I tell myself, and punch his number into my phone.

"Hi, this is Josh."

"Hi, Josh. I'm Alex Fox. We talked a few months ago on the phone. I'm writing a book about your brother."

"Oh, yes. What can I help you with?"

"I'm sorry to call you out of the blue after all this time, but I wanted to see if you're still up for that interview we talked about?"

"Um, sure. When?" I hear kids yelling in the background.

"I'm available the next two days if you can squeeze me in?"

He takes his time to answer. "Did you see my brother?"

"Yes, I did. I visited him today."

"How is he?"

"Better than you'd think."

The line goes silent again before I hear Josh's voice. "Does he show any remorse?"

"No, but we only touched on basic stuff today. Things like his childhood, his relationship with his parents. We didn't talk about the Parkers and Tyler Malone yet."

Josh takes his time to answer again. "I can do tomorrow at two if that works for you."

"Done. Where would you like to meet?"

"Why don't you come to my house. It's more private here. I'll text you the address."

"Perfect! Thank you, Josh. I'll be there."

"All right. I'll see you tomorrow."

"And Josh," I say quickly to catch him before he hangs up the phone, "I want you to know that whatever happened in your house, whatever the reason you asked him to leave, Paul didn't tell me yet."

"Um. Okay. We'll talk tomorrow."

After I set my phone on the kitchen counter, I pour myself a healthy glass of Honey Jack Daniel's to celebrate the final ending of a disappointing day. I drop onto the secondhand futon I picked up from Craigslist and tell Alexa to shuffle my "liked" songs. I close my eyes and pretend the apartment has a built-in surround sound system and not the small portable Bluetooth speaker I bought on sale at Costco. When the buzz hits, I order a pizza on DoorDash, and while I'm waiting, I check my emails even though I know that I won't see any messages that would interest me.

JENNIFER

I wake up at the crack of dawn to find Tyler's sleeping bag empty. The scent of fresh coffee lingers in the air. The door is closed, but the lock hangs undone. The curtain on the window panel is drawn, but I can see a figure moving outside through the thin fabric in the awakening sunlight.

Noah is lying on his back next to me, taking up most of my sleeping bag. I was out last night, dead to the world, and didn't notice how uncomfortable of a position I'd been in. I can now feel in my neck and back the consequences of sleeping in a twisted form.

I crack my bones and rub my face, trying hard not to wake my youngest.

My father would be proud of me if he saw this place. He's been telling me that money changed me, that I've become soft and entitled. My mother assumes that by me hiring help to clean the house and landscape the yard, I was robbing my children of learning hard work and the sweet sensation of achievement that accompanied it.

"Chores aren't designed to punish children, Jen," she would tell me when I countered her criticism on my mothering style with stories of how much I hated working around the house as a kid. "We task our children because that's how they learn life skills, a sense of contributing to the family and neighborhood, doing things they don't want to but that must be done nonetheless. Equally important, they see the result of their hard work, and it gives them a sense of achievement and self-worth."

"So, the reason you guys used my sister and me as free child labor was to make us feel worthy?"

"You're mocking me, but look at you now. You are a hardworking, dedicated woman with integrity, and your children see it. Children pay more attention to what we do rather than what we say. Connor understands this. You used to know it too. Now you are simply throwing money at everything—like that ever solved anything—and letting your kids be lazy."

Look at us now, Mom! I think with a grin. *We are living like early explorers.*

I slip out of bed without waking Noah. I check on Emily in the top bunk. She's sleeping with her mouth open, drooling, the blanket tucked to her chin.

Not Jay. He is hot-blooded, and at some time during the night, he took off his shirt and is now sleeping bare-chested.

It's chilly in the yurt. While we were sleeping, the fire died down. It seems none of us thought of getting up in the middle of the night to feed the fire with more wood.

I take the blanket from Noah's futon and lay it on Jay. He doesn't stir.

I fish out a cotton hoodie from my bag and pull it over my head. I'm still chilly, so I throw on my North Face jacket too.

I check the French press on the stove for coffee. There is enough left in it for me to pour myself a full cup.

I gently open the door and slip outside to join Tyler on the balcony.

"What are you doing up so early?" I ask as I set my mug on the railing and zip up my jacket. Despite the morning sunlight, it's bone-chilling cold out here. I can see my breath.

Tyler kisses my forehead. "I didn't sleep well last night. I was restless. How did you sleep?"

"Like a rock." I lean against him and sip my coffee. "What kept you up?"

Ty gazes toward the mountains and inhales thoughtfully, as if considering whether to tell me the truth or lie.

"I don't know." He chose neither.

"Are you thinking of your mother?"

He looks me in the eye. His lips stretch into a strange smile. "We talk every day, and it's just weird I haven't talked to her for days now."

Tyler is a sensitive man. I like this about him, but I'm not used to competing with another woman for attention. Connor never talked about his mother. We took the kids to visit her, had Easter egg hunts and Christmases together, but she wasn't an ever-apparent part of our lives. After a year together, I still can't figure out how to handle Tyler's obsession with his mother. Should I ignore it? Or snap him out of it?

"I think I know how you feel. I've been sharing my life with my followers for years, and now I feel detached too. It's like we're going through the same kind of withdrawal."

Tyler stiffens. "Surely, it's not the same. You do your channel to earn money. I'm talking about my mother."

I'm not ready for another fight, so I won't tell him how ridiculous he sounds. His pain is not the only pain out there. I have followers with whom I've been in contact for years. They aren't nameless avatars on my screen. They are my friends. We rely on each other. We feed off of each other. Maybe if his mother had done a better job raising a man instead of raising an admirer, then Tyler may have been more fit for real life. He has never been alone. He went from his mother to me, with a few occasional girlfriends in between.

"We need to restart the fire. It's freezing inside," I say to change the subject.

"I can do it," he says.

"I know you can." I don't know why I always feel the need to say encouraging words for every little thing he does as if he were just another child of mine, but it's getting tiresome.

We set down our coffees and walk to the woodpile below the yurt to get more logs.

"I saw a bunch of deer in the clearing this morning. Over there by that tree." Tyler stands tall, pointing at the lower parts of the valley.

"We should go on another hike today," I suggest, because the prospect of having countless empty hours ahead of us is looming over me.

We carry the logs in our arms back to the yurt. After placing our haul on the stone slab by the fireplace, I visit the outhouse with my umbrella. I walk calmly, not feeling yesterday's anxiety. The air is thick with dew, and the sounds of nature surround me. Twigs snapping. Birds chirping. Squirrels squeaking. Frogs croaking. But I'm not scared. I'm actually enjoying the symphony of life.

On my way back to the yurt, I glance at the barbeque area and notice a doe with a fawn grazing on the fresh grass. My presence petrifies them both, and we stare at each other for a while. I can hear my heart thumping in my chest from the excitement.

As if something from behind them in the shadows had startled them, the doe and the fawn jump with fear and rush across the clearing. I stand still, scanning the dense woods with my eyes. I hear a branch snap, and that's enough to send me racing back to the yurt.

Jayden is crouching by the fireplace and poking the fire. Tyler is sitting in the chair, watching him.

"How about I start on breakfast," I offer as I wash my hands in a small plastic tub. My heart's still racing. "I got eggs and bread and jam."

I kiss Jayden's head and smile at Tyler, who drains his coffee and stands up. "Maybe a little bit later. Jay and I are going on a walk."

My back stiffens. "I thought we'd all be going together."

"We'll be back in an hour. I'm sure you girls need extra time to get ready. With no fire last night, the shower water cooled off again, but I'll bring in more water for you to heat up."

I don't object because Jay looks ready to get out of the yurt and burn some energy and because I do need some privacy to clean myself up.

I run after them as they leave. "Don't forget the bear spray."

"It's a short walk," Tyler says, but Jay takes the can from my hand.

Emily and Noah are still sleeping, so I can get some kind of privacy to wash up.

I'll need a new batch of warm water for the outdoor shower, so I heat a pot of water on the stove. I don't let it boil. I only need it to be lukewarm to make sure I don't melt the plastic shower bag. I drain the cold water from the bag and refill it from the pot.

Underneath the house, where the firewood is stacked, there is a storage area for tools. I hang up the contraption on a hook on the ceiling, strip naked, and attempt to take a shower. The water pressure is low, and the thin stream quickly cools on my naked body. My skin soon becomes prickly, and I begin to shiver. I soap up as quickly as I can. Rinsing the foam off seems to be taking forever. I can't wait to wrap myself in a towel.

Back in the yurt, I boil water for tea. While I wait, I get dressed and put extra wood on the fire. When the tea is ready, I sit down on the futon and start reading *Rebecca* by Daphne du Maurier, which may not have been the best choice when alone in the middle of nowhere.

An hour passes. The boys aren't back yet. The kids are still sleeping.

I step out the door and cast my eyes along the horizon, hoping to spot them somewhere at the edge of the woods that encircle us.

All I see is blue skies and a blinding green forest.

I have a sixth sense when it comes to my children. When Jayden was only eighteen months old, we went away for a long weekend to Las Vegas. Jay was watching cartoons on the TV in the hotel room while Connor and I were in the bathroom getting intimate.

In the early days of motherhood, Connor loved to seize any opportunity when he could get some action, but as a new mom, I wasn't really into it. I'd ripped badly during birth, and it took a long time for me to heal. Then I was breastfeeding, and my tender nipples would shoot milk at will from three holes like water cannons. I was always tired and felt fat and ugly. But after a year and a half into motherhood, I was ready to get my marriage back on track.

So, when we had a chance to get away and enjoy our son and each other, I supported the idea.

One moment I was submerged in amour in the bathroom with my husband, and the next, a jolt shot through me like an electric shock. "Jay!" I called out.

"What's wrong?" Connor asked, kissing my neck and keeping me in his embrace.

"I don't know, but I need to see Jay."

"He's fine. He's watching cartoons," he murmured against my skin.

I went mad, like a confined animal trying to break free. "Let go of me!" I yelled at Connor, startling him.

I yanked the bathroom door open and blasted into the bedroom to find the bed empty. The TV was on, but I couldn't see Jay anywhere.

My heart dropped into my stomach. My first instinct was that Jay somehow managed to open the balcony door and fell to the ground.

I tossed the panels open and tried the handle. It was locked tight.

"The door," I heard Connor say through the haze of alarm in my head.

The room door stood open with the lock tongue preventing it from closing.

I snatched a towel from the hook in the bathroom and rushed out into the hallway. I was butt naked, only holding the towel in front of me. I spotted Jayden going into someone else's room about ten doors down the long corridor.

Ignoring the security cameras, I sprinted after him, calling out his name. He stopped, holding the door and looking at me with those innocent big eyes. I put my foot in the gap and grabbed his arm. As I pulled him to my chest, my towel fell to the ground. Connor appeared by our side, wearing only boxer shorts. He picked up Jayden, holding him tight. I quickly wrapped my body back in the towel.

I spent the rest of the morning rocking back and forth on the bed, trying to comprehend what had happened and what might have happened if I hadn't sensed the danger.

Connor suggested it was time we tell Jayden about the bad people in the world who snatch little boys and girls. That was the first time we burst our son's pink bubble with a dose of reality.

I could share other stories about times when I sensed danger around my kids, but what I felt now was nothing serious. I'm a bit worried, like how I worry when Jay takes the car and drives on the freeway alone, but the feeling isn't strong enough to alarm me.

The boys are fine. They're simply taking their time.

I make breakfast: cream of wheat with almond milk and bananas. I peel a few tangerines, too.

Two hours have passed, and the boys still aren't back.

Emily won't shower in the shed because she hates spiders. I convince her to wash up at least with a pan of warm water. I hold a towel as a curtain around her, but she makes me angry by screaming at me that I'm looking at her every time I turn my head.

I'm on edge, and my patience decreases in equal proportions with my rising anxiety. No electric shock yet, but I feel uneasy. What if the boys are lost?

Noah doesn't want to take a shower either. He says boys aren't as delicate as girls. I don't have enough composure left to argue with him right now.

The kids eat breakfast, but not a bite goes down my throat. I sit at the table wordlessly, staring at the door.

"When did you say Jay was supposed to be back?" Emily asks before she drinks her last sip of chocolate milk.

"They should have been back two hours ago," I tell her, trying hard to keep the panic out of my voice.

"You wanna go look for them?"

"Or we can play soccer," Noah says, ransacking the room. "Oh, shoot! I left the ball in the car."

"I'll get it for you," I offer, because any little distraction now is welcome.

I rummage through Tyler's stuff but can't find the keys.

"Did you guys see where Ty put the car keys?"

Emily shrugs. "Probably in his pocket right now."

"Great!" I snap. "How can he be so irresponsible? If they happen to be lost, then now I can't even drive to town for help."

"Check his bag," Emily says while she upturns Tyler's sleeping area.

I find chargers, his laptop and phone, a book about self-improvement, and a notepad. On the cover sheet, the word *Jay* catches my eye. I lift it to read the handwritten note. *You can only be the head of the family if you show Jay who is the boss around here.*

On any other day, this note would mean nothing alarming to me, but now, considering the situation, it makes my hands shake. Did Tyler lure my son into the woods to teach him a lesson? Did his attempt at showing Jay who the boss is go awry?

I feel my heart beating in my throat.

Noah crosses his legs. "I need to go pee. Can you come with me?"

I nod absentmindedly and hand him his jacket. "Put it on. It's still chilly outside."

I stand by the outhouse with my arms crossed over my chest, shuddering and scanning the forest. I find the dark paths into the woods suddenly more ominous and uninviting.

"Do you think you could stay with your sister for a little while?" I ask Noah, who is walking toward me with a piece of toilet paper stuck to his shoe. "I'm going to look for your brother."

"And Ty?"

"Yes, and Ty."

I use a stick to remove the piece of toilet paper and drop it into the toilet. Noah runs up the slope and back to the yurt, and I follow behind, dragging my legs like lead.

I stop for a moment and close my eyes. I focus on my hearing out of all my senses, hoping to pick up a call for help or the voices of the boys. Tyler would never hurt my son, I tell myself. He is a mama's boy. He is a gentle soul. Something else is keeping them from coming back to me.

This late in the morning, the forest is bustling with sounds as its inhabitants are awake and going about their business. I imagine a bear's growl travels far on the wind and would rise above the ambient noise. I fear a predator attacked my boys, but my sense tells me that at least one of them would have escaped. Plus, Jayden has the bear spray for protection. He's an athletic kid and his father's son. He knows how to handle himself in any situation. I keep encouraging myself with positive thinking.

After my unsuccessful attempt at using my feeble human senses to locate the boys, I return to the yurt to join the kids. I take a water bottle, a hunting knife, another bottle of bear spray, a first aid kit, and a few fruit bars and put them in a backpack.

"I need you to be vigilant until I return, okay?" I tell Emily. "Close the latch behind me, and don't open it until the boys or I get back, understood?"

"Can we go with you?" she asks, her face a mask of panic.

I kiss her forehead. "No, Em, I want you to stay here. If we are not back by nightfall, I want you to take your brother in the wheelbarrow and go down to the city for help at first light. It will take a few hours to get there, so make sure you pack enough food, water, and protection for you two, all right?"

Tears glisten in her eyes. "Mom, I don't like this. Why wouldn't you come back?"

I glance at Noah, who is playing with sticks by the fire. "I need you to be an adult right now, okay? I will come back, but if I don't, we need a plan B."

"They've only been gone three hours. Don't you want to give them more time? What if you get lost too?"

"I won't, don't worry. I'll mark my path with piles of rocks so I can find my way back, okay?"

I take a long gaze at Noah. I want to hug him so badly, but I don't do it. He doesn't know what's going on, and it's better this way.

I put on the backpack, round the yurt from the outside, and drop down the slope into the valley, taking the same trail the boys took. I look back at the yurt from the edge of the forest one last time. "Please, God, let us all be okay," I pray.

I pray more as the forest swallows me because I have a new fear now. I fear Tyler may have hurt my son for stomping on his pride. How could I be so stupid to let them leave alone together?

ALEX

Due to a traffic accident on Ventura highway, I'm running late for my meeting with Josh McKeehan. Once I get off the exit for Woodland Hills, I race through the aging streets lined with single-story houses. Five minutes after two o'clock, I roll into the driveway of the McKeehans' and stop at an ornate wrought-iron fence that encloses a two-story Spanish-style home. This part of the city was developed in the late fifties and early sixties, when single-story homes with an attached front garage were in demand, making the McKeehans' home stand out like a sore thumb. Back in its heyday, this area must have been a highly desirable haven for those who wanted to escape the cramped inner city of Los Angeles, craving more space and less crime. Now, seventy years later, the contrast between the remodeled, modernized houses and the neglected, crumbling homes is stark—a real estate investor's dream.

I get out of my car and press the button on the intercom. The gate opens without giving me a chance to introduce myself. Someone must have seen me from the window. I pull inside and park next to an electric BMW in a small courtyard adorned with palm trees and other tropical plants and get out of my car.

The air feels damp, almost jungle-like. The lawn is as wet as a sponge from overwatering. I pass a two-car garage that's used for storage and packed to the brim. It's not unusual in California to see expensive cars parked outside, unprotected from the elements, while cheap plastic toys are stored safely in the garage.

Josh emerges from the front door to meet me.

"Let's go around the back. The family's inside," he says, somewhat agitated.

I understand his lack of willingness to explain to his family who I am and what I'm doing here, so I follow him dutifully.

We sit on beach chairs by a kidney-bean-shaped pool, our voices muffled by the splashing sounds of the overspill waterfall from the hot tub into the pool. From a nearby ice chest, Josh produces two bottles of Modelo and offers me one.

"Does Paul know you're here today?"

"No, I didn't feel the need to tell him. He doesn't know we connected some time ago either."

"Good. It's difficult enough for me to say the things I'm about to tell you about my brother. I'd rather not get involved with your book, but if I don't tell you the truth, you're likely to make something up using the information you find online anyway. That's what I've seen most journalists do." There is anger in his voice. Pain. Regret.

"I'd rather fill the pages with the truth. That's why it was so important for me to talk to you."

He takes a sip of his beer, licks his top lip, and leans back in his chair. "All right. Ask away."

"I'm aware that Paul spent some time with you in his early twenties after his mother threw him out of the house for the third time. How would you describe him? What kind of man was he back then? Why was everybody turning their back on him? Why did you kick him out?"

Josh scoffs and rubs his eye. "Is that what he said? That we kicked him out?"

"Yes, but I would assume he knows he was the one who screwed it up between you guys."

"He sure did. We tried to help him get back on his feet, but he only wanted to hang out, enjoying the benefits without the responsibilities. At times, I thought he was confused by the situation. As if he considered himself one of our kids instead of a full-grown adult who needed to take charge of his own life."

"Before he moved in with you, you hadn't talked to your brother for years, right? So how did he end up here with you?"

"Yeah, I had been out of touch with my mother and Paul for about five years. But when I heard from my wife that Paul was living with a friend, but they gave him an ultimatum, and he had no place to go, I asked my wife to reach out to him on Instagram. She got his number, and I called him. He told me what went down with our mother, and I believed him because she was just as crazy when I was a teenager."

"What do you mean she was crazy?"

"You need to understand that our mother is extremely selfish and has an explosive personality. She belongs to a generation of people who grew up with very little and whose parents worked all day just to put food on the table and didn't have much time to pay attention to their children. When she started to get older, the deep divide in lifestyle, especially in California, became shockingly apparent to her. She wanted all the nice things other people had in the community. It caused her a lot of anxiety trying to break the socioeconomic chain around her neck. But it couldn't be done easily. When my sister and I were little, we didn't have much either. In those years, a family's life didn't revolve around the children, as it does now, at least not in my family. Our father worked twelve-to-fifteen-hour days, and our mother used us as an accessory to her life. Everything was always about her. When she was sad, we had to comfort her. When she was in a good mood and wanted to go on a trip, we had to drop everything and go with her. If she wanted to party, she'd leave us home alone without adult supervision for the weekend. And if she wanted to play a board game with us, then Lord have mercy on you if you didn't jump for joy at her idea. I'm not going to lie, it was tough to be subjected to her mood swings. But she did cook for us, even baked for us if she was in the mood. We had a roof over our heads. A bed to sleep in. A school to go to. So, we had it better than many other kids in this world."

"That sounds a lot like Paul's story." I keep my response short. Josh didn't need any encouragement to continue speaking about his past, so I'd rather not break the pattern.

Josh gets out of his chair and removes a few leaves from the pool before continuing.

The backyard is an authentic yet small re-creation of a tropical island oasis with densely planted queen palm trees, birds of paradise plants, and banana trees. A wall of vegetation traps the heat and creates a humid climate as if we were sitting inside a greenhouse. I feel the sweat rolling down on my spine.

"I don't know what Paul is complaining about," Josh says as he returns to his chair. "He had it much better than my sister and I. Nobody bought *us* cell phones and computers. My parents didn't pay for *my* car. They made me wear ugly hand-me-down clothes and shoes to school. I hated it. I remember being embarrassed in front of the other kids. They would make fun of me for how I was dressed. We frequently went behind grocery stores to fish for expired cereals in their garbage containers. It wasn't a pleasant experience. But Paul's childhood was different. By the time he came around, Mom and her current husband had money. They went on lake vacations where they used their jet skis and boat. All I had for a vacation when I was a kid was a cheap tent on the forest floor of a local shitty campground."

I wipe the sweat from my forehead with the back of my wrist. "So Paul is lying about his tough childhood?"

Josh finishes his beer and grabs a new bottle. I'm not even halfway through my first beer, so he doesn't bother asking me if I want another one. "Look, I wasn't around when my brother was a kid, but he was close to my son, Mark. What I can tell you is that Paul lived a much more comfortable life than I did. All Paul had to do growing up was to go to school and help around the house. But he was too lazy to do even that. He started things but never finished them. He played baseball for a year or so. Then he gave it up. He started playing guitar, but only a few months after my mother bought him a guitar, it was in a corner collecting dust. He had this incessant idea of becoming famous on the internet. He always found someone new and famous to follow and tried to copy them. He was like a leaf in the wind, floating around."

"How do you explain Paul's lack of interest in sticking with things?"

"I don't know. My sister and I wanted to do so many things when we were kids, but we either didn't have enough money to do stuff or didn't get any support from our parents. They were too busy building their own lives to focus on ours. On the other hand, all Paul had to do was say the word and he got it. He was in Boy Scouts his entire childhood. I wasn't even offered a chance to join."

"Boy Scouts? Paul didn't mention that."

"Of course he didn't. He enjoys playing the victim. In reality, he is a manipulative, lazy person who betrayed the people who tried to help him, including us."

"I noticed that he likes to think he can manipulate the situation."

"Oh, is he doing it to you too?"

"He tries, and I don't mean to sound snobbish, but his attempts are rather pathetic and obvious."

"I know. Paul isn't as smart as he thinks he is, and that's a very unpleasant trait in a human being."

The opening of a sliding door at the patio stops our conversation. A cute girl about ten years old and with big eyes pokes her head out. "Uncle Josh, when are we going to the park?"

"In a little bit," Josh yells over the roar of the waterfall.

"Yeah, but when exactly? Auntie's asking."

"Thirty minutes or so."

My stomach drops at the thought of not having Paul's brother for the entire evening. He sounds to me like someone who has stories for days about Paul—stories I desperately want to hear.

"Sorry about that. My wife's sister dropped off her daughter earlier. Nicole and I usually take her to the park and get her ice scream when we are looking after her," Josh explains once his niece is back in the house.

To get another angle for my book, I decide to ask about his wife. "How was Nicole's relationship with your brother?"

"She was always cool with Paul." Judging by his tone, I can tell he has a deep love and appreciation for his wife. "When Paul was living with us, Nicole spent the most time with him because I was mostly at work. She tried to support him in his efforts to finish high school and to drop some weight. My mother would cook for my sister and me when we were kids because we couldn't afford to eat out, but Paul grew up mostly on fast food. By the time he was twenty, he was at least forty to fifty pounds overweight. Nicole would take him on walks to help him lose weight. They wrote up an exercise and diet plan together for my brother. But he didn't follow any of it. Don't get me wrong, he was excited to do these plans with us and made big promises about how he wanted to change, live healthier, and be productive in life. He had big goals, but when it came time to execute, he always fell short."

"He is still on the heavy side," I say.

"No surprise there. Paul was always trying to get out of work or anything that required a little bit of effort. While my family was up at seven in the morning, he'd sleep till noon. He never helped around the house. Even if I asked him to help my kids and me clean the kitchen or the backyard, it was like pulling teeth with him. He certainly was a terrible influence on our children."

"Sounds like it. So how long was Paul living with you?"

"Oh, gosh, it's been years, but I'd say about two months or so."

"Apart from him not helping around the house and sleeping in often, did he do anything else that may explain how he started down the road he took later in life? Using drugs, getting mixed up with a bad crowd, or being addicted to watching inappropriate content online, or something to explain his behavior?"

"He was in trouble with the law a few times for minor thefts; I know that. He got caught for shoplifting, I believe. He had trouble with drugs too. I don't believe he was using anything in my house, but I can't be sure. He would disappear for days, then show up without a text or call. When we questioned him about his whereabouts, he'd get mad, saying that he was an adult and he didn't need to report to us. He didn't seem to grasp the fact that we were doing him a favor and our home wasn't a free motel where he could come and go as he pleased. One night he showed up in the middle of the night and started rummaging around in the kitchen. My wife almost had a heart attack because she thought an intruder was in the house. Paul seemed to be missing the common sense most young men have growing up. He lived in a dream world, often so detached from reality it was scary."

"Did you try to help him get a job or do something with his life?"

"Yes, of course. I wanted him to join the military or LAPD, but he detested those ideas. He only wanted to be a millionaire entrepreneur or an Instagram influencer. He had no intention of working long hours, but he had no education or skills, and certainly not enough charisma to influence people online. I'm not sure where the inflated image of himself came from, but he certainly didn't see himself in the same light as others did."

Well, looking around this slice of heaven, I understand why Paul aspired to be a wealthy businessman instead of working a blue-collar job. But by looking at Josh's hands and the shed full of used garden tools, I could tell he did a lot of the work at home himself. Paul wanted to take shortcuts, and that approach might work for some people, but it certainly didn't benefit Paul.

Josh's niece shows up at the patio door again, urging her uncle to hurry up.

Slightly red-faced and distracted, he ends our meeting. Talking about Paul is painful to him and something that still brings him regret.

As I pull out of the driveway, I watch the family gathering in the front for a walk to the park. Cute kids on bikes and skateboards. A smiling wife that radiates confidence and kindness. A successful man who bulges with pride yet is humble. And I wonder how the same mother could have raised two completely different men.

JENNIFER

As I advance deeper into the woods, shame descends on me for having ill thoughts about my boyfriend. Tyler would never hurt Jayden or any of my children. I would have never brought him into my family if I had an inkling of suspicion that he wasn't a decent man. I had vetted him thoroughly before I accepted his first dinner date invitation. I googled his name and searched every social media site for his profile, but no alarming news popped up. His virtual biography displayed him as a middle school English teacher, a dog lover, and a man who worshipped his mother. He volunteered to coach baseball at his school, had a Goodreads account with over three hundred books shelved as *read*. When I compared our book lists, I discovered that we had a similar taste. We both love historical fantasy and crime fiction.

He isn't as active on social media as I am. He does have a Twitter account, but he only shares other people's tweets on liberal politics. He has less than two hundred friends on Facebook. Before we started to get serious, his profile picture was a selfie of him eating at a restaurant. Now, it's a snapshot of us taken at his cousin's wedding.

He is on Instagram and Snapchat, too, but he shares little about his life apart from a few family event photos.

I never found anything that raised a red flag, and not for my lack of trying.

No, Tyler was not going to hurt my son. He took Jayden on a morning walk to only give him the man-to-man talk. They must have lost their way in this giant maze of trees. We are not outdoorsy people. We are not used to an endless expanse of thick forests that can swallow us. I'll find them, I promise myself. And everything will be all right.

I arrive at a fork in the dirt road. My heart draws me to the right. I build an arrow with rocks that points me toward the direction of the yurt. It could also guide Tyler and Jayden if they came across it.

On second thought, I carve a short note into the dirt with a stick: *Back to the yurt. Jen.*

The rustling sounds in the bushes behind me make me jump. I put my finger on the trigger of the bear spray and aim it in front of me. Whatever caused that noise must now be watching me cautiously. The air hangs suspended between us. Over my racing heartbeat, I pick up every little sound around me. The songs of birds. The whispering of the wind. The squeaking of the trees. The buzzing of insects.

I came here with the idea that I will conquer nature, but instead, nature made me bow down to her. It's humbling to understand how powerless I am against Mother Earth.

Despite my fears, I have to move on. I must keep going.

I check my watch to see how much time I have left until sunset. In less than four hours, darkness would swallow me—swallow us all. I won't be able to wander for more than two hours before turning around and heading back to my children in the yurt.

I know I have to get going, but my legs don't move. "Jayden!" I shout into the air against my better judgment. "Tyler! Where are you?"

If only it were that easy to find them.

Driven by maddening mother instinct, I press on, still gripping the bear spray.

In about twenty minutes, I hit another split in the path. While setting a stone arrow as my road marker, I notice fresh bear prints in the mud and a pile of scat filled with red berries. Disturbing images from survival documentaries flash before my eyes. In one episode, a teen boy was mauled by a bear after he was separated from his father on a hunting trip. The boy escaped, but he was seriously injured. Chunks of flesh were hanging from his thigh, and his arms and face were scratched to a bloody mess. Against all odds, he managed to drag himself down the hill, where he luckily encountered a Marine on an endurance camping trip in the woods. The man slung the boy over his shoulders and ran with him to the nearest town to get help. They both displayed extraordinary superhuman strength that resulted in the boy's survival.

Tyler would never be able to carry Jayden. Connor would, even if it was the last thing he did in life.

I feel ashamed for wanting my ex-husband to be here with us on this trip and not my boyfriend. I hate myself for being so weak emotionally. I'm usually more in control of my thoughts, but I haven't felt exhaustion and hunger like this for a long time, and the effects are starting to set in despite my resistance. I need to find the boys before panic takes over me completely.

I loop toward the left to slowly make my way back to the yurt in one big circle to cover more area. It's been over two hours since I set out on this rescue mission, and I've already pushed farther than I planned.

Desperation starts to take over my mind from not seeing a trace of my son and boyfriend, and I begin to call their names repeatedly, ignoring the possibility of drawing too much attention to my presence. If a bear attacks me, there is no way I'll have the strength to fight it off and walk away with my flesh hanging in pieces.

I don't do well with the sight of blood. When Emily was eleven, she fell on the running track at school. Pebbles from the decomposed granite shredded her knee like a cheese grater. Watching her getting stitched up, I became pale and light-headed in the urgent care center. The doctor asked me if I wanted to leave the room. I nearly did, but I stayed for my daughter.

I'm not sure I could stay strong for only me.

As I set another arrow made with sticks and stones, a jackrabbit jumps onto the path. The surprise makes me fall back, and I watch the rabbit hop across with my heart hammering in my chest.

"Jayden, where are you?" I cry out again from the dreadful feeling of helplessness, but there is no answer.

I bring my hands forward to wipe off the mud when I notice something red on my skin. I look down at the dirt to see patches of crimson that appear to be coagulated blood. Do people hunt in these woods? The ranger would have notified us if they do, wouldn't he?

I jump to my feet so fast I'm barely able to maintain my balance. I hold my hair behind my ears as I search the ground for more traces of blood.

I find footprints—two different sets. I have no idea what prints the soles of the boys' shoes would leave, but I hold my foot over one footprint, and I judge it to be a shoe three or four sizes bigger than mine. Tyler is a size ten and a half. Jayden is an eleven. I'm a nine. The person who left these shoe prints wore a bigger size than any of us. These prints may be unrelated to us, but I can't ignore them.

I follow the blood trail to the other side of the dirt path, where I lose it in the undergrowth. I start running through the woods. Branches and leaves tear into my jacket and pull my hair. The soil is moist and soft, and my hiking shoes sink deep in the decomposing forest floor. Every step is a struggle through this mucky land.

I don't venture far from the fire road. If I lose my way in the dark, I'll never make it out of here alive.

Every ten minutes or so, I stop to yell Jayden's name and wait for his answer.

He is not here.

The road next to me splits again. One fork goes higher up the mountain, and the other seemingly leads back to our clearing. My shoes are damp and heavy with mud and leaves, and I can't feel my legs from the dozens of cuts and bruises on my shins, but what other options do I have?

I get back on the fire road. I take deep breaths, trying to keep my emotions at bay with little success. I crouch to the ground and start crying. *Please, God, don't let anything bad happen to my son. And Tyler.*

I feel a big ball of emotion gathering in my stomach, and I release it with a thundering call of my son's name.

Almost immediately, I hear a feeble voice: "Mom."

My heart stops. I focus my eyes on the woods behind me, then in front of me.

"Jayden!" I call out again.

"Mom, I'm here!" This time I'm certain that I didn't imagine it. But the voice drifts through the air, and identifying which direction it's coming from seems impossible.

"Jayden, where are you?"

"I'm here. By the tree."

By the tree? There are millions of trees here.

I step off the path and move into the woods in front of me. "Which tree?" I ask with urgency. I close my eyes to focus on my hearing, but my blood is pulsing fast and loud in my ears.

"Here!" He is banging a piece of wood against a tree trunk, and I pick up on it.

Stepping on plants and leaves, I force my way through a thicket to get to him.

Soon my eyes behold his body against a thick pine tree. I'm so relieved to see him that tears well up in my eyes and roll down my cheeks.

I fling myself onto my knees in front of him and wrap my arms around him.

He winces.

"What's wrong, honey? What happened? Why didn't you come back?" I bombard him with questions as I search his face and body for apparent injuries.

"I'm shot," he says, gripping my arm with his fingers. "Tyler is dead."

"What? Shot? Who shot you? What do you mean Tyler is dead? I don't understand." I speak fast, almost incoherently. My mind races far ahead, and my mouth can barely catch up.

He is crying now as he leans against my shoulder. "A man shot him."

"What man? Why?"

I understand the words that come out of my son's mouth, but I can't comprehend them. Why would anyone be here with a gun?

"I don't know. Some dude came up to us, and without a word, he shot Tyler in the chest."

I'm shaking my head in confusion. "I don't understand."

"We were walking, and this guy showed up out of nowhere. He asked if we had a smoke. I said we didn't, but Tyler stopped to chat with him anyway." He pauses to catch his breath. "He pulled a gun and shot Tyler. He dropped to the ground immediately. I started running. He shot me in the back of my leg. Look!"

He turns over, hissing, his face flushed with pain, and shows me his bloodstained pants.

I feel dizzy. The strength is draining from my limbs. I take a deep breath while I examine Jayden's wound. There is a bandage wrapped around his thigh that seems to be a part of his T-shirt.

"How bad is it?"

"I can walk, but it hurts like hell. I think it's just a flesh wound. It didn't hit an artery, but it was bleeding pretty good."

As I try to wrap my mind around the situation, I notice that he doesn't have a water canister. He must be dehydrated. "Here, drink some of my water."

He licks his dried lips and takes the bottle from my hand. He drinks thirstily. When a sip goes down the wrong pipe, he starts coughing.

I tap him on the back gently but effectively.

"I survive being shot to then die choking on water." He smiles, but it's not an expression of joy, only relief.

I stand up and look around to evaluate our situation. The sun has moved lower in the sky, barely hanging above the jagged ridges of the mountains. We will start losing daylight any minute now.

Clouds of insects hover near the ground, buzzing and zipping by us, looking for a safe place to settle for the night. The temperature is dropping fast. I can feel the cold air's touch on my face. "We need to get you back to the yurt."

"Didn't you hear what I said? Tyler is dead," he says to me in an alarmed voice.

I squat down again and cup his face in my hands. "I understand, honey, but all I can think of right now is to get you to safety. Then we can figure out what happened. I can't start panicking now."

"Are you kidding me? This is the perfect time to panic. The man is still out there somewhere. I've been hiding from him all morning."

"Is he hunting you?'

"I don't know what his deal is. We barely even talked to him, and he shot at us. I don't think he was a hunter because he had a handgun, not a rifle."

"Is it possible that Tyler said something? Or he knew Tyler?"

"No, Ty was nice. You know him. He called him 'brother.' Maybe he got offended because of that. I don't know."

"What did he look like?"

"He was pretty big—heavy I mean. I don't know. I didn't have enough time to memorize his features. Maybe he got mad at Tyler for calling him 'a brother,' I don't know."

"All the more reason to get out of here. Can you walk?"

As Jay struggles to get back to his feet with my support, I think of the Marine who carried someone else's son, and I feel dreadful for not being able to do the same for my own son. Once again, I wish Connor were here.

"Can you give me that piece of wood?" He points at a limb on the ground. "I've been using it for a crutch."

I loop one of his arms over my shoulders to take some of his weight. He tucks the makeshift crutch under his armpit.

He winces as we move toward the fire road.

"Maybe it's better if we walk through the woods," he says as he stops to catch his breath. "That dude will see us on the road."

"When was the last time you saw him or heard him?"

"Hours ago, but he could still be here."

"He probably gave up on chasing you. We need to take the road. Otherwise, we won't make it back to the yurt before dark."

He looks into my eyes with desperation. He is scared. So am I. But we need to be brave for each other and get back to Emily and Noah. What if the man's path leads him to the yurt? I can't let my mind go there.

The journey back to the clearing is a long and tiring one. Once the dark sky has fallen on us, the big dipper is our only guide. In the distance, a coyote or wolf howls. I do my best to ignore the terrifying sound.

I feel Jayden's body trembling underneath my arm, probably from the combination of cold, fear, and exhaustion.

He comes to a sudden halt. "Mom, I can't go on," he says breathlessly as he stoops over, his shoulders drooping.

"We're almost there. We can't stop now."

"Go on without me. Bring back the wheelbarrow when you can. I'm gonna sit down here and wait for you."

I make him drink water. Most of it trickles down his chin. I kiss his forehead. "Do you remember that soccer game where that kid cleated your calf and gashed your skin?"

He looks at me, puzzled.

"You went down, and your teammates surrounded you. They were freaking out because they thought you might be out of the game. They practically begged you to get back on your feet and keep playing. You were in excruciating pain, but you pushed yourself back up and finished the game. The blood had soaked through your sock, and you were limping, but your team won the game. I was furious at the coach for allowing you to play injured like that. But you told me that it was okay because you wanted to push through the pain for your team. Once in the back seat of my car, you finally relaxed and allowed yourself to cry, but you found the strength to play with pain somehow. You remember that game, don't you? You were only twelve."

Jay wipes the sweat from his forehead. "Why are you telling me this now?"

"Because I need you to find that strength in you now as you did in that soccer game. I need you to get up and keep walking. Can you do that for me?"

I offer him a protein bar, but he shakes his head.

We stand for a moment in silence. The trees crack and sway in the breeze around us. An owl hoots.

The pain is taking everything out of Jay, I can see it on his face, but he bobs his head at me and purses his lips. "Okay, let's keep going," he says and puts his arm back over my shoulder.

We are moving again, slowly but still moving.

To keep his spirits high, I tell stories of beach days and funny family mishaps. I don't stop reminding Jay that his efforts will pay off.

By the time we reach the clearing, I no longer feel my body. I walk like a zombie. I use every ounce of my remaining energy to drag Jayden up on the last hillside to the yurt.

I consider asking him if he needs to use the outhouse before we go back inside, but he had soiled his pants sometime before I found him, most likely when the stranger shot him. I decide not to bring it up. I can take a pan to his bunk bed after I clean him up. The most important thing for him now is to warm up by the fire before he gets hypothermia.

Golden light spills from the windows of the yurt, and a funnel of smoke rises from the chimney. I feel a profound warmth toward Emily for stepping up her game while I was gone. I also feel relieved that they are okay.

I sit Jay on the bench on the patio and knock on the door. After the third knock, the curtain moves and Emily looks out the window. As she shakes her head, her face is distorted with terror. Suddenly she disappears as if someone has jerked her away from the door. I hear the lock turn. The door slowly opens.

"What's going on, Emily?" I ask, but before she can answer, the door swings wide and a mountain of a man with dark hair and rough, tanned skin appears in front of us. He points his gun directly at my forehead.

"Get inside."

JENNIFER

The first thing that races through my mind when I see the stranger greeting me at the door of the yurt with a gun pointing at me is that he is not a friend, not even an acquaintance, but I've certainly met him before. There is something familiar in those dark, beady eyes that spark an unpleasant flashback.

"Hello, Jennifer," he says, smiling, holding the door open like a visiting family member who just dropped in on us as a surprise.

Emily is standing by the table. Her arms are crossed over Noah's chest as he presses his back against his sister. From one glance at her pale face and tear-washed cheeks, I gather this is not a friendly visit. We are in trouble.

I hear a thud behind me, followed by a series of rattling sounds on the patio.

"Don't get any ideas, boy," the man says over my shoulder.

I look back at Jayden sitting crooked on the floor. The veggies are still rolling around him in every direction. He must have knocked over the grocery bag when he fell off the bench.

"It's him," he says breathlessly. His face is shrunken with terror. His eyes are wide with fear. "He shot Tyler."

My first instinct is to protect my children from this intruder, but his presence makes no sense to me, and I'm not reacting as I should.

This yurt sits on a secluded mountainside away from civilization and prying eyes. This man is not supposed to be here—nobody is supposed to be here, apart from us. I never heard a car engine or a motorcycle roar. How did he get here?

"What do you want?" I ask the broad man towering over me, trying hard to keep my composure. I need to eliminate this threat by disarming the intruder, but I know my own strength. If I attack him, I better knock him out cold with one blow because if not, the next will be his turn. If he takes me down, then who will protect my children? I need to remain calm and alert, just as I always advise my kids and followers.

The man takes a step back to allow me more space to enter the yurt. "What I want from you is to come inside to warm up by the fire. It's cold outside." He lowers the gun. His polite manners and soft tone don't fit the situation.

I hear a soft trickling sound and a short whimper. I notice a growing puddle of liquid underneath Noah's right foot. He's peeing himself, and the urine soaks through his pants.

"Jayden needs to come inside, too. He's hurt. He is the one who needs to warm up, not me. I need to tend his wound." My lips are shaking as I talk. The man picks up on it, because he assures me that I have no reason to be nervous.

I'm not only nervous. I'm deadly terrified. I know this man. I know I do. But from where?

I get weird messages online from men sometimes. When you share your personal life and intimate moments with the whole world, people get attached to you. They feel like they know you—as if they are part of your life. I used to respond to those messages as kindly as possible without egging them on, but I haven't done so in a while. Did I connect with this man online? No, that's not it. His smell. His look. It all feels more personal. We've met in person. I'm certain of it.

"Here, let me help you," the man says as he rushes to my side to carry Jayden inside the yurt.

Jayden jerks away from him. "Don't you fucking touch me," he yells.

My insides knot up in anticipation, expecting the man to retaliate for Jayden's tone. Connor didn't allow him to be disrespectful at home. Tyler can't stand it when he talks back with venom. I doubt this stranger will welcome it.

"I got him," I carefully say because the man watches my son with speculating eyes, and it's the scariest thing I've seen in a long time.

"Chill, bro," he says. "If you don't want my help, fine. But get inside. It's fucking freezing out here."

I glance over the railing, contemplating the possibility of ramming into the man and pushing him over the four-foot barrier. He must be at least 250 pounds of fat, muscle, and bone. From my fixed starting point, the reality of my gaining enough momentum to nudge him over is negligible. If I had more space to gain speed, I might try, but it seems too risky now.

Jayden pulls himself up by the bench and lets me support him.

"Get a move on!" the man grumbles, tapping my skull with the barrel of the gun.

"We're going," I assure him, rubbing the spot he hit.

Jayden opens his mouth, but I shake my head at him, indicating he shouldn't say another word.

The wooden floorboards creak underneath my feet, and I'm aware of the flimsy construction now more than ever.

As I advance inside the room, I can't stop looking for a possible weapon or a helpful idea to overcome this maniac. He's not a weary traveler who needs a bowl of hot soup and seeks the heat of the fire. He is here to hurt us. I feel it in my bones. If he touches my daughter, I swear—I rage in my head, but I can't finish my train of thought because the man notices the urine on the floor by Noah and starts yelling, "What the fuck is this? What did you spill here?"

"It's nothing," Emily says. She is reticent and submissive. How long has this man been here with my children that Emily has had time to learn what kind of tone is acceptable with him?

I scan Emily's face for injuries, but I don't see anything alarming apart from her red eyes and chapped lips. The rest of her body is clothed. If she has bruises, I won't learn about them until we have a chance to talk.

"Well, clean it up." The man pushes my daughter to the ground. I lurch at him out of mother's instinct, but the stranger shoves me back and threatens me with the gun again.

Emily grabs a rag from the pail we use to wash the dishes and starts dabbing at the wet spot on the floor. Noah is quietly crying.

"I'm hungry," the man says casually, as if he is our guest. "What do we have to eat?"

"What do you want from us?" I ask again as I help Jayden onto my bunk bed, which is the closest one to the fire.

The man pulls out a chair and sits down by the table. "I want you to make me something to eat. You know, toss something delicious together like in your videos."

I was wrong thinking I'd met him in person. If he knows about my lifestyle vlog, then he most likely follows me online. But what is he doing here? What are the odds of running into a follower of mine here in the middle of nowhere in Montana? I try hard to recall the attendant's face at the gas station yesterday. Was anyone else there? Was this man there?

I feel dizzy with a rush of confusion and fear on an empty stomach.

When I don't move, the man aims the gun at Emily. She whimpers. "I'm not asking. I'm ordering you to make me something to eat."

I put my hand up, my fingers shaking. "Please don't hurt my daughter. I can make you a..." I rub my forehead as my mind draws a blank. "Um, chicken soup. Or I can make you a sandwich," I say as I shuffle through the grocery list in my head.

The man sets his gun on the table. "A soup sounds nice."

In a grasp of dread that had been with me all day, I rush to the cabinet where I keep all the ingredients I need to create the meal: chicken broth, canned chicken meat, canned peas, a bag of noodles. I organize them on the counter with rigid, cold fingers. This whole situation seems unreal, as if I'm still dreaming, not quite awake from this nightmare.

A bread knife is within arm's reach. It doesn't have a sharp point I could drive into this intruder's flesh, but the serrated edge can cut through the hardest crust of a loaf of fresh-baked bread. Could I slash the man's throat before he shoots me? I look back at the short distance stretching out between us. It can't be more than eight feet. He'll see me launch an attack on him before I could even pose a threat. I need to get closer.

"How's your leg, boy?" he says, and I turn to see Jayden's reaction. He doesn't answer, only purses his lips and shakes his head. The contrast between our lovely family day in the yurt and this jarring shift is so incongruous it almost seems like different realities.

"I need carrots and celery from the bag outside," I say to draw the man's attention away from Jayden. If this animal indeed shot Tyler in cold blood, who can say he won't do the same to my son for talking back to him.

Tyler.

My stomach churns. The terrible reality of his brutal murder threatens to overcome me, but I push back the feeling. I won't accept his death until I see his cold, lifeless body.

The man uses his gun to wave permission. "Go get them, then."

"I also need water." I lock eyes with Emily. "Can you go to the tank and bring in some fresh water—"

"The boy goes." The man cuts me off.

"He's injured," I say. "He can't walk alone."

"Not him. The little boy."

My plan to have Emily run for help has backfired. "He's too little."

The man scoffs. "You make him do more difficult tasks than this in your videos."

"So, you know who I am. Do I know you?"

His surprise is genuine. "You don't remember me?"

We are in dangerous waters again. If I hurt his ego, he may resort to violence. If I flatter him, he may get the wrong idea. "I do," I say carefully. "I know we've met, but the details are a little hazy. I'm exhausted. I barely ate today. I feel a little light-headed, and I'm frightened."

"Whatever. Just get what you need and start on the food. I'm starving." He puts his feet up on the table. I recognize the pattern of the soles. There are the same footprints in the mud where I found blood.

"You, kid. Grab a jug, and go get some water."

I open the door. "Can Emily go with him to help?"

"Do I look stupid to you?"

He looks big and burly. A pair of bent skinny legs support his round upper body. The waist of his black jeans is tight, and his stomach spills over his belt like a mushroom top. His skin is dark enough to conceal the scars of his bad teenaged acne, but when he turns and the lantern light illuminates his cheeks, his skin looks like a pot-holed road. Above his meaty lips, a giant nose sits crookedly, covered with open pores, huge blackheads, and skin bumps. He looks like an aged alcoholic, yet he appears to be in his mid- to late twenties.

His posture is an orthopedic's dream case. Years of hunching over a videogame controller or cell phone can warp a kid's spine, creating a Quasimodo-size lump at the base of the neck on someone's back. I've seen boys develop this deformity from hunching for endless hours and lack of exercise, but the curve in this guy's spine is the worst I've seen. When I realize he may have spent his entire childhood in front of killing games, he scares me even more.

"I didn't say you were stupid," I say. He does appear to be uneducated and simple-minded, but it's not the time to be honest.

He rolls his eyes. "The boy goes alone. Am I clear?"

Noah hides behind his sister, holding onto her legs. "I don't want to go," he whimpers.

I crouch down. "Come here, Noah."

"I don't want to go," he cries.

I spot the head-strap flashlight on the futon. I reach for it. "Hey, buddy, I know you're scared of the dark, but look, we can play a little game, all right? I'll put this lamp on your head, and it will light your path."

Emily turns to face her brother. "It will only take a minute. Fill up the jug with water, and come back quickly. We'll be here waiting for you."

"Please don't make me go," Noah cries, and his tiny voice makes my heart bleed.

"Look!" I stand to confront the stranger. "I'll get the damn water. There's no point wasting time. You're hungry, aren't you?"

He doesn't say anything, only gawks at me. There is no intelligence behind those beady eyes. I judge him to be a high school dropout. The way he talks and moves tells me that he is a small-town burnout with limited people skills.

"I'm not going to run away. I promise. My kids are here. I wouldn't leave them."

The man pops a few peanuts into his mouth. "The boy goes."

I heave a deep breath and sigh. "Noah, come here, please."

He sniffs and wipes his nose.

"It's okay."

He shakes his head.

I turn on the light and put it on my head. "Look. It works. It's just a game. Like a scavenger hunt. You remember where the water tank is, right?"

He nods.

"Just turn the valve and fill up the jug. You'll be back here in no time. I promise."

"Go!" Emily nudges him.

Noah chews his fingers as he starts toward me. He takes a wide berth around from where the man is sitting.

"Boo!" the man snaps.

Noah winces and sprints to me.

I hold the man's gaze. "That was unnecessary."

I hug my son until his crying ceases, then I strap the headlight on his head and hand him the jug. I walk him out the door, but I can't pass the bench where the vegetables are scattered because the man is aiming his gun at Emily again.

"Just keep going," I tell Noah.

"I'm scared, Mom," he whispers as he holds the jug against his chest and inches away from me.

"I'm right here, sweetheart. Don't think about anything. Focus on getting the water and coming back."

I glance at the stranger as I gather the vegetables and put them back into the bag to buy me some time. He is holding my daughter at gunpoint while watching me. He beckons me to get back inside. I put the last onion back into the bag and straighten back up. I see the stream of light from Noah's headlight. He is dashing down the hill. The light goes all over, zigzagging. "Are you okay?"

"I fell," he yells back. "But I'm okay."

"Just hurry back, okay?"

Now the man is tapping his gun against the table in rapid, short bursts. The sound of metal on wood is both threatening and unnerving. His need for control is pointless since there is no place to run to here in the middle of the night in the dark forest. No mother would leave her two children behind to save one. Whatever this stranger wants from us, I have to figure it out. If I stay calm and obedient, he won't have a reason to kill us.

I go back inside, as he asks, before he does something rash.

I start on the soup while Emily is ordered to feed the fire with more wood.

My head is buzzing as I debate my next step while chopping the carrots into small pieces. It's hard to focus on the task at hand when I'm fighting the urge to look back and check on the intruder.

My cutting is hectic—fast and uncontrolled. The knife slips on the rigid, cold carrot, and the knife cuts deep into the flesh of my left index finger. The pain is sudden and sharp and jolts from my finger through my arm and down my spine, making me hiss. I suck the blood from the narrow gash, looking for a first aid kit. I see a red box with a with cross secured on the wall by the door.

"Can I get a bandage?"

"I thought you were skilled in the kitchen?"

"I am. But I'm a bit stressed, considering the circumstances."

He shrugs. "But no funny business."

I find a box of bandages in the first aid kit and wrap one around my finger. I'll use the opportunity to ask the man to allow me to treat Jayden's gunshot wound. If he wanted us dead, he'd have killed us already.

When I look up to make the request, I see Jayden fastening a rope between his hands and pulling at it, testing its strength. The blood drains from my limbs. A feeling of panic creeps upon me fast. The words of a mother's warning echo in my mind, but I can't say them out loud. The stranger is between us, paying attention only to me.

My only hope now is that Jayden reads my face and listens to reason.

But he isn't listening. He scoots to the edge of the bunk bed, closer to the stranger, and keeps wrapping the rope around his hands.

My chest begins rising and falling with my rapid breathing. The unfolding events don't escape Emily's attention either, and she puts her hands together and silently begs her brother not to do something foolish.

A feeling of impending doom looms within me. Jayden doesn't seem to be preparing to stand down. He is stubborn like his father. He's seen too many stupid action movies where the hero kills someone with a single blow to the head or chokes someone to death in a matter of seconds. In reality, killing someone with a rope takes much longer and incredible effort. If he fails, the man will kill him.

"Stop!" I shout out of reflex when Jayden lifts the rope. "I mean, the bleeding stopped. I'll start on the soup again."

I correct myself with haste, my heart beating in my throat. *Please don't do it!* I pray in my head.

A beam of light crossing over the patio floor next to me grabs my attention. Noah bursts through the door and slams into me as if someone were chasing him, hyperventilating. Water from the jug spills onto my pants and soaks the planks around us.

Breaking eye contact with Jayden for a split second was enough for him to turn his idea into action. By the time I manage to refocus my attention on him, I catch him lurching at the man. He flings the rope over the man's head and pulls it against his neck, but it's not a noose, and he has difficulty getting a tight enough grip to disable the man. This brute's neck is thick and short, and he is pulling at the rope with his strong fingers.

He pushes himself back on his chair against Jayden.

The rope goes loose.

Jayden tries to regain his advantage by tightening the rope, but it's not working.

Noah's screaming fills the room, paralyzing me.

Emily seizes the moment to help her brother disarm our attacker.

The stranger reaches back and jerks Jayden over his shoulder and drops him against the futon, and he pistol-whips Emily on the forehead. She collapses onto the ground and hits her head on the leg of the table. The man jumps back to his feet and kicks Jayden in the stomach. Hard.

He folds over, crying out in pain.

Noah is screaming at my feet, and I've been holding onto him protectively. Everything happened so fast, but the time to act is now.

I jerk my head around, looking for a weapon. I remember leaving the bear spray on the bench when I settled Jayden down to rest after we got back to the yurt. If I'm fast enough, I could get to it. But Noah has his arms locked around my legs, and he trips me as I try to move. That moment of hesitation costs me the opportunity to take back control. The man bellows like a lion as he paces by the table. If he is hearing some inner voice telling him not to kill us, I hope he listens. Now that he's back in control, some sort of punishment will surely follow.

He rubs his neck and kicks at Jayden a second time. "What the fuck, man!" he yells at him.

The muscles on his face are twitching. Thinking about what to do next takes all the effort he can muster.

He kicks at his chair. "You got some fucking dumb kid here, you know that?"

"I'm so sorry. He saw you kill my boyfriend. He's confused. Please don't hurt him."

He stops pacing but still breathes heavily. His face is a mask of surprise. "That fucking clown? I did you a favor. He was getting all too cozy and friendly with your son."

I feel woozy and lean against the countertop. "He would never."

"You think I'm lying? Ask your son. He was all touchy, and, you know…inappropriate."

"Shut up!" Jayden screams at him. "Just shut up!"

"Jayden, please." I look at him pleadingly.

"Whatever." The man flicks his hand and picks up a black travel bag from the floor by the futon and pulls out a roll of duct tape. "Come here."

"No, please," I beg.

"I said come here," he repeats sternly, shaking his gun.
I obey.

He hands me the duct tape. "Tie them up."

Ignoring his order, I say, "Please, Jayden is shot. He needs medical attention. Please let them go."

He taps the gun against his forehead. "Stop begging me. It's not like you. What the fuck are you, a dog?"

"What do you mean it's not me? Of course it's me."

"I want the Jennifer from your videos. I want you to make me food, and laugh with me, and…and dance with me like you do with your boyfriend."

His words scare the shit out of me. Not because of how he says them, but what they mean. This man knows me. He is a fan of mine. It's not a coincidence he is here on this behind-God's-back mountain. He followed me here. Which means he has an agenda. He has plans for me. He already killed my boyfriend. It didn't matter to him. Tyler was collateral damage because it's me he wants.

What if my children are collateral damage too?

JENNIFER

In the stunned silence, the crackling of the fire fills the space. The flames have eaten away at the center of the thick log in the woodstove, and the limb splits in half, the pieces rolling off the top of the stack, sending up sparks.

I don't know why I stare at the fireplace when my children and I are being kept hostage by a maniac, who is also a cold-blooded murderer, but the fire draws my eyes to it. It could be a defense mechanism of the mind. My brain needs relief from the massive wave of stress that's been pounding away at me all day.

"What's your name?" I ask the man with a sigh of anguish.

He stops his pacing, and I lead my eyes to his face. "You know who I am," he says.

The enlarged eyes, slightly gaping mouth, and slouching posture betray his sense of being offended. He acts childishly, like a man who has lived a sheltered life and could not mature into adulthood.

I'm terrified to answer him. If I say I have no idea who he is, he might blow a gasket. If I lie and he catches me, the result could be similar.

"I do," I say without distinguishing if it's a question or statement.

He sits down to level his six-foot frame with mine. "We've been messaging back and forth for two years now." He taps his chest with the barrel of his gun. "It's me. The Persian Prince."

I sense my children's fear around me. My body soaks it all up, making my bones feel weak. I'm ten times as nervous as I was back in school when I had to give a speech in public, where one wrong answer would drop me out of the competition.

"Yeah, I remember you." My voice is shaking. My statement lacks conviction. If he is an active fan of any of my social media sites or YouTube channel, then I certainly don't know him. I haven't answered any comments or messages for years. I have an assistant do that for me.

A wave of relief washes over his face, and he smiles. His mouth is small, with weird meaty lips, squeezed between bulging, puffy cheeks. His controlled expression of joy makes him look like a gaping fish. "Your messages changed my life," he admits convincingly. "You encouraged me to follow my dreams. You said if I can dream it, I can have it. I've been dreaming about meeting you for a very long time, and look at us now. Here we are. Together."

Out of the corner of my eye, I spot Emily dabbing a piece of paper towel against her bleeding temple. On the other side of the room, Jayden lies on the ground by the futon where the man threw him, wincing and moaning in pain. Like a terrified puppy, Noah is cradled by his brother's feet, seeking protection. I'm their mother. I'm supposed to protect my children. What should I say to this man to get us out of this situation unharmed? What has my assistant, Zoe, talked about with this stranger? I warned her not to get too personal with fans. She was supposed to answer comments and messages with a polite tone, emulating basic responses of courtesy. I warned her to stay neutral and not to express any specific opinions. Whenever you take a stand on an issue, you'll have people who love you for it or turn on you because of it. And never, ever, was she supposed to build a long-lasting, intimate relationship online—especially in my name.

"I'm glad we could finally meet in person," I say to play this absurd game. I even force a smile. "It's good to hear that you are achieving your goals."

He cocks his head—another childish response. This man must be at least twenty-five, but he acts like a sixteen-year-old boy, irrational, hasty, overly passionate.

"Well, I wouldn't say I achieved my goals, but you know, you said yourself in your video that it takes time to build an online business. Rome wasn't built in a day, right?" His face flushes as if embarrassed. "I signed up for your online class on how to get a million followers. And I wanted to ask you in person about what I'm doing wrong because I followed everything you said. I'm consistent with my postings, and I use targeted hashtags. I try to be personal and share goofy videos instead of doctoring my videos to look perfect, but I've only gained 342 followers. I don't get more than a couple a week." He leans forward on the table and talks casually to me as if this weren't a hostage situation but a friendly business meeting.

"Tell me more about your videos?" Now that we are sociable, I get the courage to attend to Jayden's injury. I inch toward my boys, sideways, crablike, not dropping my attention from the intruder.

"What was your last post about?" I ask him as I kneel by Jayden and start rolling up the leg of his pants to check on his gunshot wound.

I make sure I feign interest in what the man has to say, but he doesn't appreciate my divided attention. He becomes antsy and keeps changing his sitting position. I have to be careful not to push his patience with me farther than he can endure.

"Well, you know, I'm posting videos of cooking simple meals in a bedroom on a portable electric burner. It's for college kids who live in a dorm or people who rent a room and have no money to eat out."

I bob my head understandingly as I grab a cloth, pour water on it from a water bottle, and start washing off the dried blood from Jayden's thigh. Noah wraps his arms around mine. His fingers are ice-cold. "I need you to be a big boy now, okay?" I whisper to him.

"What was that?" the man asks.

"Nothing," I say quickly. "How many people liked your video?"

"Not too many. And I don't understand why, because I followed what you said in your video." His stomach growls. "Shit, I'm starving. Are you gonna make that soup or not?"

I look piercingly into Jayden's eyes to make him understand that I don't want another heroic yet stupid attempt at disarming our capturer. He looks away at the floor. He understands.

I get back to the cooking area and resume cutting up the vegetables. I heat water in an old pot on the burner and add the chicken stock.

The intruder pulls out his cell phone from his pocket and starts recording me.

I don't object.

"You said you'd look at my page and give me some advice, but you never got back to me. I kept sending you messages. Why did you ignore me? Because of your new boyfriend?"

I struggle to focus on the cooking because I keep looking over my shoulder to see if he is still recording me or messing with my children again.

The blood from the cut on my finger shows through the bandage, but I ignore it. I have more pressing issues at hand. My frustration with my assistant, Zoe, makes my blood boil. I'll have a serious word with her when I get home—if I get home.

The man puts the phone into my face for a closeup.

"I'm sorry. I've been swamped with my channel lately and my volunteer work at the shelter. Planning family trips, and other things, you know? I didn't mean to ignore you." I add four cans of minced chicken meat to the soup and stir it with my shaking hand.

He leans his back against the counter and folds his arms over his chest. "You think this video will be authentic enough for my followers?"

"There is no reception on the mountain. You won't be able to share it."

He shrugs. "I'll share it when I get home." He lowers his phone and leans closer to me. "By the way, you don't have to worry about wasting all your time on that stupid baby cow anymore. I took care of that worthless animal."

Emily's whimper pierces the air. My hand nearly drops the wooden spoon. I can feel my heart pounding underneath my fingers as my other hand touches my chest.

"It was you?" I say, battling for air.

"Yeah," he says matter-of-factly. "I got tired of watching you spending all your time with that dumb animal. I mean, what kind of world do we live in where a fucking baby cow gets a hundred thousand followers? All those fucking idiots, wasting their time watching a fucking cow eat grass! I practically have to beg my friends and family to like my posts."

I look at him with pleading eyes. "Can I go to Emily? She is in shock."

He puts his arm over my chest and stops me. "No, you cannot. She is fine. She's a big girl."

My jaws clench painfully. I want to strike this idiot on the head with a frying pan so hard his brains splatter onto the wall. Who the hell does he think he is, barging in on our family vacation and telling us what we can or cannot do?

"Let me at least give her a glass of water. She must be dehydrated. You don't want her to die, do you?" I glare into his eyes.

He blushes again. "She knows where the water is. She can fetch it for herself." He takes a piece of carrot from the cutting board and pops it into his mouth. "I want you to answer my question. What am I doing wrong? I want to be an entrepreneur, a social media influencer, but nothing I do is working. Why?"

My patience is wearing thin. "Look, I don't know. Maybe the content you share isn't something many people relate to." I shrug. "I appeal to stay-at-home moms who struggle with balancing family and keeping their identity at the same time. We exercise together. We cook together. I don't lecture people. I don't tell them how to live their lives. I only invite them to share their day with me, so none of us feels alone," I say all this in one breath, through clenched teeth.

The man nudges me on the shoulder. "The soup is overboiling."

I grab the pot's handle on the burner with a rushed movement, and it burns my hand. I nearly drop the whole thing. A splash of soup spills onto the hot plate. It sizzles, sending up steam.

"Look at you! You're a hot mess. I thought you were this awesome cook."

My patience has reached its limit. I look at him with so much hate that I might attack him myself. "These are different circumstances, don't you think? You come here and threaten us with your gun. You hold us against our will. You killed my boyfriend." I spit the words into his face.

He leans to me and puts the gun into my temple. "No! I saved you from that sick fuck."

"Please don't hurt my mom," Noah screams. "Please! Please!"

I messed up. I should have remained composed. My low blood sugar is messing with my nerves.

"If you touch my mother, I'll fucking kill you, you fat piece of shit!" Jayden is on his feet. He has become a threat. The man takes note of it, and as he moves toward my children, I grab his arm. "Let's all calm down. Here, the soup's ready. Let's eat."

"I'll eat once I handle this bigmouth."

"He didn't mean it." I'm holding onto the man with both hands. I can smell his stench. It's a revolting combination of body odor and cheap deodorant. Sickening. I think I might puke. "Tell me more about your business. You said you're an entrepreneur? I want to hear more." I sound desperate. He knows I'm lying.

He switches directions and goes to the table, where he grabs the duct tape and hands it to me. "Tie them up. I'm not asking again. Now. I'm done playing nice."

I put my hands up. "Okay! Okay. I'll do it."

He starts pacing again while tapping the gun against his forehead. He looks as if he has another personality he's consulting with before making a decision.

I go to Jayden first. "Hold out your hands."

Something hits my back. The man threw a peanut at me. "Not in front. Tie his hands behind his back," he orders. "And his ankles too. And make it tight."

Jayden's expression betrays a mix of his emotions—fear, disappointment, even anger. I nod at him to ask for his cooperation, then I turn him around and wrap the duct tape loosely around his wrists. "Sit down on the futon."

He does, and I rip off a piece of tape from the roll with my teeth and attach it over his ankle socks.

A force pushes me to the side, and the space is so small that I slam my hip against the edge of the tabletop behind me. I yelp in pain, but I manage to stay upright.

"What the fuck is this?" the man yells, pulling on the loose tape. "You are truly disappointing me, woman," he says with disgust, twisting his lips. I see his arm move. A flash of black. A numbing pain in my temple. Then nothing.

JENNIFER

My mouth is dry, and I taste blood. My eyelids feel heavy hanging over my itchy eyes, and it takes a great deal of effort to keep them open. With every blink, the details of my surroundings become less hazy, yet my throbbing brain struggles to create a complete picture. It appears I'm in a dim room, bathed in golden light from the glow of the fire.

My face is lying on the floor in a pool of saliva. The smell of ash and smoke tingles my nostrils.

Groaning, I attempt to move my arms to support my effort in sitting up, but they aren't responding. I try again with more focus and force. A stinging pain shoots up from my wrists as if something was pulling on the fuzzy hairs on my lower arms.

I groan as I roll to my right, blinking rapidly to clear my vision. My eyes are so itchy they are killing me, but I can't rub them because my hands are bound.

From one glance at the lantern on the table and the three soup bowls in the pool of light, my memories rush back to me.

Wriggling in panic, I cast my eyes around the yurt. I spot a dark mound of a body in my bunk bed on top of the sleeping bag, covered with a blanket, but I don't see anybody else. When I try to open my mouth to call for my children, I realize that my mouth is taped just like my hands and ankles. My attempt at yelling ends up in a feeble, muffled whimper.

Like a caterpillar, I inch my body to the futon, where I push myself into a sitting position with incredible effort.

I'm naked and aching. My first instinct is to check for signs of being violated. I find blood on my thighs.

As my heartbeat speeds up, so does my need for oxygen, and I suck the air through my nose in terror. Where are my children?

I crane my neck in the hope of seeing over the table at the other side of the room, but salty tears are stinging my eyes, blurring my vision. I bang my back against the futon to make some noise, hoping to elicit a response.

A muffled whimper rises from the other side of the room, but from this angle, the dining set obscures my vision. I drop back to my stomach to look underneath the table. Between the legs of chairs, I see Jayden, Emily, and Noah sitting on the ground next to each other across the room, bound by duct tape.

I start worming my way around the table to get to my children. Splinters from the wood floor etch my skin, and soon my knees feel raw from the unfinished floor. When a tiny broken-off sliver penetrates the naked skin on my right breast, I see stars in white places. The duct tape contains my scream, and the sound gets stuck in my chest like a piece of unchewed food swallowed too hard and fast.

Emily's face is the first one that comes into my view. Her eyes are dark-circled, sunken, and red from crying. Head movements are the only means of communication between us, and there's not much we can share, but we both must understand that we are in trouble. She is fully clothed, and I feel a shard of relief for that.

Jayden sits next to her, their shoulders touching. The moment he sees me naked, he looks away and forces his eyes shut tight. He's never seen me without clothes, not even when he was a little boy. My sister likes to bathe with her young children, but I never found that necessary.

I see Noah's legs on top of each other parallel with the floor, but before I can inch forward enough to see his entire body, the stranger wakes up and tosses his legs out of bed and onto the floor next to me.

Despite our predicament, I sigh in relief. My children are alive.

"You up?" the man says, yawning. "Finally."

He stretches his arms and cracks his neck. "The soup was good. Want some? You must be hungry after the night we had." He smirks, and I have to hold onto every bit of my self-restraint not to throw up in my mouth, which would undoubtedly result in me choking to death on vomit.

I nod at him, mumbling my request that turns into a throaty groan.

"What?" He points at his ear. "I can't understand you with the tape over your mouth." He makes a gesture of feigned ignorance.

Emily is crying again, and I want to go to her and hug her so badly.

I don't hear Noah's voice. He isn't moving. Please, God, let him be sleeping.

I mumble again, wiggling my body. This time the man gets up from the bed and comes to me. He rips off the tape from my mouth with one swift movement. White pain blinds me for a moment.

"Can you cover me up, please?"

He smirks again. "Why? You have a beautiful body. I love looking at you."

I want to tell him that I can't have my children see me like this, but I'm worried he would rather get rid of them than allow me to dress.

"I'm cold. I'm shivering," I say instead.

His smile disappears. He leans over my head and pulls off Noah's blanket from the futon. He squats in front of me, holding the blanket in a ball in front of his crotch. He watches me, and I stare back at him with my mind void of thoughts. I've never been so humiliated like this in my entire life.

He reaches out with his right hand and cups my left breast. He rubs his dirty thumb against my nipple. My need to stand up for myself screams at me, but my self-preservation silences the voice.

He removes his hand from my breast and puts his thumb into his mouth and sucks on it. He puts his wet fingertip against my nipple and starts rubbing it again until it turns hard. "You like that, don't you," he says, looking at me with a sick desire in his eyes.

I try to wriggle away, but he stops me by pinning me against the futon with his knees. He runs his hand up to my face and forces his thumb into my mouth. I want to bite down on it with all my might, and I need every ounce of my willpower not to do so.

The rough skin on his dirty thumb rubs against my tongue as he shoves his finger deep into my throat.

I gag, unable to breathe. I struggle to lean away because the intruder takes hold of the back of my head and pulls my mouth to his. He pushes his tongue into my mouth, and I taste my salty tears mixed with his sour breath.

On the edge of my peripheral vision, I see my children. Jayden's eyes are still closed. Emily is watching us, tears washing down her face, her chest heaving. Noah still isn't moving, and I can't see his face to confirm that he is okay.

I close my eyes and try to keep my tongue away from his invasive piece of slimy meat in my mouth, but his tongue is aggressive and there is no escape from it.

When I feel the man's hand rubbing me between my legs, my eyes pop wide open. I protest with a groan, fighting him to get away, but in vain.

When his fingers penetrate me, his nails scratch me. I've never felt so hopeless and helpless. I want to die.

At last, he unlatches his vacuum-sealed lips from my mouth.

"Please, not in front of my children," I beg as my heart sinks to my stomach.

"They already saw us earlier," he says, breathing into my face. His breath smells like sour wine. "Kids don't care. I saw my mother doing her boyfriends many times. I didn't care."

I need to stop appealing to this man's common sense. He doesn't have any. "Can you cover me with the blanket? I'm freezing," I say, because he does seem to care about me in some very twisted and sick way.

"Let me warm you up." He lifts me from the floor and lays me onto the futon. I hear him undo his belt and zipper, but I can't bear to watch. I look to the side at Noah's blanket still in the man's grasp. It's his Dodger throw he sleeps with at home. I close my eyes and transport myself back to that day when we were at the stadium in Los Angeles, watching a game. We were posing in baseball caps and team jerseys. We were so happy. I recorded the whole day and shared it online. This sick bastard probably watched it.

My body tenses up from the man's weight, giving me trouble breathing. I can't block out his wheezing that's warm against my ears. Connor will kill you for this, I think as I clench my jaws harder from the disgust and pain.

JENNIFER

I don't know what time it is, but I assume it's well into the morning, judging by the amount of sunlight penetrating through the windows and the skylight. I never thought I'd be able to fall asleep in a hostage situation, especially if my children's lives were at risk, but my subconscious takes no orders from me. After the man had finished with me, drained a bottle of Tyler's wine, and made sure all of our restraints were tight and secure, he turned the lantern off and went to sleep.

So did I.

I remember fighting the darkness as long as I could, but I had little chance of winning against the raw aching of my body, the hunger, and exhaustion.

Now I'm slowly waking up, a throbbing headache behind my eyes making me nauseous, and when I turn toward my bunk bed to ask the man to allow me to drink some water, my heart leaps in surprise.

The bed is empty.

I wriggle myself into a sitting position to let my children see me. I find only Jayden sitting in the spot where he was last night. No signs of Emily or Noah.

Jayden's expression is blank and distant. His eyes are aimed at me, yet I feel he looks right through me.

I roll off the futon and force my way to the edge of the table, which I use to scrape off the duct tape from my mouth. I feel a scratch. I must have cut my lips, because I taste blood.

"Where are your sister and brother?"

Jayden shrugs, his head unmoving. My son is always full of spirit and life. But now he appears to be broken and catatonic.

"Jayden, where are Emily and Noah?" I ask again in a more assertive voice.

He lets out a series of frustrated gurgling sounds. Yes, of course. His mouth is taped.

I drop back to my side and slither to him like a snake. He looks away from me again as if he's ashamed of seeing me naked. I press my face into his upper body to use him as a guide to sit up. I rip off the duct tape from his mouth with my teeth.

"He took them," he says once his lips are free.

"He took them where? When?" Nothing matters at this moment, not my exposed body, not the horrors he'd seen last night, nothing but to work together and get my children back and into safety.

"Emily needed to pee, and that bastard took her outside."

"Where is Noah?" As much as I feared the answer to the question, I had to ask.

"He went with them."

I lean my head against Jayden's chest and sigh in relief. Noah is alive.

Jayden winces, and I move to adjust my position.

"We need to get out of here," I say against his T-shirt. He doesn't smell like my son. The odor that surrounds him is alien to me. Maybe we release different pheromones when we are scared, changing our scent.

I straighten away from him and look into his face. He focuses hard to keep his eyes on mine.

"Can you lean to the side? Let me see if I can untie you."

He does, and I inspect the rope behind him that connects his chest to the leg of the bunk bed.

"I'll need a knife or something to cut this rope. Help me stand up."

I lay my head on the bunk bed mattress, and Jayden uses his knees to push me up. From the sudden change of position, I become dizzy and I need a moment to still myself. When the buzzing subdues and my vision returns, I hop toward the kitchen cabinet for the bread knife. I turn around and push my back against the edge of the counter, trying to reach over the countertop, but my arms can't bend high enough. I rise onto my tippytoes, but it's still too high.

"Try to stand on a chair," Jayden says, and I'm glad to see that he is focused once again. He might blame himself for his failed attempt to disarm the intruder, consequently causing me last night's humiliation. But I know it wasn't his fault. He didn't cause any of it. That man didn't follow us to this mountain top to play patty cakes. I'll explain all this to him later. Now is not the time for a heart-to-heart chat.

I hop back to the table and use my hip to push a chair toward the cabinet. It flips over and lands on its side. With my ankles and wrists bound, I have no choice but to use my hip to move the chair. Sitting down on the floor without the unrestricted use of hands and legs is extremely difficult. I end up dropping hard to my butt like a giant bag of flour, and it hurts.

I make a few attempts at pushing the chair back into a standing position with my shoulder and then with my face, but it's pointless. I use my hip to move the toppled chair toward the cabinet. That seems to be working.

Garbled voices coming from outside stop me in my tracks. I can't make the words out, but a man is talking.

"Hurry, Mom!" Jayden urges me, and I'm moving again frantically, beating my body against the chair.

At last, I hear the back of the chair slam against the front of the counter. I still need to stand it up, but it's a milestone getting this far.

The words spoken outside of the yurt are becoming clearer and louder. I may have only moments left to free myself.

I roll onto my knees, using my teeth to attempt to pull the chair toward me. It moves but not enough to stand it up.

"Mom, leave it and get back to the futon!" Jayden warns, but I can't give up yet.

I hook my head underneath the seat and try to turn the chair upright.

Footsteps on the patio are getting closer, and I'm worried fear will soon paralyze me.

The third attempt brings the result I'm looking for as the chair wobbles a few times and lands on its four legs.

Using the chair as a crutch, I pull myself back to my feet. I hear Noah's voice right outside the door.

My eyes are on the serrated edge of the bread knife. I sit down on the chair, pull my legs to my chest, and set my feet firmly on the seat. Standing up on the chair seems impossible without hands, but I won't give up, being this close to my goal. We may never get another chance at escaping.

"Leave him be!" I hear Emily's voice slipping through tiny cracks in the structure.

The chair tilts a few times but remains upright. I repeatedly bang my knees against the edge of the countertop before I can straighten my legs enough to stand up. Without hands, I must use my teeth to grab the knife, so I bend forward and place my face on the counter. The knife is right there. I can almost bite down on it.

"Mom!" Jayden's voice sounds desperate.

With all my might, I push myself forward, my face sliding against the smooth aluminum surface. My tongue touches the handle of the knife, and I pull it closer until I can feel it against my teeth. My jaw clenches hard over the handle. Now I only have to get off the chair, get back to Jayden, and cut off his restraints.

The door squeaks, and my panic reaches its height. From a wrong move, I fall off the chair and land on my back. I hit the back of my head on a knob on the cabinet door, and I feel my elbow bleeding from scraping against the edge of the chair seat. The impact has knocked the wind out of me, but at least I didn't stab myself. The handle of the knife is still clasped in my mouth.

When I manage to push the pain aside and open my eyes, the intruder is standing over me, holding Noah's hand. The grasp is so tight that my son's little fingers are white from the lack of blood.

Emily has a noose around her neck. The other end of the rope leads to the man's left hand. He is leading my daughter like a horse.

"What the hell are you doing?" the man asks me almost nonchalantly. "Are you trying to kill yourself?"

I know he expects an answer from me, but I can't bring myself to release the knife.

The man drags my kids around the table and sits them down by Jayden.

"I take your kids to the outhouse as a courtesy, and instead of thanking me, you do what?" He shakes his head at me vehemently as he works on tying the kids back to the bunk bed. "Play with knives?"

I don't move. I watch them in silence as millions of thoughts race through my head.

After checking the ropes and tape, he cuts his way through the space between the woodstove and the table. He kicks the knife out of my mouth. It slides underneath the cabinet. He bends down, grabs ahold of my elbow, and pulls me to my feet. From the rapid rise, my head swims again. I wobble. He steadies me with both hands. "Jeez, you stink!" He pinches his nose. "You need to bathe."

I'm a hygiene freak. I shower every morning, every night, and after every workout. I use shampoos and lotions that smell good. I never wear the same clothes twice without washing them first. I use natural fragrance-free laundry detergent and add jasmine oil to the laundry to make my clothes smell nice. I brush my teeth at least twice a day. My mother taught me to take care of my hygiene and never leave the house in a state that would embarrass me if I ended up in an ambulance. I live my everyday life by that rule, especially since I was involved in a fender bender when Connor was driving us home from a hike. It wasn't a serious accident, yet the handsome firefighters carried me into the ambulance for a check-up regardless because I was pregnant with Emily. When the paramedic took my shoes and socks off, I noticed how dirty my feet were. Connor and I had been hiking on a dusty trail that morning. I almost died of shame.

But given my current situation, I don't care what this animal thinks of me. I smell bad? Good, at least my stench will keep him from touching me again.

Regrettably, my hope for becoming repulsive to my attacker is premature. The man turns to my children. "I don't want to hear a peep while I take your mother to the shower. Got it?"

Noah starts crying again, and he keeps wiping his eyes with the backs of his hands. My heart breaks from seeing him like that.

I stay silent and go along as he drags me and pushes me out the door. He throws me over his shoulder and carries me across the patio and down the slope the yurt is built into to get to the part underneath the patio. His shoulder bone presses into my stomach, and I hiss at every movement he makes as he balances my body.

We arrive at the shed, where I'd hung the shower bag when we were still enjoying our family vacation.

I stand on the platform, shivering with cold. "You need to untie me. I can't shower without my hands. I can't even walk."

The man's eyes travel up and down my naked body. "I can wash you down. But here, let me record you. I'm sure my followers would love to be part of this." He sets his phone on the top of a beam, checks the angle, and presses record. "Come closer. The tube doesn't reach that far."

I move to stand underneath the showerhead he holds out for me and close my eyes, expecting freezing water to saturate me when I'm already shivering.

I gasp when the first touch of ice water hits my chest. It's a slow trickle, not a cascade, so I expect this shower to be excruciatingly long.

The stranger uses the hygiene items I left here earlier to wash my hair and body. He keeps smiling at me and poses for the camera while he rubs my naked body with his meaty hands. I close my eyes and force my mind to conjure up better pictures to survive this humiliation, but my brain isn't cooperating.

Suddenly the water stops while there is still soap in my eyes.

"Fuck! The bag is empty. Wait here," the man says, as if I have the choice to run away with my hands and legs bound.

A few minutes elapse until I hear his muffled footsteps on the wet ground again. I hear the sound of the faucet turning on and water filling a bucket.

My teeth are rattling from the cold as I wait for what comes next. I can make out the sound of water sloshing in a bucket and the soles of heavy boots squeaking on the wet grass. Then shock paralyzes my body and chokes the air in my lungs. This idiot poured a bucket of cold water over me.

My eyes and mouth pop open. I breathe heavily as I watch the man holding his phone and recording me through a curtain of water that rolls down from my hair onto my face in streams.

"Wow! You are sexy as hell," he says, laughing.

I want to attack him and bash his face into his skull. I've never had violent feelings like these before in my life. Like many mothers, I'm sure, I've had thoughts of what I would do to a person who hurt my children, but this is a whole new level of savagery in me.

"Oh, shit!" the man says, slipping his phone in his pocket. "You must be freezing. Here." He throws a towel at me that's been hanging out here in the cold. I manage to clamp it with my chin against my chest, but with my hands tied behind me, I won't be able to wrap it around my body.

"Let me help you." He leans against me as he reaches behind me with the towel. There is that acrid smell again that makes me hold my breath.

He picks me up and carries me in his arms to avoid my feet getting dirty. What a gentleman.

By the time we get back to the patio, it's starting to snow.

JENNIFER

When my captor releases me from his arms and sets me on my feet, the loosely tied towel around me falls to the ground. Once again, he makes me stand naked in front of my children, and it's not okay, so I immediately turn away in shame.

"I'm going to get dressed now," I say assertively, not leaving space for a discussion. If he only wanted to kill me, he'd have done it by now, but this man has a plan for me. The endgame for me could still be death, but I'm important to him for the time being. I feel I can leverage that.

"Go ahead," the man says without looking up from his phone. The smirk on his face betrays the amusement he gets from watching the video of me showering. It's scary how detached he is from reality. He's like a kid with a toy.

Watching him eat makes my stomach turn. Tiny flakes of breadcrumbs drop from his mouth onto his shirt from the soft bun he is devouring. I haven't had any food for over thirty-six hours, and the kids only ate a small bowl of chicken soup last night. I must get into this man's head and make him more aware of our predicament. Even sociopaths must have some empathy.

I bump into him to get his attention. "I need you to cut the tape off of me. I can't put clothes on with my hands and ankles tied."

He casually removes a switchblade from his pocket and slices through the duct tape between my ankles. I turn around, and he frees me from my bounds over my wrists next. His actions are so natural, as if we've been living like this for years.

The moment my arms move free, my shoulders flare up with stiffness and strain. I cover myself with my hands as much as possible as I make my way to the bunk beds. I stoop down at my travel bag and dunk my hand inside of it. I packed my clothes at home meticulously, so I know where I will find each item I need. I pull on some underwear and slip my legs into a pair of sweatpants.

"Wait! Wait! Wait! Slow it down!" the stranger barks at me. He is holding his cell phone up in front of him. I'd hoped that his battery would have died by now as ours did, but now I see that he has a portable charger connected to it. He came prepared. "I want to record you getting dressed. You're so sexy."

I keep my head down as I put on an undershirt and pull a hooded sweater over my head. I'm still shivering. The cold has seeped into my bones.

I put on a pair of hiking socks and a knitted hat. My kids are watching me.

I look up at the skylight. The snow is falling in giant flakes. I try to rub the tension out of my shoulders to get the feeling back to my arms, but they are weak and heavy.

"Is it okay if I put more wood on the fire?" I ask the man, blowing air into my hands and rubbing them together.

"Yeah, sure," he says without paying much attention to me. He is in a good mood. He must have had a good night's sleep, but I decide not to push my luck with him.

I pick up a few logs from the basket and open the door on the woodstove. The heat that bursts out of the chamber envelops my face. My icicle hands and feet are warming up, bringing the inevitable sensation of hot needles prickling my skin from the inside.

"How's your leg?" I whisper to Jayden.

He shrugs. He can't look me in the eyes. Not even when I'm dressed.

After I feed the fire with two more logs, I run my fingers along Noah's cheek. I want him to know that I would never let anything bad happen to him.

"Come here." The intruder taps the seat on the futon next to him. I recognize that look in his eyes. I saw it last night.

"I was about to make us something to eat. You must be hungry," I say as I stand up and walk to the cooking counter.

"Come here and sit on my lap." He is tapping his thigh, holding out his phone to the side, recording us.

"I have a few cans of clam chowder soup. It would go well with those bread buns you like." I'm stalling because it's too bright in the yurt and the kids have a straight view of the futon. They're already traumatized by the events of the past twenty-four hours. I have to avoid adding to their trauma.

"We can eat later. Now come here." There is a hint of impatience in his voice. I don't know him enough to judge how far I can push him before he breaks. Everything I say or do is a gamble.

"The children haven't eaten anything since last night. Can I please make some food first?" I plead, pulling the lid back from the first can to show him the soup could be done in no time.

The phone lowers in his hand, and his shoulders drop. A dark veil descends over his face. His hand moves so fast that at first, I can't even make out what's happening.

I hear the sharp sound of something penetrating wood. He's thrown a knife at me. The blade has sunk into the cabinet door a few inches from my face. Emily screams, but the tape over her mouth muffles most of it.

"I'll count to three." He holds up his fingers. "One, two…"

I put the can down and approach him, screaming inside my head. I don't want him to touch me. I don't want to smell him. I don't want to be near this man. Oh, God, please help me.

"Come on! Hurry up!" His phone is on me again. It's on selfie mode. I see myself on the screen. Sunken eyes. Dark circles. Matted hair.

"Can I please send the kids outside? We need more wood. More water."

"Forget about the kids. Just come, sit." He is undoing his pants. Red, hot excitement flushes his face. "Take your pants off."

"I just put them on."

He rolls his eyes and reaches for his gun. He presses the barrel hard against my temple. "Don't piss me off, woman. If you took your pants off for that fruitcake loser, then you better jump out of your pants for me. I'm not gonna ask you again."

I hold his gaze without blinking. "I'm putting the headphones on Noah first." I pull away, turn my back, and walk away from him. He wants me. He won't shoot me in the back. I know I have some kind of power over him, but my heart is hammering fast, and I feel pins and needles poking my chest. My left arm feels numb as I search the room for the headphones.

"Come back here right now!" He is shouting, but he hasn't left the futon.

My breathing accelerates, yet there is not enough air in my lungs. My vision alternates between clear and blurry.

I find the headphones on the floor under Tyler's bunk bed. I put them over Noah's ears. There is no music connected to it, but these expensive headphones are designed to block out ambient noise. I clamp his little head between my hands. "I need you to close your eyes again until I tell you to open them, okay?"

Tears roll down his cheeks.

"Close them now, please. You don't need to worry about me. I won't let this man hurt me, okay?"

He nods and shuts his eyes so tight they turn into a wrinkled line on his face.

I focus my attention on Emily and Jayden. "Look away. I'm so, so sorry."

They are crying too. I can't bear the sight of my children like that.

As I stand up, I suddenly feel a cramp in my chest. I press my fist against my sternum, taking deep, ragged breaths. Jayden notices that something is wrong with me, and he starts wriggling against his restraints, whimpering.

"We will survive this. Stay calm....please," I tell Jayden, but every word is a struggle to get out of my throat.

"Okay, that's enough! You are pushing your luck, bitch. Get over here right now. Don't make me ask you again."

A roaring thunder rips through the air. I jump, my ears ringing. I feel as if a horse has kicked me in the chest. Panicking, I inspect my children. They don't seem to be hurt. "Did he shoot me?"

The pain in my chest intensifies. I'm losing consciousness.

I rotate my head to face the man. "Did you shoot me?" I ask, trying to rise to my feet, but I'm wobbly.

"No, I shot in the air!" The man jumps beside me, examining my clothes. "Are you bleeding?"

"I don't know. My chest."

Jayden is in a rage. The entire bunk bed is rattling as he pulls on his rope, growling like a madman.

"What's wrong with her?" the stranger asks Jayden, but he can't communicate without words.

"Here." The man rips off the duct tape from Jayden's mouth.

"She's having a panic attack! Get her pills! Hurry the fuck up!"

"Where are they?"

"In her bag somewhere, you fucking idiot!"

"Shit! Where?" The man stands up and scratches his head.

"There, hanging on the hook by the door, you rapist piece of shit," Jayden roars almost incoherently.

I roll onto my back, holding my chest, taking rapid, small breaths. I think I'm having a heart attack. I watch the blanket of snow that has settled on the round skylight above me. A dull light cuts through the layer of white fluff, and tiny dots sparkle like diamonds. I feel myself fading. This is it. *Please, not yet, God. My kids need me. I can't leave them here alone with this monster. Please give me a few more days. I'm begging you. Let me save my children.*

Someone sits me up and shoves pills into my mouth. Liquid trickles down my chin. I nearly choke on water. The man slams me on the back hard, and I cough a few times.

"Don't you die on me now! We have one more day!"

"Mom!" I hear Jayden's voice. "Mom, please, look at me."

I want to look at him, so why isn't my head turning?

I feel the edge of a glass cup against my lips, and this time I'm ready to drink. I swallow the water. I blink a few times.

"Mom, take a deep breath. If she dies, I'll fucking kill you!"

I'm taking deep breaths. In and out. I can do this.

"Is she gonna die? What should I do?"

I detect genuine worry in our captor's voice. I turn my head slowly to look at him.

"Untie me, let me help her! Are you listening to me, you dumb fuck?" Jayden's voice is full of urgency.

The man is squatting a few feet away from me, banging the gun against his forehead. My heart rate is slowing down. I move my fingers.

"I didn't want her to die. I didn't want this," the man murmurs, confused.

The bunk bed near me is rattling uncontrollably. "Untie me! Untie me now, you hear me!"

"I'm okay," I say, or at least I think I am. "I'm okay," I whisper again. I want to move, but I don't feel my legs. My whole body feels leaden. There is pressure on my chest as if someone is sitting on it.

I manage to stretch my arm far enough to reach Jayden's ankle. I give it a weak squeeze to let him know I'm okay. I've had a few anxiety attacks before, but never this severe. My eyes wander to the orange prescription bottle on the floor. The man gave me hydroxyzine. In less than thirty minutes, I'll be asleep for a good eight hours. *No!* I scream in my head. I can't check out now. I need to stay awake. What would help me counter the effects of the drug? *Caffeine.*

I moan as I roll to my side. Finally, I get on all fours. "I need coffee," I tell Jayden.

"No, Mom. Stay still! I don't want you to die." Jayden's face is a mask of agony, anger, and hot tears. We have a very close relationship. Despite Connor's insinuation, he isn't a mommy's boy, because I encourage his independence, but he knows he can always count on me, that I'd walk through fire for him. Unconditional trust and love are the most powerful tools parents can offer their children.

I open my eyes wide to stay awake as my nails dig into the wood planks from desperation.

"Is she going to be okay?" I hear the man ask, but I can't bring myself to look at him. I must fight the drowsiness.

Jayden is struggling to break free. Noah's face is wet with tears. Emily is leaning against her little brother. I can't imagine what will happen to them if I'm not here to take the heat from this monster.

"I can't stay awake," I whisper, blinking slowly. "My stomach is empty." I get to my knees and pull myself up on the table. I shuffle to the cabinet, my eyes set on the can of clam chowder. Putting some food in my stomach may buy me some time.

"Where do you think you're going?" The man grabs my waist and pulls me back to the futon.

"Please, I need to eat something."

"Okay, fine." He is confused and off-kilter. He sets his gun on the counter and finishes what I started. Moments later, I can smell the soup in the air and hear the bubbles pop as he heats the clam chowder on the stove.

My eyes stay closed longer than I can keep them open. I see a hazy image of the mountain of a man approaching me with a bowl and spoon in his hand, but before I can take my first bite, I slip away into dreamland.

CONNOR

The hot sun is beating down on me from the clear sky, burning the back of my neck and scorching the already drought-stricken land around us. At least it's a dry heat and not that sticky shit they have in Florida or up north in the summer months.

Last August, my crew worked slightly east of Santa Barbara, replacing poles and parts on electrical lines. The city reported record heat that month we were there. And as if the high temperatures weren't enough, the ocean layer brought moisture to add to our misery. We were sweating like pigs in a pen on that job. On trying days when Mother Nature seems to conspire against us, switching to a shirt-and-tie office job looks tempting. However, the feeling is fleeting. After a long day in the field, I go home, jump into my pool, and grab a cold one, and I'm a happy man again.

Today we're working close to the Mexican border near Tecate. There's nothing out here but desert, snakes, and chaparral bush.

I watch the lineman rechecking the connections one last time before re-energizing the lines my crew has been working on all day. I keep an eye on their every move because this site is my responsibility. I wish I didn't have to hover over them as if they were children, but last week, one of my linemen grounded a line into a nearby house instead of the main ground, and the whole transformer damn near blew up. It was quite a fireworks show. When it's a contract job with one of the big electric companies, we can't afford to make clusterfuck mistakes like that. I haven't decided yet if I'll recommend the lineman that made that mistake to be let go or not. A weak link in a crew can ruin the reputation of the entire team, as there's little room for error in what we do. But he is a family man with mouths to feed, so I'm conflicted about what to do.

When the lineman's voice comes through the radio telling me he's ready to energize the line, I bring my hand to my brow to block the glare from the sun and give his work one last inspection. I nod and give him two thumbs-up. He pushes the fuse back into place and activates the line.

No sparkles.

That's good.

After the guys check the voltage, I yell at the groundsman to lower the crane and bring my people to the ground.

We are done for the day. It's about damn time.

As I load the tools into my truck, I spot Tim, one of the groundsmen, by the edge of a slope, gulping water out of a bottle. His face is caked with dirt, and black rings line his neck. When he is finished drinking, he wipes the spilled water from his thick manicured beard. His trendy facial hair is the most envied feature among most of the younger men.

Most of these guys on the job are here from Kansas or Missouri. They spend three to four months away from their families, roasting under the hot Southern Californian sun all day without complaint. They make excellent money because not many people can, or will, do the job they do, although I'm not sure how much of that money makes it back home. These guys aren't famous for making the best life choices. But if a war ever breaks out on our shores, these are the type of men who will have my back.

"Don't move, man!" I hear Rodney, one of the crane operators, shout at Tim. "There's a fucking rattlesnake in the dirt again. He's cruising right toward you!"

Tim freezes on the spot according to his training. On the first day of the job, I explained the dangers we face here in the Californian desert. We often encounter snakes when we clear out brush from an area so the trucks can put down their outriggers, but this big boy is slithering across the uneven dirt like he owns the place.

I grab a shovel from the back of my truck and head toward Tim. But Bubby, another lineman from West Virginia, steps expertly in and snatches the rattler behind its head and along its body with one swift move.

"See, boys, ain't no reason to be killin' this poor fella. He wants to live too, ya know," Bubby says as he walks the snake away from the site and releases it back on the slope.

Tim removes his hard hat and wipes his forehead in his sleeve, leaving a dark smudge on the neon yellow fabric. "Thanks, Bubby. That's, like, the eighth time you saved my life."

"Don't worry about it none, bud. It woulda passed by without bothering us, you know. I just don't see no need to be chopping the poor fella's head off. But I'll take a beer on your tab." He winks and snaps his fingers.

I grin at Bubby in appreciation.

Tim steps to me. "Why don't you join me and the boys today, boss. We're grabbing a cold one after we unload at the yard."

I hesitate to agree. I'm the foreman, and if I start drinking with my men, it will be harder to reprimand them or let one of them go. It's a rookie mistake I'd made before I wised up to what my job entails.

To win some time to respond to the invitation, I pull out my phone from my back pocket and check for text messages from Jayden and Jen. They should have been off the mountain yesterday, and I've been calling and texting both of them all day, but I can't get through. Not hearing from them puts me on edge. It makes me nervous to know that that foolish mommy's boy Tyler is in charge of my family. I wouldn't trust the dude to walk my dog around the block.

Going to the mountains was my thing. When I was a kid, I spent every summer on lake vacations and camping trips. That pansy-ass Tyler only knows all-inclusive hotel vacations, yet now he wants to go to the mountains? It's not enough that he stole my wife; now he is trying to replace me in my family completely.

My head is buzzing with frustrating thoughts again. I'm a divorced man, free to do anything I want. I can't be anchored to my old life forever. If my family doesn't want to talk to me, well, so be it. "You know what, Tim. A cold one sounds damn good to me right now."

It takes forty minutes to drive back to the main yard, unload the old fuses and lines, and switch trucks. I get into my 4Runner. My car was parked in the sun all day, and the trapped air inside the cabin is hot and dry. I can barely breathe, let alone touch the burning steering wheel. I turn the AC on full blast.

The boys won't shower or change before hitting the bar. We'll go as we are. Sweaty. Dirty. Tired.

As I wait for the cool air, I look down at myself. My daughter, Emily, used to tell me that I look like a traffic cone when I go to work. She meant no offense, but I think deep down she was embarrassed by me in jeans, work boots, and a neon orange or yellow job shirt.

Her best friend's dad owns an online newsletter and social media company. He drives a Tesla. Eats at Curry Leaf. Drinks Starbucks coffee with all kinds of drizzle and whipped cream on top. He still dresses like a college kid. He recently adopted a kitty from the pound. He is involved in his community and goes to protests. I know all that because Emily reports on him every time I have her for the weekend.

Yet, without crews like us, there would be no electricity, no cell phone connection, no internet. And after a wildfire blazes through the lands and burns down powerlines, guess who the first guys in after the firefighters are? We are the unsung, or even unknown, heroes of society.

At times, I feel the urge to explain all this to Emily, but I never do. I simply listen to how cool Tina's dad is and smile.

Maybe that's why Jennifer left me. She was embarrassed to be married to a traffic cone.

Tim knocks hard on my window. "Ready, boss?"

I offer him a thumbs-up, but before putting the car into gear, I try to call Jayden one more time. The call goes straight to voicemail again. I ring Emily, then Jennifer. All I get are voicemails. As a final attempt, I click on Tyler's number in desperation. I get the same result.

I rub my face, thinking what the hell is going on. Are they having so much fun in that yurt that they don't even think of checking in with me? Jayden wouldn't do that, would he? I'm mad at myself for encouraging Jennifer to go with the kids on this off-the-grid vacation. I wanted to appear as a cool ex-husband by supporting her, be more like Tina's dad. But I'm furious now with my decision. It should be me on that mountain with my family, not her lousy boyfriend.

Fuming, I shift into drive and follow Tim's truck to an off-Yelp local dive bar, where a raspy-throated old bartender lady seems genuinely happy to see a bunch of hardworking, dirty men. As we enter, she smiles and says, "Welcome home, boys!"

JENNIFER

"Mom! Wake up!" The words are sharp against my ears, accompanied by a violent shaking that's so intense it rattles my brain.

I struggle to open my eyes. The will is there, and I'm trying, but it feels as if someone has glued my eyelids shut.

"Mom! Someone is here!" I recognize Emily's voice, and I'm doing everything I can to make my body obey my mind's command and bring me back from this drug-induced coma.

"Splash cold water on her face." It's Jayden talking now, I know, I recognize his voice, but I still can't see.

"Mom! Someone's here. What should we do?" Emily is shaking me again. I feel her cold fingers against my skin.

She is trying to peel apart my eyelids. A cloudy image of her face comes and goes, in and out of focus. I feel like I'm underwater, drowning.

"Leave her!" Jayden groans. "Give me a knife or something."

I can sense Emily's presence leaving my side.

"There are no knives here."

"Whatever, find something."

Why are my children looking for a weapon? What's going on? Where is our attacker? Wake up, dammit!

"There's nothing here." Emily's voice buckles. She's panicking.

I clench my teeth and strain my body. I feel the muscles stretch in my neck and the blood rushing through my veins, pushing into every capillary, every cell. I'm restarting slowly, like an old, neglected engine.

"There! Break the bottom of that beer bottle and hand it to me." It's clear now that Jayden is readying himself for an attack. He is in danger. I can't lose him too. "Noah, splash Mom's face with that water. There, on the table. Hurry!"

From the cold liquid that slaps me on the face, my eyes pop open and my muscles seize with a jolt. Gulping a mouthful of air, I grab the top of the backrest of the futon and pull my heavy head off the pillow.

Smoke hovers in the room mixed with the stream of sunlight breaking through the skylight and the blinds. My eyes behold all my children: Jayden, Emily, and Noah scattered in the room. An overwhelming mixed sense of gratitude and relief touches me. The joy of seeing my children alive and seemingly unharmed is making me cry. My love for them floods my heart, and I become more emotional than rational. They need my help to defend themselves. They need a parent who can fight for them, yet I'm drowning in these strong emotions. *Damn these stupid mind-numbing pills. I'll throw them all out when I get a chance.*

"You're not tied." I manage to push the words out of my mouth. "Run! Save yourself!"

"Mom, we need you, please," Noah pleads with urgency. "We heard voices. There are people here."

He is kneeling next to me. His little body is pushing against the futon. He reaches for my hand, and his fingers grasp mine.

"Emily, look." Jayden's voice has lowered to a whisper.

I see him pointing toward the window. I turn my head in the direction he is indicating, but the effort it takes is so great, it's as if I'm wearing an iron helmet. I focus all my energy to pull myself out of the haze. Emily is by the cooking area, holding the bottle, whole and unbroken. Jayden is sitting on my bunk bed. They are all looking toward the door, focusing on the approaching footsteps outside the yurt. There are conversing voices—a woman's and a man's.

"Lock the door." I breathe the words.

In my head, I picture myself running to the door, closing the latch, and arming myself with a broken bottle, but when I look down at myself, I see I haven't moved.

"Where did that fucker go?" Jayden's anger manifests itself in a way that's a lot like his father's. I'm always asking him to put a lid on his anger and act civilized, but this time I'm grateful for his rage. "Maybe that animal brought some friends. Noah, give me that stick," he orders with a sense of authority that launches his little brother into immediate action.

Noah reaches for the sharpened branch Jayden had carved the first day we arrived and used as a spear. He isn't tied up either. None of my children are. *What did I miss?*

Emily locks the door, then retreats behind the table.

"Oh, great! Look at all this stuff. These assholes didn't clean up after themselves," a man complains. He is outside on the balcony, but his voice is loud enough for me to hear.

My children and I hold our unified breaths, joined by a common hope. We need these people to be here to help us and not to hurt us.

"Take pictures, because I'm not cleaning this mess up," a woman says, irritated. "We should go back to town and get someone to come up here."

"I think these are the people who rented the yurt after us," I whisper.

The days blur together in my head, but the presence of these visitors can mean only one thing: it's Thursday afternoon, and we are supposed to be gone by now.

"He's outside somewhere. He must see them too. Should we warn them?" Emily sounds so mature as she talks. I use my love for her as a driving force to move, fighting my drowsy brain's lack of cooperation. If I hadn't brought hydroxyzine on this trip with me, I'd be lucid right now.

I had a few anxiety attacks in the past year brought on by family issues and stress. I had nights that I couldn't sleep a minute without taking a pill. When I took two, I was dead to the world for ten to twelve hours. But that was my choice. I never thought that someone would use these pills to incapacitate me.

"Maybe they have a gun." Jayden sounds hopeful. "If Dad were here, he would have brought his Smith & Wesson. That fucker would never have had a chance against Dad."

"Noah, go under the bed," Emily calls out to her younger brother. "Here, hide."

"Don't leave me here," Noah whimpers as he climbs under the bunk bed where Jayden is sitting, his injured leg stretched out in front of him.

A man's face appears in the glass window of the door. He looks surprised to see people inside the yurt.

My brain doesn't compute with the required speed needed to analyze the situation. The buzzing in my ears is further numbing my senses. The noise is so intense, as if I've stuck my head inside a beehive. I need something to jumpstart me. A cup of strong coffee would do the trick, but the counter where the kettle is seems to be at an unreachable distance from me.

The door handle rattles. The tension around me is palpable.

A woman with long brunette hair presses her face against the glass. "Excuse me. Can you open the door, please? You're not supposed to be here."

Emily looks at me for confirmation. I nod at her as I try to get off the futon but immediately fall back into its cradle.

Jayden's grasp tightens over the spear, which he points at the door while Emily releases the latch.

A couple in their mid-thirties steps inside the yurt. "Hi," the woman says, unsure, suspicious even. "I think there's been a mistake. We have a reservation for this yurt for a week from today. What are you still doing here?"

"Lock the door quickly!" Emily screams at them, only to deepen their confusion.

I'm the mother here. I should handle the situation, but the dark arms of unconsciousness won't let me go. I'm not in control of my body. I'm only an observer of the events unfolding.

The man steps in front of the female and sets his backpack on the floor. "What's going on here?"

They must smell our stench—the combined odors of blood, urine, and ripe body, but their annoyance at the unexpected change in their plans seems to stump their common sense.

"I'll tell you, but first, close the door quickly!" Jayden says so fast I can barely understand.

The couple isn't listening. They are not the type of people who take orders from strangers, at least not until they have assessed the situation and made up their minds. Their probing eyes are sweeping the inside of the yurt, searching for answers. When she notices the blood on the floor where Jayden has sat for days tied to the bedpost, the woman gasps. "Honey! I think…" she says, but our captor's appearance in the doorframe cuts off the rest of her sentence. Holding a shovel, he towers over the couple with his height and body mass.

"Hello!" he says, almost playfully. Then he slams the shovel against the man's temple. The man collapses on the spot. The woman's screaming fills the room. Emily screams too. My ears are so sensitive to sound that my head twinges with a stabbing pain. *How many pills did that asshole shove down my throat?* I'm a worthless lump. A pile of blob. Useless. Powerless.

The shovel comes down a second time and dents the forehead of the woman. Her screaming stops instantly. She falls on top of the man and remains there, unmoving. The pool of blood underneath them expands and slowly moves toward us like an alien organism. I never knew blood was so dark and thick.

Our captor crouches down and puts a finger on the woman's neck, then on the man's. "I was a Boy Scout, you know," he says to us, amused. "I know how to check for a pulse and do CPR. Oh, fuck. They're dead. Why did they have to come up here in this God-forsaken weather?"

"Don't come any closer." Jayden points his spear at him, balancing on one leg.

Emily is biting her hand to choke her screams.

The intruder cocks his head and pulls his handgun from the back pocket of his jeans. He turns the barrel to the side like a wannabe gangster and points it at my son. "Put that stick down before I put a bullet in your head."

Fighting against the drugs with all my might, I extend my arm toward Jayden. I even manage to scoot a few inches forward on the futon. I can't reach him no matter how hard I try to stretch myself.

Emily sees my effort and puts her hand on Jayden's thigh. "Put the stick down, Jayden, please. I don't want you to die," she cries.

"Smart girl," the man says. "Smart, like your mother." He steps over the bodies and walks toward us. Jayden fidgets, unsure, and Emily recoils toward me. I don't hear a peep from Noah, so I assume he is still hiding underneath the bed.

"I thought I could trust you guys, but I guess I was wrong. Now look what you made me do. These two bodies are on you guys. Not me."

"You are an animal," Jayden says, his head hanging in defeat.

The man's face darkens. "Don't call me that." He leaps to my son like a steaming locomotive and pushes the barrel against his forehead. "Don't fucking call me that. You understand?"

I scream as I watch Jayden holding the man's gaze with defiance. "Don't you dare hurt my son!"

The man tilts his head and looks at me. His calculating eyes bore into mine.

"Please, I'm begging you," I plead, tears rolling out of the corners of my eyes. "Please don't hurt him. I'll do anything you want."

After a moment of silence that seems like forever to me, he clicks his tongue and shoves the gun back into his pocket. "Emily, get those ropes and tie up your bigmouth brother. You guys just lost your privileges."

He steps to me and kisses my forehead. His lips burn against my skin like the kiss of the devil. "Now look what you guys did. You woke up your mother." He pets my hair as if it were a genuine, loving gesture. The acid in my stomach swirls from the hatred that coils inside of me. I've never experienced an utter loathing like this before in my life.

While Emily's working on the ropes, the man looks around the space, seemingly searching for something. He grabs my medicine bottle, pours out two more pills, then picks up a bottle of water from the table and approaches me.

I shake my head, whimpering, but he pushes the pills into my mouth with his bloodstained fingers and forces water down my throat.

"I need some time to clean up this mess. I can't deal with you right now," he tells me and kisses my lips.

My eyelids flutter a few times. I see him checking on the knot Emily tied. I see him pulling Noah out from underneath the bed. But I can't do anything to stop him.

From a pang in my chest, my body tenses. I moan as I press a fist against my heart.

The man leaps to me so fast that I can feel the wind of his movement on my skin. He shakes me, breathing so hard his rancid breath fans against my face. "Don't you dare die on me now!"

I'm not dying. I can't be dying. God gives us as much as we can handle. He knows I'm strong. He'll allow me to prevail. He'll give me a chance to fight back. He must, mustn't He?

CONNOR

I pray for my company to leave my bed because I have to get up at five to get to work, but her arm lies across my chest like a strap. Her warm breath brushes against my shoulder as she softly snoozes next to me.

The air conditioning kicks in, and I welcome the cool breeze beating down on my naked body. I'm tired and mentally drained. A good night's sleep would do me good. But even if I fall asleep now, I'd be lucky to get six hours in before the alarm goes off again.

I look at the face of the stranger in my bed. She is way too sexy for a guy like me and the complete opposite of Jennifer. This chick's body is a road map of tattoos and piercings, while Jen's skin is smooth like alabaster. When my mind swam from beer and tequila, I tentatively listened to the stories behind every patch of inkwork on her extremities last night. Now, when an irritating pounding and buzzing torments my head, I want to grab a sponge and rub off the black images until her skin is red and raw.

This chick is cool. We had fun. But I have a feeling that if I fall asleep, she would rob me blind by the morning. It wouldn't be the first time a girl conned me.

I stir enough to wake her.

"Hey," she says, smiling.

"Hey," I say back with less charm. I think I smiled, but it may have been a grimace. "Can I get you something before you leave?" I know this isn't the most subtle approach, but there is no point in stretching out the inevitable all night. I'll be a dick. She will hate me for it and promise to leave and never come back. The chicks that are attracted to me always seem to follow a similar playbook.

The woman's face flushes with understanding. I brace myself for the yelling and insults, but she only sits up in the bed and starts getting dressed. Her quiet compliance makes me feel self-conscious and somewhat worried about what may come next. I like it more when they turn into a dragon than this calm-before-the-storm tension. It's easier to dislike them when they throw books and shoes at you and call you an asshole. I don't need this guilt right now.

"Look, I had a great time, but I need to get to work early tomorrow. I need a few hours of sleep." I lean in and kiss her to prove that I'm not trying to be mean. The whole situation is strangely amicable, and I feel the pressure to excuse my behavior.

"I get it. Don't sweat it. I didn't mean to fall asleep," she explains as she is getting dressed. This woman has a pretty face and a body that's round in all the right places. She keeps tucking her long black hair behind her ear every time she bends forward to pick up a piece of her clothing. In another stage of my life, I might have asked her to stay.

"Are you sure I can't get you something? Do you need me to call for a taxi?" I'm hovering now as guilt gnaws at me. She looks hurt and sweet, maybe even embarrassed. I may have misjudged her. This girl knows neglect and bad treatment from men. Fuck. I'm an asshole.

I hand her a bottle of water and ask for her number. It's cruel because I know I won't call her. I'm not ready for a relationship. If I call, I'll give her hope, only to take it away later. That damn divorce has ruined me.

She takes the water from my hand and punches her number into my phone. We kiss one last time, and I shut the door behind her.

I call Jayden again. I still can't get through to him.

Despite my desperate need for sleep, I spend an hour staring at the ceiling fan spinning. Then I put my hand under my boxers and relieve myself one more time. After that, sleep comes fast.

* * * * *

The sharp sound of the alarm pierces my ears. I wake with a start, my head full of nightmares. I slide my legs across the mattress and sit at the edge of my bed. As my head sinks low, I feel the tension in my neck. An invisible force is gripping my body, squeezing hard at my muscles, and making my heart beat fast and out of rhythm. Something isn't right. I can sense it.

I go to the bathroom to wash my face. Fragments of images from last night's dream flash in my mind. I only recall bits and pieces, but I know Jennifer is the main character in every story. There are other memories too. They are from the movie *The Mountain Between Us*. Emily made me watch that survival story with her a few weeks ago.

I pick up my phone and open Qwant to check the weather forecast for Norris and Branham Peaks in Montana. An unexpected heavy snowfall has dumped on the area.

I feel a cramping pain in the pit of my stomach. I'm worried that that city boy Tyler didn't prepare for harsh weather conditions in the mountains. I remember Jennifer telling me that they checked the weather forecast before they left, and it promised to be seventy degrees Fahrenheit and sunny. I tried to warn her to prepare for the worst, mountain weather can change unpredictably and fast, but she called me a paranoid pessimist.

I punch the wall, groaning, "That idiot can't take care of my family."

They're probably snowed in and can't leave the mountain to call for help. I hope Jennifer was smart enough to pack adequate food supplies.

I search for the name of the closest police station to Branham Peaks. Ennis Police Department's headquarters pops up in the search engine. I call the listed number. A tired voice answers at this early hour. At my inquiry, she tells me that snowplows have been clearing the roads all day and night, and an Audi SUV shouldn't have any problems leaving the mountain.

"My wife and children are in the Bell Lake Yurt for a vacation, but I haven't heard from them for days. Would you mind driving up there to check on them?"

"Oh, yeah, I remember. A young man came in here yesterday. He said if someone calls us about Jennifer Parker and her kids in the yurt, they're fine. They decided to stay longer on the mountain and camp. There is no cell phone service in the area. But they're fine."

"Was it my son Jayden?"

"How old is your son?"

"Seventeen."

"No, this young man was more like twenty-five. About six feet tall. Kind of heavy-set."

A jolt of pain stabs my stomach. Tyler is what, thirty-five, and certainly not heavy-set.

"Did he say his name?"

"I think he did, but I don't remember. I'm sorry."

"That's okay. Would you still mind checking on my family to be sure they're doing okay?"

"They are no longer in the yurt because a new couple checked in yesterday. If there were any problems, I'm sure we would have heard back from them by now," the officer assures me.

This neglectful behavior is unlike Jennifer. She would never have changed her plans without checking in with me. The weekend is my time with the kids. If they are still on the mountain in Montana, it means they won't be back by Saturday. She would never deny me my weekend with the kids without asking me first.

"Can you just drive up and check anyway?"

"Who did you say you were? The husband?"

"The ex-husband. My wife went to the mountain with her boyfriend and *my* kids."

"Oh, okay. Look, sir. I have no reason to believe there is foul play here. That must have been the boyfriend who checked in with us yesterday. He was polite. He didn't seem nervous. I can't go around harassing people on their vacation."

"Humor me, please. Better safe than sorry, wouldn't you say?"

I hear a sigh, followed by a moment of her silence. A printer is going in the background. Phones are ringing.

"It's jam-packed here today with the big dump of snow, but I might be able to send an officer to the yurt later today or tomorrow."

"I'll come up there and check on them myself. This is my family we're talking about, lady. I can feel something is wrong. Thanks for the help."

I hang up the phone and go straight to Expedia to book myself on the next available flight to Bozeman, Montana. I also reserve a Toyota 4Runner to be ready for me when I arrive.

After calling my boss and asking for emergency leave, I pack a bag with clothes and survival essentials, some nonperishable food, and my old bowie knife and race to the airport.

JENNIFER

Someone is calling my name. I'm almost sure it's a real voice, not a dream. "Mom! Moooom!"

The single voice evolves into a chorus of voices penetrating the haze in my head. My children are calling for me. They need me. I have to go to them. They wouldn't sound so desperate if they weren't in trouble.

Clenching my teeth, I push myself upward and force my eyes open. Every movement takes a great effort. My mind is languid, unwilling to react. "I'm here," I whisper. "I'm here."

It's dark around me. Ominous and cold. I feel the chill on my face, nibbling on my skin. Above me hangs a sea of black in the shape of a circle, dotted with bright stars. A sinister feeling touches my neck, and like running tiny cold feet, fear glides down my spine, making me shiver.

"Mom, wake up!" Jayden's panic-stricken voice penetrates the darkness.

My body is alien to me, so foreign and senseless, like moving sticky, rubbery octopus arms instead of my limbs.

My efforts meet with no resistance. I'm shocked to realize that my hands and legs are free. The ropes and tape are gone. I look at my children with bubbling hope. "I'm awake. I'm here,"

"There is something in the room," Emily whispers. She must have had a nightmare. No wonder, after spending two nights in this place with a violent attacker and watching people die, what child wouldn't? I need to get to her and offer her comfort and support, even if it warrants punishment from the animal that's holding us hostage.

My legs drag like blocks of lead on the wooden floor, but my mind is focused on reaching my kids. I move stealthily, trying not to wake the beast that must be slumbering.

When I reach the bunk bed, I squint over the mattress and find my sleeping bag empty. I expected to see the mountain of a man lying in my bed, and now my nervous anticipation morphs into fear. I become aware of my heart beating in my chest as I pull myself to a standing position and check Tyler's sleeping bag and both top bunks. The man is not sleeping in any of the beds. Then where is he?

My entire body goes into defense mode from the unknown. I take deep breaths to calm myself because I can't afford another episode. To relax my racing mind, I tell myself that this is an opportunity, not a setback.

The moonlight casts a cloudy sheen on my children, who are sitting in the same spot where they have been confined these past two days, though the duct tape is gone from their mouths.

"Where is he?" I ask in a restrained voice.

"He left," Jayden says. His voice is weak.

"Did he go to the outhouse?" I want nothing more than to free my children and bring them to safety, but I fear the danger I'd put them in if we get caught trying to escape again. What if the man becomes fed up with my children and considers their presence more trouble than it's worth? It takes a particular sort of demon to harm a child, and I don't think our capturer has it in him, but let's not underestimate the hazards of a crime of passion.

"I don't think so. He left hours ago. It was still light. You were out for a good ten hours," Jayden explains. His face and lips look pale in the moonlight.

"He was pacing up and down for hours. He ate all the peanuts and the bread," Emily adds. "He kept saying that he didn't want to hurt you."

The words stick in my mind. I comprehend their meaning. But the possibility that the man abandoned his plan and left us sounds too good to be true. Trust but verify.

"Let me check if he is roaming around outside."

"Be careful, Mom!" Emily whimpers.

I nod at her with pursed lips, though I'm not sure she can see my face in the dark.

With short, controlled breaths, I poke my head around the table, expecting to see the dead bodies on the floor. My nose must have gotten used to the stench of the room because I can't make out any distinct smells, but as miraculous as it is, my foggy mind remembers the murder of the couple.

I see a dark oval shape on the floor, clearly distinguishable on the light wood, and some lines that could be drag marks.

"He took the bodies," Emily says as if reading my mind.

"Be quiet. Let me see where he is," I warn, moving my feet softly on the floor.

"I'm telling you he's gone." Jayden's sharp voice startles me.

I spin around so fast I lose my balance and need a chair to steady myself. "Shush!"

He shrugs and looks away. I can't blame him for losing patience. While I was sleeping, he was tied up, most likely without food and water. His gunshot wound must hurt like hell. Unused muscles tend to stiffen up and ache with a harassing pain. Not to mention the rope must burn over his wrists and ankles.

I try to step over the blood, but it's quite vast and my bare feet land on something slimy and cold. Blocking the reality from my mind, I pull aside the curtain on the door window and look outside, but I can't see a thing in the pitch dark. I grab the serrated bread knife from underneath the kitchen cabinet where the man kicked it, and slowly open the door.

Noah's sudden panic-stricken voice gives me shivers. "Mom! Please don't go. I'm scared!"

I turn back from the door and put a finger over my mouth. Emily shushes her brother.

I step out onto the patio to be confronted with a winter wonderland. The wood planks moan under my feet, but the layer of virgin snow muffles my footsteps. The half-moon plays hide-and-seek with the sparse clouds, and I walk through a realm of alternating complete darkness and silvery moonlight.

It's so quiet around me that I can hear the wings of bats flapping in the distant night air. An owl hoots somewhere in the valley.

I look toward the outhouse, but it's concealed in darkness. I can't see any artificial light coming from the woods that would suggest our captor is out there, walking with a flashlight or lantern.

Relieved just as much as terrified, I turn to head back inside the yurt when I hear a squeaky sound followed by some scratching on wood next to me. It sounds like an animal trying to get into the yurt.

"Mom! It's here again! Come quickly!" Emily yells.

Three giant leaps take me back to the yurt. "Stop screaming. He'll hear us."

"He's long gone." Jayden talks as breathlessly as before. He must be in incredible pain, and guilt fills me for having a deep, long sleep under the spell of my pills.

"What makes you think that?"

"Just a hunch. He ate a lot of food, ripped the tape off our mouths, took his bag, and walked out the door hours ago," Jayden explains impatiently.

I lock the door behind me and wedge a chair against the door handle. I cut my children free. Noah jumps onto my neck, and Emily joins in the hug, but Jayden remains on the floor, rubbing his wrists, hissing, and moaning.

"How's the leg?"

"It doesn't matter. We need to get out of here."

I lean to him to pull him into a hug, but he winces away from me.

"All right," I say, ruffling Noah's hair, who is still clinging to me. "Do any of you know where Tyler put the car keys?"

Emily stops gulping down water from a bottle. "It's not in here?"

"I don't think so. I already ransacked this place when I went to look for the boys two days ago."

"Then he has it in his pocket," Jayden concludes as he pulls himself upright by the bunk bed. I try to support him, but he refuses my help.

I suck in my lips and look down. There is no time to talk out our feelings. We need to move. We need to get off this mountain. But to achieve that, we need a car. The thought of Tyler's cold body on the forest floor being ravaged by wild animals makes my stomach turn.

I turn to Jayden again. "Do you think you can lead us to Tyler? We need to search his pockets for the keys."

He shakes his head. "Maybe in daylight, I might be able to find the place."

I stand in silence as I process the situation.

"I can go out with a flashlight and look for him." He steps away from the bunk bed, teeth clenched tight, projections of pain dancing on his face. My heart twitches from seeing my son like this.

"All right. We can't wait till morning," I say, grabbing the bag of nonperishable food to inspect its contents. "We need to eat something. The hike back to town will be long, and we need energy. All of us." I talk fast, not leaving time for argument and opposition. "We'll put Jayden in the wheelbarrow. I can push him down the mountain. Emily, you think you can carry Noah?"

"I can walk, Mom," Noah interjects, talking with a full mouth as he is downing the last chocolate chip muffin.

I look at him smiling. "I know you can."

I find a bag of trail mix, three apples, four boxes of nonperishable milk, a half a bag of beef jerky, but all the other food items are gone. The fat pig must have taken everything else with him.

As I stop to think for a second, the scratching sound intensifies, and Emily jumps onto a chair. It's wild to comprehend that after all those days and hours I spent worrying about being attacked by big game, it was the human element and a rodent that we should have feared the most.

"It's only a mouse or a rat. Look at this mess—food on the floor everywhere. Let's hope that idiot didn't leave any leftover food outside. The last thing I want to do now is to confront a bear."

"Only a mouse or a rat?" Emily scolds. "I read somewhere that they can chew off your toe without you waking up because they have a numbing agent in their saliva."

"Well, good thing we aren't sleeping."

From a sudden turn, I'm light-headed again. I steady myself for a few moments. Then I pop a handful of trail mix in my mouth to up my blood sugar. "Guys, hurry up. Make sure you dress warm. Grab every flashlight, pepper spray, and sharp knife you can find. Fill up our water containers. Get a few blankets, and let's go. We have an opportunity here, and I don't want to waste it."

Emily jumps off the chair and stills me by my shoulders. "Are you okay, Mom?"

I'm not okay. I'm sore. My limbs are weak. And fear, like a tumor, has invaded my body. But I can't tell her any of that.

I can't look her in the eye. "Yeah, but I'll be better when we get to town."

"Aren't you gonna shower, Mom?"

Jayden's question stops me in my tracks. "No. I can't."

"Don't you want to wash that nasty animal off of you?" His eyes are gazing and glossy.

"More than anything, but my body might be the only evidence we have to identify my attacker. I can't risk removing his DNA until I get a rape kit."

Jayden's jaw clenches, and he looks away. "If Dad doesn't kill him, I will."

"Let's worry about getting home first, okay? Now, please, do what I asked. I want to leave this place in five minutes."

CONNOR

Nervous energy grips me when I enter the airport and holds me in its grasp during the flight. It feels as if I never woke from my restless sleep. I know the intense light pouring inside the airplane will soon give me a headache, so I pull down the window blinds to block it out. A boy Noah's age groans next to me as he leans back into his seat and crosses his arms.

I close my eyes and press my head against the backrest to relax and calm my nerves, but I can't find peace. The boy whispers to his mother, pleading with her to ask me to pull up the blind so he can see outside.

Noah loves to look at the clouds and guess their shapes when we fly. He enjoys watching the landscape change beneath us, from mountains to plowed plots to small towns and big cities. I remember how his face used to light up during a plane's landing. I feel a pang in my gut at the memory.

I turn to the boy. "You can sit by the window if your mom is okay with it," I offer.

He puts his hands together in prayer. "Please, Mom. Can I?"

I switch seats with the kid and his mom for their benefits, not mine. The aisle seat is my least favorite place to sit on the plane, and soon I'm reminded why that is. During the entire flight, people bump my elbow on their way to and from the lavatory. These days, most of them don't even offer a half-hearted courtesy apology.

Luckily the trip is only four hours with an hour layover in Salt Lake City. I grab a coffee and an overpriced turkey sandwich while I wait by the gate to board. I try to call Jennifer, Jayden, and Emily again, but the failed attempt only heightens my worry. I can't stop replaying the words of the police dispatcher at the Ennis police station in my mind. She said the roads were clear, and new vacationers had already arrived at the yurt. So, where the hell is my family?

After I land in Bozeman, I rush to pick up my rental car and drive to the hot springs, where I hope to gather information about Jennifer and the kids. There is no traffic on MT-84, and I speed between the endless stretches of uninhabited lands, cutting the expected forty-five-minute drive to a little over half an hour.

I feel somewhat relieved when I spot the unique architecture of an orb-shaped building I was already familiar with after an online search of this place. I take a sharp left to get off the main road and slam into the parking lot, my tires kicking up dirt and pebbles. When I get out of the car, a cloud of dust descends on me, and I cough into my fist a few times as I follow the signs to the campgrounds. According to their website, the campground is located next to a natural hot spring engineered to fill a rectangle-shaped pool.

Since that person who claimed to be part of my family mentioned camping to the police officer, this place seems as good as any to search for them. I know for a fact that they had no camping gear because I was the one helping Jayden pack. Unless Tyler decided to throw in a little surprise and packed a tent and somehow convinced my comfort-loving wife to spend a few extra days in the woods after a three-day survival adventure in a yurt, I can't see how they could pull it off. The idea of mommy's boy Tyler stepping up his game doesn't sound conceivable to me. Besides, they would have let me know about the change of plans. Tyler's only motivation for this trip was to show me that he now completely replaced me in my family. I'm sure he'd grab any opportunity he had to rub it in my face.

Or at least Jayden would have called me. He always keeps me in the loop. Always.

Jennifer is aware that I'm supposed to pick up the kids at her place in Woodland Hills tomorrow. She would not risk violating my rights over an unmade phone call.

But if they indeed decided to camp for a few days, I imagine they would have picked an organized campsite like this over staying alone in the wilderness. I check my phone. There is reception here. Something must be stopping them from calling me.

My mind won't stop firing ideas as I pass two white trailers that have seen better days hooked up in designated spots. I search for my wife's—I mean my ex-wife's—Audi as I walk around the parking lot. I see a Toyota Camry, a Mini Cooper, a few pickup trucks, and SUVs, but not Jennifer's car. My anticipation sinks back into the pit of my stomach and sits there like a stubborn garden gnome waiting to pounce.

Time has sunk its teeth into the whole place. I know Tyler made a reservation for the family to soak in these natural hot springs two days ago, and I can see that after having cold showers at the yurt, an hour in these hot mineral waters would be tempting to my family. But I can't see Jen staying here longer than necessary. My hope goes out the window.

I head toward the office to try my luck there. Someone must remember seeing a family from California in the past few days.

The admission is free, but I'll have to pay if I want to soak.

Inside the fenced area, the air is saturated with the greasy smell of hamburgers and fries. Amplified, garbled voices echo off the water's surface, and a band is playing inside the dome. I take a moment to scan the patrons' faces.

A soft female voice calls out to me from the ticket booth. "Can I help you?"

"Yes, my wife and children were supposed to come here two days ago. The reservation was under the name of Tyler Malone."

The young woman glances at her computer screen, then back at me as if a thought has occurred to her. "Are you Tyler Malone?"

"No, I'm the ex-husband. Tyler is my wife's boyfriend."

She puts both of her arms on the table. "I'm sorry, but I don't think I should give out any information about our customers." She is eyeing me as if I were a disgruntled ex who is here to make trouble.

I search for an open spot on the plexiglass that separates us that isn't plastered with state mandates and notifications. "I'm sorry, miss. I know this is unusual, but Tyler Malone brought my family up here from California for a short vacation, and I haven't heard from them for days. They were supposed to check in with me days ago, and now I'm worried." My voice has an uneven ring to it. I can sense her opinion about the situation is shifting. She is becoming a recipient of the nervousness radiating off me. "I wouldn't bother you if it wasn't important," I press. "I know they had a reservation with you guys for Wednesday, and I only want to know if they made it here or not."

"Did you think about calling the police?"

"Yes, ma'am. I did call them. They are my next stop. I just got off the plane and drove straight here."

The girl looks behind her as if checking to make sure we're alone. Then she nods at me and spins her chair to face the computer screen. "I'm sure they are okay, but let me check for you."

"I appreciate your help. Thank you." I roll the key ring around my finger while I wait.

"Yes, I see their reservation here for one p.m., but it's marked 'canceled.'"

A rush of energy hits me. "Who canceled it?"

She leans closer to the screen, then looks up at me. "Nobody. They just never showed."

JENNIFER

It takes us over twenty minutes to get to the main road where Tyler parked when we first arrived at the mountain. The fresh snow sticks to the wheels of the wheelbarrow, and combined with the weight of Jayden, moving forward is a challenge. My car could get us to town in thirty to forty minutes, but even if we knew how to hotwire it, we find the tires slashed.

I look back at the smoke trailing from the chimney of the yurt, glance at the car one more time, then, with an abandoned hope of having no other options, I usher my family down the plowed path.

It's enraging to consider that someone was clearing the roads so close to us but we had no means to call for their help. It's incredible how the little things in life can make all the difference in someone's luck or demise.

The handles of the wheelbarrow rattle in my hands from the uneven surface, and the mere thought of traveling like this for the next three to four hours is daunting. I think of the story of the Marine carrying someone else's teenage boy off the mountain to stay strong. It's working for now, but I don't know how long my depleted body will cooperate.

Noah walks in front of me without a word, following the path the flashlight in Jayden's hand shines ahead of us. I imagine families leaving their war-ravaged homes walk the same defeated way we do. I think of the times when I complained about waiting too long for our food in a restaurant or when the grocery store was out of my favorite ice cream. I remember the arguments I instigated with Connor for keeping guns in our home. If he were here with us, this would never have happened. He'd have pulled his gun and shot that stinky pig in the face.

Anger is good. So is remorse. I use these powerful feelings to find the strength I need to put one foot in front of the other.

The darkness surrounding us makes us all uneasy, but none of us is addressing it. If we get attacked by a mountain lion or bear after what we've endured in the cabin, then we will be the most unfortunate souls on earth. No one is that unlucky.

As we move slowly down the hill, Jayden looks at me frequently. I know he feels helpless and angry because he always had a sense of justice ever since he was a little boy, and he always took care of his share of the work. But I am his mother. I am still the adult here. If I can't bring my children to safety, what good am I to them? I didn't protect them before, but I will do it now if it's the last thing I do.

"Mom, do you want me to push Jayden?" Emily asks in a soft, considerate voice.

She is holding Noah's hand and carrying the water bottles and whatever food we could salvage from the cabin in a bag on her back. I can't ask more of her.

"How long have we been walking?" I ask, brushing her offer aside.

Jayden checks his watch. "About an hour."

"Let's stop for a second and catch our breaths."

I veer the wheelbarrow onto the shoulder between two oak trees. With a deep sigh, I sit down on a rock. Noah comes and lowers himself onto my thigh and leans his head against my chest. I bury my face in his hair. It smells smokey, but I couldn't care less. One whiff of his scent is enough for me to feel grateful to be alive.

Emily holds out the canteen for me. "Want some water?"

I send a few gulps of the cold liquid down my throat, watching Jayden and Noah drinking at the same time. Emily's grasp on the situation makes me so damn proud of her.

"Mom, I can walk. You don't need to push me like a baby," Jayden complains.

One look at his pale face and pain-stricken eyes is enough for me to recognize that he is not honest with me.

"I know you can, honey, but it'll be much faster if I push you. Let me rest for a moment, and then we can get going again."

I hand the canister back to Emily, who puts it away in her backpack. I crack my neck and stretch my spine. Amazed by my lack of panic at possibly having forest predators around us, I massage my face to keep myself awake. Then I push down on my thighs and stand up. That's when I see headlights flaring up in the dark at the lower part of the mountain. It could be someone who could help us or the man who held us captive. I can't risk staying here and waiting to find out.

"Hurry. We must hide in the woods." I rush the words as I get ahold of the wheelbarrow.

"What's going on?" Emily asks, scrambling to get her stuff.

"Someone's driving up the mountain. We need to hide."

Jayden cranes his neck to see out of the wheelbarrow. "What if it's the police?"

"Why would the police come up here at this early hour? I fear it's the man who attacked us." Pushing the wheels over the lumpy, moist forest floor makes the undertaking nearly impossible. Both Emily and Noah join me, and together we move Jayden's carriage.

As we advance farther away from the road, I can't stop looking over my shoulder, expecting a car to roll up behind us at any minute. That's when I notice the marks we leave in the snow.

"Emily, grab a branch and brush away our tracks." I take over her side of the wheelbarrow and push it with an erupting strength from an unknown depth within me.

She stays behind to follow my instructions. Now it's Noah who lifts some weight off of me as we struggle to move Jayden into a part of the woods that offers us concealment.

"Don't let him see you," I shout after Emily. "Hurry!"

I'm like a puffing bull in the arena, ready to face the matador as I push my son. My eyes are set on a cluster of bushes I want to reach. When we do, I see a little valley walled by giant boulders creating a secluded, cavern-like space. I don't stop at the mouth of the narrow canyon. Instead, I keep pushing to get as far as we can from the main road.

"Mom, let me help you." Emily pushes her way next to me.

"Did you get rid of the tracks?" I ask her as we lift the wheels over a flat rock with great strain.

"Most of them," she says, grunting from the exertion. "I couldn't clean the main road because I saw the headlights, and I got scared."

"That's all right. It's dark, anyway. Maybe he won't notice."

On the other side of a massive boulder, we arrive at a small ditch lined with bushes, and the wheelbarrow turns out of my hands and rolls into the trench. Jayden falls onto the ground, and the rest of us stagger on the uneven ground and fall in like bowling pins. I get to my feet fast and start ripping branches off a nearby bush to cover the wheelbarrow.

"Jennifer! I know you're here!" The voice from my nightmares rings in the air. I cross my lips with a finger to hush my children. I slowly pull Jayden's makeshift spear out of the pack.

Emily grabs my arm. I look at her. She shakes her head, indicating she doesn't want me to go.

"How does he know we're here?" Noah whispers.

"He must have seen the wheel marks in the snow leading off the main road."

"I covered our tracks. He can't find us."

"I hope not." I shush her again. Then I climb over a boulder and flatten my body onto its curve, holding the spear next to me. We could use some fresh snow to cover our tracks, but it's not coming down now when we need it.

I see the headlights beaming straight and unwavering on the road and a sweeping flashlight searching the area near the car.

"Jennifer, your son needs help. Look, I got a car. I can take him to the hospital."

"Don't listen to him."

I snap my head back and hush Jayden.

"You don't want him to die, do you?" The man's voice is like nails on a chalkboard to my ears. I must fight my impulse to run at him and stab his heart with this pointy stick. The best tactic now is to stay quiet.

The flashlight moves closer to us, scanning across the forest. I slide off the boulder and become one with the undergrowth. My fingers land on a sharp rock in the snow next to me. I shove it into the pocket of my parka, promising myself he will not be taking us back to the yurt.

"Jenny, come on. I know you're mad at me, but you must be hungry. Look, I brought you food." He lifts up a white plastic bag and holds it in mid-air. "Chicken fingers and fries. I have milkshakes in the car for the kids, too."

I'm surprisingly calm and collected. I take long breaths through my nose and exhale with a sense of purpose. I use a special box-breathing technique I learned from a yoga teacher who I once invited to collaborate with me on a video.

I don't move. I'm determined to blend with nature. There could be millions of critters around me, but I don't fear them anymore. I fear the worst predator of all—this soulless monster.

"If you come out now, I'll forgive you, but if I have to find you, I'll shoot your children one by one in front of you, you hear me?" Rage is seeping into the man's voice. Every syllable he emits is an assault on my ears. The trembling terror begins to well up inside me again, but I won't waver because we are at a great distance from him and still have the advantage of surprise.

The flashlight's beam swipes right and left as the man searches for us, making me believe that he doesn't know where we are. He is only baiting us, driven by his desperation. The track marks in the snow may have betrayed our movements, filling our attacker with the suspicion that we've passed through this area once, but there is no way he can determine how old the prints are. The question is will he venture far enough into the woods to reach us? I guess we'll see soon enough. If he does, this time, we won't go down without a fight.

CONNOR

Less than twenty minutes after I left the hot springs campgrounds, I arrive at the next small town called Ennis. The nervous energy that's been eating at me for days has spread into my entire core, and it nibbles at my insides like a piranha. Maybe some food or a cup of good coffee would help settle the sharp pain, but the mere thought of sending anything down my throat makes me nauseous.

This little Montana town has a quaint charm with its authentic Wild West saloon-style shops lining the main street. The rustic wood-siding-covered police department blends in perfectly. The brown building sits on the corner next to a dirt lot where scantly parked confiscated vehicles create a junkyard appearance.

I stop at the pinboard by the main door to read the notifications. I see a few community announcements, one wanted poster, and a picture of a stolen car, but not a word mentioning my missing family.

My hand shakes as I shove the door open and enter the hall. The impatient voice of an angry man fills the room as he is arguing about a citation over a loose dog. The uniformed female officer behind the desk handles the angry citizen, twice her size, with expert calmness.

I wait for my turn for a solid five minutes, but then I lose my patience because finding my missing family trumps this idiot's argument about dog leash laws any day.

"Hey, pal. Why don't you pay the fine and get the hell out of here? She doesn't make the laws."

"Who the hell are you?" His handlebar mustache quivers over his cracked lips between words.

"Gentlemen. There is no need for this kind of language. Let's all calm down."

It's too late. I haven't been calm for days. And I doubt this ass-wipe knows the first thing about proper etiquette. I used to be him not so long ago—getting riled up over every little thing. Always fuming. Always picking fights.

I throw my hands in the air. "I don't want to start anything here, bud, but while you were wasting your breath yelling at this lady, someone backed into your truck in the parking lot." I point toward the window. "That black Ram truck is yours, right?"

The man pulls his baseball cap deeper into his forehead. "Are you shitting me?" he snorts and, with big stomping feet, storms out of the building. Watching him is like looking at my old self. No wonder Jennifer left me.

The officer grabs her notepad and a pen, getting ready to write an accident report.

"No need. I was lying to get him out of here." I put my hand on the counter. "My name is Connor Parker. I called in this morning inquiring about my family."

"He'll come back twice as angry when he finds out you lied to him." The officer's face is flushed red. But I suspect that she isn't upset with me—more amused, rather.

"I'll cross that bridge when I get to it. Back to my family. Was I talking to you this morning?"

"No, it wasn't me. You talked to Adela. She mentioned your call at shift change. She said you were worried your family got snowed in on the mountain?" Her eyes glaze over to the side as if she were trying to do a quick head calculation to see if I had enough time to get from California to Montana since my morning call. If she deems my trip plausible, that would somewhat verify the authenticity of my story.

"Has any officer gone up to check on the yurt?"

She starts fidgeting on her spinning stool like a child who got caught doing something naughty. "You know, I was going to send an officer up today, but we're short-handed. The first few days of fresh snow are always busy for us. Lots of fender benders. But as Officer Cornes told you, the roads are clear and drivable."

The edgy way I grind my teeth tells me that I'll turn into an asshole like the man before me here if I don't get some straight answers soon. "I understand that the roads are plowed, but my wife and children would not go offline for days. They know I'd be expecting a call from them. Something is wrong."

She consults with her notes. "You mean your ex-wife?"

I glance at her name tag on the counter. Elaine Sapp. "I feel like we're going in circles here, Elaine. I understand you guys are busy. I can see you are the only one here right now. So, let's focus on how we can solve my problem so I can get out of your hair." I scratch my head, running ideas through my mind. "Do you guys have a long-range radio I could take with me? I could drive up to the yurt, see what's going on, and radio back to you."

She tucks in her chin in surprise. "We do, but it's department property. I can't just give it to a civilian."

I reach for my wallet in my pocket and pull out all my credit cards, cash, and my driver's license. "Here. Take them all as collateral. Now you know I'll come back."

She is still unsure.

"Do you have a better option?" I push the items toward the officer behind the counter.

She gathers the cards and cash and shuffles through them before handing my driver's license back to me and placing the rest of the pack in a drawer underneath the desk. "All right. Fill out and sign this form. I'll give you a radio, but this has to stay between us. I don't want to get into any trouble, but I do want to help you find your family."

I press my hands together like the boy on the airplane. "Thank you, Elaine. I promise to bring it back."

"Here, go to channel three. I'll keep mine next to me. Make sure you check in with me when you get up there."

I take the radio to test it. We are on the same channel. "I will bring it back. I promise," I say and move toward the door.

She rounds the counter and follows me. "Sorry, we are a small town with limited resources. On days like these, we're always running around like chickens with our heads cut off."

"I understand."

I reach for the door, but she stops me. "Let me go first. No doubt Luke will be waiting for you for a little payback for the trick you played on him."

"I think I can handle myself. Besides, I can't let a woman take a punch for me."

She puts her hand on the butt of her gun and smiles. "Nobody's taking a punch here today."

JENNIFER

"Mom, I'm freezing." Noah's whispering voice buzzes around me.

He's been such a big boy, facing each challenge without complaint and to the best of his abilities. He understands the evil of men—he's seen all the *Avengers* movies with the rest of us. He is also the third child, prone to growing up faster and in a smaller bubble around him. Living with older siblings has exposed him to conversations that are not particularly suited for a young child's ears. Teenagers will try to display their budding power over their parents and siblings by slipping in cuss words whenever they talk or argue, with little regard to their audience's age. Jayden and Emily can go for days without saying a single nice word to each other. Noah is too often caught in the crossfire, observing and absorbing. To Noah, *hate* must be an empty word. He's heard his sister yell it at her brother and her brother say it right back. But he's also witnessed Jayden jump every time Emily asks for a ride. And Emily, despite her frequent verbal expression of dislike toward her older brother, would bake chocolate chip cookies at home simply because they're Jayden's favorite. So, the word *hate* confuses Noah, but that's not necessarily a bad thing. A young kid should not have to learn about soul-eating feelings. Hate begets more hate. If we ever survive this night, I'll have to hire a therapist for my children to help them process these horrific events.

I turn my head to look at Noah lying in the snow underneath the starry sky. I can't see his lips, but I hear his teeth rattling. "I know you're cold, honey, but we need to be very quiet now, okay? Just a little bit longer."

Emily rolls onto her brother and envelops him in her arms. The idling engine sound of the car should cover our voices, but it's not the time to take chances, especially when our attacker is dangerously close to us.

It's been twenty minutes since we've been hiding behind the rock formation, exposed to the low temperature and the moisture, and I've been shivering for most of it. I can no longer feel my fingers. My face is numb too. But my survival instinct gives my hands a powerful grip, and I hold onto the spear like a hunter waiting for its prey in the tall grass of the savanna.

"Jayden!" The man shouts my son's name with a temper. "You want your little brother and sister to freeze to death? What kind of man are you?" His words echo through the woods. Our attacker has already learned about Jayden's rage and pride, and he's trying to manipulate him. I hold my breath, listening to any little noise behind me, hoping that my son is too smart to walk into a lame trap like the one this animal is setting.

I glance at Jayden to make sure he doesn't take the bait. There is not much I can see in this darkness, but I notice his blood dripping onto the snow beneath him. He must have ripped his bandage open when he fell out of the wheelbarrow. I need to find him help. I've been saying this for days now, but this morning is my first real chance to get him to a doctor. God, will this maniac ever give up and leave us be?

"You know, I used to idolize my mother too when I was your age. Then I realized that the woman wasn't worth dying for. You'll learn it too. She doesn't love you. She only uses you to make herself more popular online. You are only a pawn, Jayden. Don't die for her. Come out now and let me take you to the hospital." The man steps on a branch, and the sharp snapping sound sends a jolt to my heart.

Daybreak will be approaching soon, and the light will betray us. But there is no plan B. We have only one option: it is to stay quiet and not move. I must trust in the common sense of my children and their endurance. And I pray and pray for strength, but there is not much else I can do now. My mother always says that even a hardcore atheist finds God when in peril. How right she is.

The man has made his way to within fifty yards of us. His flashlight casts a halo of light around him as he checks the time on his watch. I notice that he isn't wearing a jacket. He must be freezing like the rest of us. Where did this guy grow up? Alaska?

"I'm not playing. This is your last chance. Show yourselves. Now!" His raging voice echoes in the woods.

I watch him raise his right hand overhead, holding a black object. A crashing thunder blasts into the air, assaulting my eardrums. I hear a whimper from behind me, followed by muffled sounds. Emily is holding Noah's mouth.

My nails dig into my palm as my fingers tighten around the spear. It feels like we've reached the endgame. If he decides to cover the last fifty yards or wait for the first rays of sunlight rising over the horizon, he will win. If he gives up in the next few minutes, then my prayers have been heard.

I clench my teeth and close my eyes to pray harder for divine help.

When I open my eyes, I see the man's back. A moving shaft of light points ahead of him. He's walking back to his car, no longer scanning the woods for us.

Hope surges within me, but I can't celebrate yet. Our attacker may be leaving or simply getting his coat.

Minutes later, I hear the car door slam and the engine roar. The beams of the headlights sweep right and then left as the car rolls back onto the lane leading up the mountain. The streams of lights shrink against the black backdrop of the night until they vanish altogether.

Are we safe? Or is he trying to trick us?

I roll to my side and crawl to Noah. With a glance of appreciation toward Emily, I pull my youngest into my arms. I blow warm air onto his freezing little hands.

"Is he gone?" he asks through rattling teeth.

"For now, but we will stay put for a little longer in case he's nearby and waiting for us to show ourselves. He seems to know a lot about the outdoors. He might be a hunter. We can't play into his hands."

"He said he was a Boy Scout," Jayden says.

"All right." I blink at Jayden and hand Noah over to Emily. "Let me check your brother's wound."

Emily sits her little brother on her lap and wraps her arms around him.

Jayden pulls away from my touch. "I'm fine."

"I know you are, but it's time to change your bandages. You don't want your wound to get infected, do you?"

He makes a face as he relaxes his leg. I help him turn to his side. He unbuckles his belt, and together we pull off his khakis to below his knees. Blood has soaked the fabric over his thigh. I remove the dirty rags and pour some water onto his gaping gunshot wound. I place some snow around his red flesh to ease some of his pain. At the same time, Emily searches the backpack for the clean T-shirt that I packed in the yurt. She hands it to me, and I rip a long shred from the bottom of the shirt and wrap it tight around Jayden's leg. I tear off another piece to add more layers of protection to his wound. He is a tough guy, but losing blood is dangerous, and I'm angry and worried at the same time, which is good because these strong feelings help me fight the hangover drowsiness.

He won't let me help him pull his pants back up. He is like his father. They both refuse to show weakness.

I pull out the bag of beef jerky from the backpack and hold it out to Jayden. "Eat this."

"I'm not hungry."

"You need protein and iron to make up for the lost blood. I'm not asking you; I'm telling you. Eat this." My voice is stern, leaving no room for discussion. I've been trying to treat him as an adult by allowing him to make up his own mind about things and handle his own business, but I won't compromise his health.

He rips the bag out of my hand, takes a piece of jerky, and starts nibbling on it.

I offer Atkins bars to Emily and Noah, and I eat half a bar myself.

"How long will we stay here?" Emily asks between bites. "I can't warm up. My whole body is shaking."

"Okay, all of us, let's get up and do a few pushups to get our blood flowing."

Jayden is the first one to move.

"Not you, Jayden. You stay still and save your energy." I take the blanket from the wheelbarrow and lay it on his back. Then I lead us into the exercise.

I know that I'm beyond exhaustion when I don't even feel the workout in my muscles. My entire body is disoriented and on autopilot.

After ten pushups, I shut down like a robot that has run out of power. I feel some warmth dispersing in my veins when I sit down, so risking our exposure wasn't for nothing.

We stay hunkered down between the trees and boulders for another twenty minutes, but when the morning dawn breaks through the line between earth and sky, we all agree it's time to get moving.

Returning to the main road where it's easier to push the wheelbarrow is out of the question. We can't risk getting caught with this maniac driving up and down the mountain. Our only way is through the forest.

The wheelbarrow is no use to us on this terrain, so Emily and I loop an arm under Jayden's thighs, and we carry him despite his resistance.

As the distance grows between the yurt and us, we must stop more often than I'd like. Jayden is heavy, and Emily and I often reach the point where a strong will isn't enough to carry him.

Walking through ankle-deep virgin snow is a challenge. Noah once again makes my heart burst with pride as he hikes in front of us without complaint, the giant backpack perched on his back like a fairytale gnome hitching a ride.

We still move slower than I'd like.

When we take our next break, I search the area for something Jayden can use as a crutch.

The forest here is mature and in its ancient, untouched state. It's not unusual to see dead trees or broken limbs lying on the ground or piercing into the dirt. After a short search, I find a thick branch with a Y splitting at one end. I tie a sweater on the curve to cushion the rough edges, and Jayden uses it for a while to help me support his weight as he drags his feet.

When I can't take another step, Emily takes over for me, and we keep dragging on, step by step, on our way to town that stretches dauntingly in front of us. I'm plagued with moments when I feel we will never reach it. I'm sure I'm not the only one.

As the forest slowly comes to life around us, I understand the meaning of the proverb, "Beauty is in the eye of the beholder." We drove to this mountain to experience nature, yet when we are drowning in it, not even magical moments like watching the sunrise through the limbs of majestic trees can get our attention. Not even Noah—who was the most excited for this vacation—points out the cute little rabbits on the melting snow, stunned frozen by our presence, or the family of deer leaving their resting place and crossing paths with us. We are exhausted and oblivious to the beauty surrounding us.

Today will be a warmer day judging by the clear sky overhead. The snow is already melting on the forest floor, and the soft, wet ground makes our journey more difficult. Without having eaten anything of substance for so long, we will run out of steam soon.

Jayden learned about edible plants that grow in the woods at a survival camp he took with his father, and he points out edible greens to Noah.

"I can't eat this," Emily says, holding out a mountain sorrel leaf pinched between her fingers.

"Fine. Then can you please top up our canisters with clean snow before it's all gone?" I impatiently say while munching on a bitter dandelion.

Jayden takes the leaf from his sister and pops it in his mouth. "Maybe we can find some berries, but it's too early in the year, so don't get your hopes up."

We need to keep moving, and I help Jayden to his feet to get going.

As the hours roll on, our break times grow longer. Now we spend more time resting than moving. If we are stuck in the forest for another night, then it's game over for us. We are all mentally and physically beyond exhaustion.

"I think we're lost," Emily says as she distributes the last of the trail mix between us. "We should have stayed by the road. Now we have no idea where we are."

I split my share between Jayden and Noah. It takes some convincing to get them to accept the snack when I have nothing left to eat. "If we stayed by the road, he would have found us," I remind my children.

"Do you think we could have overpowered him and taken his car?" She looks at me with those big brown eyes, waiting for my answer.

"Maybe, but he had a gun. I couldn't risk losing any of you."

"We might still die out here."

"Are we going to die, Mom?" Noah asks, unsure.

I shoot a steely look at Emily, then turn to my youngest. "No, honey. We are not going to die out here."

Jayden locks eyes with me. His expression says it all. He is mature enough to understand that, yes, there is the possibility that we may never leave this mountain alive.

CONNOR

The police officer was right. The loudmouth idiot was standing by my rental car, hands rolled into fists, waiting for me. I brace myself for a fight, or at the very least, a battle of words. Officer Sapp's footsteps slow down next to me. I side-glance at her to see her approach. Her right arm pulled higher, bent at the elbow, but she's no longer gripping the butt of her gun in the holster. Yet her posture gives me the impression that she is ready to draw her weapon if needed.

"I don't want any trouble, man. I don't have time for this macho crap," I say to the man. Not exactly the most subtle approach, but the words pour out from my mouth as my occupied, troubled brain unleashes them.

The man watches me with narrowed eyes, the skin wrinkled between his bushy eyebrows. He steps forward, putting me on alert, and extends a hand toward me. "Sorry, dude. I lost my head in there. Thanks for checking me before I made a complete fool of myself."

Cautiously I approach him and take his hand. I try to read his body language. It's a skill I've acquired through my years of working with tough, roughneck men who redline testosterone all day. I'm usually on point when it comes to predicting someone's next move, but now I can't focus. My self-preserving guard is down as my worry for my family stands in its place.

He nods as his firm hand slips out of mine. Then he looks over my shoulder at the officer. "Sorry, Elaine, for yelling at you. It was a dick move. I got the bank breathing down my neck about the farm, and, you know…I don't want to bore you with the details. I'll pay the fine and get out of here."

There is more to that conversation, but I don't have time for it. I bid a quick farewell and jump into the 4Runner. I place the police radio on the console between the two front seats and get on the road.

Once I reach the foot of the mountain, I arrive at the last building in town, a gas station-minimart. If my family needed gas, this place was on their route. I prepare to stop and ask if they've seen a silver Audi SUV, but the lack of vehicles and light inside the store suggests the business is closed for the day. I suck at my teeth, disappointed, as I start driving up the mountain.

Leaving the town behind me, I enter a whole new world. Here the tree line becomes dense, immediately overshadowing the road and the landscape. My headlights illuminate an eerie sheen of haze in front of me that I would have found exciting in any other circumstances, but not now with this troubling worry sitting on my chest.

I hammer down the accelerator, following my printed map. I'm aware of the possibility of hitting a wild animal in the road at this hour of the evening. A full-grown male deer can kick you to death in seconds if his hooves get caught in a broken windshield. But my goal outweighs the risks.

The winding dirt road narrows as I get higher up the mountain. The combination of the last few sleepless nights, stress, and inadequate nutrition is wearing on me, and it shows in my slowing focus and jerky driving.

To prevent slipping off the mucky road, I steer the car away from the edge and hug the tall cliff on my left. The frequent need for braking and the sounds of gravel ricocheting against the undercarriage of my car suggest that I'm driving faster than the road conditions allow. This gives me another idea. Jennifer is a great driver, but she always preferred me taking the wheel on family trips. She would handle the maps, search the internet for information about places along the way, record videos, keep in touch with her fans, and feed the rest of us with homemade sandwiches and fruit. I'd assume she'd want Tyler to drive, too.

I don't trust anything Tyler does, especially not his grandma-style driving. He is not a confident driver, and a split second of hesitation can kill you on these roads.

My wandering mind nearly leads me off the cliff. The right rear tire dips into the loose dirt, and I veer right and left, trying to maintain the car's balance and keep it on the road. I end up stopping hard across the path. "Shit!" I blurt out. "What the hell am I doing?" I slap my cheeks a few times to get the blood flowing and wake myself up. This isn't an easy road to navigate. If Tyler tried to drive up and down the mountain after sunset, he might have made a mistake.

I grab my flashlight and get out of the car. I look for skid marks in the slush. Mine are not the only ones, but it's challenging to distinguish patterns on wet mud.

I walk to the edge of the cliff, where the vegetation is surprisingly scarce. There are no thick tree trunks here to stop a falling vehicle. I sweep the mountainside with my flashlight; the tug of war inside my head is driving me insane. I desperately want to find my family, yet I hope not to see Jen's car balancing on its side against a tree.

I see nothing. Thank God.

I stop at a few more spots along the road where the turns are sharp and check out those areas too, but I don't see any broken tree trunks or stomped-down vegetation that would indicate a vehicle rolling down the mountainside.

Hope comes when the road seems to plateau, and I can focus more on looking at the woods on both sides, not just driving. Then my headlights hit a reflective license plate of a vehicle on my left. My heart starts hammering so fast my fingers are pulsating. It's a silver Audi SUV parked on the shoulder.

I pull in behind the vehicle and jump out onto the crunchy wet snow. The first things I notice are the flat tires. One flat tire would make sense, but all four flats are suspicious. Something terrible must have happened.

The snow is ankle-deep here. The snowplow trucks only cleared the main road. I take out my parka from the car, grab my flashlight, the police radio, and my 9-millimeter handgun, and I start making my way into the woods toward the location of the yurt on my map. I check the snow for footprints but don't see any. It's not snowing now, but if it did an hour ago, a fresh coat of powder would have covered any tracks.

When I smell smoke in the air, I pick up the pace. My family is fine. They had a flat tire and had no way to call for help, I reassure myself.

I almost feel relieved when I first lay eyes on the dark turquoise plastic sheet coat of the yurt.

I run across the patio, my heart pounding relentlessly. I tug at the front door's handle, disregarding the warning that a new couple who rented the yurt is supposedly already here.

The handle gives way. The door opens. I burst into the yurt with reprimanding words on my tongue for leaving the door unlocked. I was going to blame Tyler for everything and hug my kids.

A thick, smoky air tinted with a sour stench engulfs me. It's dark, and I can't see a thing. I scan the flashlight's beam across the room and inspect the bunk beds, the futon, and chairs around the table. My family is not here. Nobody is here. The realization that this place is vacant hits me hard.

I brush my hand along the wall by the door for the light switch and flip it up. The brightness scares away the remaining mice feasting on dirty dishes. The first item I recognize is Jayden's duffel bag we packed together, sitting on the floor by the futon. There are other personal items in here that I suspect belong to the rest of my family. Why would they leave without their stuff? Where is the new couple the cop was talking about? I want to shout in frustration.

I ransack the duffel bag for clues. Jayden's phone is in it. He'd never go anywhere without it. Maybe they went on a hike and became lost in the snowfall. Their jackets and boots are gone. Noah's baseball blanket isn't here either. Why would they take a blanket on a hike? Nothing is making sense.

I round the table to check the fire. The condition of the burning wood may help me determine the last time someone placed a new log inside the stove. As I squat down in front of the fireplace, my eyes catch a bundle of rope and used duct tape. I pick the pile up to examine them. There are blood smears on one of the ropes. Pieces of hair are stuck in the parts of the gray tape, and there is a clean cut mark across all ropes. I'm starting to lose it. My breathing is becoming short and fast.

I frantically begin searching the bunk beds. Then I leap to the futon. I notice dark maroon drops and smudges on the fabric that resembles dried blood. I can't breathe. I need to sit down. *Calm the fuck down! Compose yourself*, I scream in my head.

A dark expanse of color on the floor by the door catches my eye. I rush there to inspect it. I dip my finger in the dark substance. No question about it. This puddle is sticky coagulated blood. A pain like a knife stab to the heart pierces my chest.

I pull out one of the chairs and sit down before I pass out from the rush of blood to my head and call Officer Sapp on the portable radio.

"Something horrible happened here," I say breathlessly. "Send dogs…a search party." I swallow hard. "And a crime scene unit."

JENNIFER

We have reached one of the worst parts of our journey. The snow has already melted, and the ground has turned damp and sticky. Thick layers of fresh mud stick to the soles of our shoes and have turned our feet into lead blocks. The tall and dense undergrowth on the slope only adds to our misery. My thighs are burning, and my calves are cramping from the exertion.

I can't stop looking at Jayden's face. His eyelids sag like those of a weary middle-aged man, and the color of his skin looks like cold ash. I worry that I may have chosen the wrong path, and staying far away from the forest road robbed us of any opportunity of being saved.

But being re-captured by our attacker or being miraculously saved by a kind Samaritan was a fifty-fifty shot. I couldn't risk walking near the road with those odds.

During the past few hours, dragging ourselves down the mountain, none of us had spoken a single word. Talking took energy none of us could spare.

Suddenly, Emily puts her arm across Jayden's chest to stop us in our tracks. "Do you hear that?" She turns her head, listening. "It's a car."

"The road must be nearby. That means we aren't lost," I observe as I touch Jayden's forehead to check for a fever. His skin is hot to the touch. I already gave him the ibuprofen from the medkit I packed back in the yurt, but he is warm again. If we don't find help soon, he might…no, I can't go there. I stop my train of thought.

Collectively, we focus our attention toward the direction the engine sound came from, listening and waiting. It sounds as if the car has stopped, leaving the engine idle.

"Look, is that a flashlight?" asks Emily, pointing.

I think I also just saw a flash of light, but I can't be sure. The forest is dense here, creating a nearly impenetrable wall around us, obscuring our vision.

Basic survival instinct would dictate we get down low and hide, but unless someone is here to search the woods with an industrial-powered spotlight, there is no way we are visible in the twilight.

Noah makes me proud as he turns his flashlight off without being told to do so, letting the darkness conceal us.

"I have a good feeling, Mom," Emily says. "I think we should follow the light and show ourselves."

I hold her back by her arm. "No, honey." I don't want to be a bearer of doom, but this is not a high-traffic area, especially in the evening. The odds are that the man is still searching for us. Who else could it be?

"Maybe it's a hunter?" Noah says, looking up at me, but I can't see his expression in the weak light.

I touch his head, smiling.

"People usually hunt at dawn, not at night," Jayden observes. His voice is so weak it's nearly a whisper.

"Okay, let's vote, then," I offer, because at this point, I'm no longer confident that I'm making the best decisions. Jayden has been to a survival training camp. My outdoor survival knowledge comes from my childhood reading obsession and my recent choices of TV shows. I can only rely on my motherly instinct.

"I vote to take the game trail we saw back there." Jayden turns, holding onto his makeshift crutch and pointing to our right.

"I vote for getting back to the main road and following it into the town. Noah, are you with me?" Emily says, pressuring her younger brother.

Noah hesitates as he switches his attention between his two siblings before taking Jayden's side.

"Predatory animals use trails at night, don't they?" I ask our expert, Jayden, before I cast my vote.

"No, not necessarily. It could be a deer trail."

I know he's lying to put us at ease. I can sense it in his voice.

"Okay, so there's an equal thirty-three percent chance we encounter a dangerous animal, or a deer family, or nothing at all. That sounds better than revealing ourselves to our attacker since we know he's out there somewhere, hunting us. Besides, I have the bear spray, but we have no way to protect ourselves against his gun."

"Whatever," Emily snaps, tosses her bag over her shoulder, and slips her other arm through the straps. I think we all are too exhausted and hungry to argue.

As we agreed, we take the game trail down the hill, but it soon becomes apparent that this may have been a bad idea. We move much faster on the beaten path, but the wall of untouched vegetation surrounding us creates a tunnel from where there is no escape if something does attack us.

The trail is narrow, forcing us to walk single file. We have Jayden walk first because he is the slowest. Noah is behind him. I'm next, holding the bear spray, ready to spray ahead or behind me. Emily brings up the rear. She turns back often to check the path behind us, making me even more nervous, as if I weren't on edge already.

Over the next hour, we make good progress and reach a clearing where the game trail widens. Lights from a town on the horizon bring us hope, and I hug my children as tight as I can with my weak arms.

We drink the remaining water from the canister, draining every last drop, and begin moving again. This time, the space around us allows Emily and me to support Jayden's weight. Feeling his warm chest against my hand fills me with strength, and I pray and pray, begging God to give him the stamina he needs to make it these final few miles to safety.

"Mom, stop!" Jayden roars, powerful and loud enough to shock me to a halt. "That's a freaking bear."

"Where," Noah asks as he sweeps his flashlight across the forest.

"Put the light down," Jayden snaps at him.

"Gimme that light," Emily orders in an urgent yet strangely excited manner.

She aims the light to our right, illuminating a long line of white fence. "I can't believe it. I think there's a farm there," she gushes, practically giddy.

My heart starts racing in my chest. Salvation seems within arm's reach now, yet there is unbelievably another obstacle thrown in our path.

"What should we do?" I ask Jayden.

He shifts his weight on the crutch. "We need to stay together and make it clear that we are human and not prey."

I pull Noah to my front, holding him close with my arm over his chest.

"Cast a light on us to make us look scary," Jayden orders his sister. "Hey, bear, get away bear!" he tries to yell, but his voice has lost its power again.

"Shine the light at the bear. I want to see him," I instruct Emily.

Jayden was right. A large brown bear is watching us in the tall grass, close enough to attack us and rip us to shreds but far enough away to escape in the other direction.

"Wave your arms and yell," Jayden says. "We must make ourselves seem big and loud, so he knows we are a threat and not food."

"Are you sure?"

"No, I'm not. But do you have a better idea?"

I do as my son says, and so does Emily.

"Get lost! Go away, bear!" I shout, waving my left arm.

Jayden pulls on me. "We need to slowly move toward the fence. But we need to move sideways. We can't turn our backs on him."

"Do you think he can see us in the dark?" Noah asks. "Maybe we should turn off the light?"

"His vision is way better than ours. Besides, he can smell us a mile away. I don't want him to jump us in the dark, do you?" Jayden says breathlessly as we struggle to walk sideways while supporting his weight.

We stumble through the grassland, and I repeatedly step on my son's foot as my legs try to carry me out of harm's way faster than Jayden can move.

"Shine the light at the bear again. Where is it?" I ask Emily.

When the circle of light finds the giant animal slowly moving toward us, blood starts to pulse hard in my veins.

"Where is that damn fence?" I groan, then start yelling at the bear with the most powerful voice I can manage.

The bear growls and then pounds up and down on the ground with his front paws.

"I wish we had food to throw at him," Emily says as she drags her brother, leading us along.

"Noah, get behind Emily," I shout.

"Food would only make it follow us closer," Jayden says.

"If he gets any closer, I'll spray him, but then we have to make a run for the fence."

"I can't run," Jayden says, crestfallen.

"Okay, you three, go ahead and get to the fence. I'll stay back to distract the bear," I offer, letting go of Jayden. "Noah, come to this side and help Jayden."

"No, Mom," Emily screams. "Don't. Please!"

"We have to stay together," Jayden urges, once again straining himself to give some strength to his voice. "We're almost at the fence."

I remove the safety latch from the bear spray, ready to fire the deterrent liquid, when a thunderous gunshot rips through the air.

The bear lets out a nerve-shattering growl, making the hair stand up on my arms. The light of our flashlight moves back and forth like a searchlight, alternatingly illuminating the bear that's now running away from us and a person standing behind the fence with a rifle in his hand.

CONNOR

I endure the most excruciating two and a half hours of my life as I wait outside the yurt for the police to arrive. The on-duty Ennis police captain had called in for assistance from nearby Bozeman, and I was left counting the minutes to their arrival. A sergeant instructed me on the radio not to disturb anything and to preserve the scene for footprints, fingerprints, DNA, or any other trace evidence that might help them find out what happened here. Doing nothing is turning out to be the hardest thing I've ever done.

Even when I stare at the pool of blood, my mind refuses to accept the evidence of a crime scene, let alone contemplate the possibility that my loved ones are hurt. I was told to stand down and wait, but the urge to venture into the valley and the forest to find my family is strong.

I zip up my jacket to my chin, blocking out the biting cold wind as much as I can. My uncovered ears and hands are still freezing. I could get my gloves and hat from the car, but I can't even think of getting comfortable when my family could be out there in the wild and the cold, lost and scared. For a while, I manage to stand on the patio and be content with looking at the circle of brightness my flashlight casts on the landscape, but when the snow starts falling in gentle but giant flakes, I give in and walk down the hill to inspect the surrounding area.

My path leads me to the storage area underneath the yurt. I find an outdoor shower setup hanging on a hook inside the little covered space.

The water bag is empty, which can suggest two things. They took showers and used up all the water, or they never had the chance to fill the bag up in the first place.

I search the floorboards for blood drops or footprints but find none. The snowflakes couldn't make their way inside here and create a white carpet that would help me identify prints, but the boards are still wet.

As I wonder what happened here, my mind won't stop playing troubling scenarios.

A narrow trail leads to the outhouse from here, and I make a point of walking off the path to preserve any trace that might have been on it. The snowflakes reflect like shiny stars in the beam of light as I walk along the trail, stepping over small plants that poke out of the smooth white blanket. The snow starts coming down thicker now. Without shelter, and exposed to the elements, no one can survive in these woods for long.

My intense worry has a grip on my heart, and the blood vessels throb in the back of my head so intensely that my vision blurs at times. I don't know what I will do if I don't find my family soon.

The probing light from my flashlight disturbs little creatures that hide underneath the bushes, and they scatter as I move along the path. The snow is undisturbed here, too, with no footprints or drag marks, which could mean one thing: this place was abandoned many hours ago.

I'm halfway to the outhouse when I pass underneath a tree. Its crown reaches over the trail and the snow seems to be thinner here. I spot a change in color in the white beneath my feet. I crouch down to examine it. Despite the warning from the police officer, I use my hand to wipe away some of the fresh snow almost mindlessly and expose a patch of what looks to be new blood. I see more discoloration in the snow ahead of me. I gaze at the back of the outhouse, praying to God for help.

I race to the small building, the beam of the flashlight in my hand throwing zigzagged lines in the darkness. The only thing I hear is my breathing as I round the outhouse from the left and encounter two sets of legs lying on the ground. They are crossed on the side and slightly blanketed with snow. I don't want to look inside the shack, but I must. Relying on every bit of willpower I have, I shine the light on the bodies. The faces belong to people I don't know.

I bend over, hyperventilating. I feel I may throw up. I stagger away from the outhouse to avoid contaminating the scene and fall against the steep slope rising from this area. Something hard presses into my palm, like a branch or stone, but I see the keys to the Audi when I pick it up.

I shove the keys into my pocket and start running toward the valley. "Jennifer! Jayden!" I shout as loud as I can. "Tyler! Emily!" I run and run. I don't stop until I'm deep in the woods and completely out of breath. Gulping air, I spin in a circle, aiming the light into the dark woods around me. I see nothing but tree trunks and bushes covered in snow. The last time I cried was when Noah was born, but I can feel the hot tears burning on my frozen cheeks.

I pull the radio off my belt to call in about the dead bodies.

"It's me, Connor Parker," I tell Officer Sapp. "I found the couple at the yurt. They're dead."

"Mr. Parker, I have someone here who wants to speak to you," she says, ignoring the terrible news I just shared with her.

"Connor, is that you? It's me. Jennifer."

At the sound of my wife's voice, my knees buckle, and I drop to the ground. The release comes on so strong that I can't stop the tears, and I cry harder than I've ever cried in my life.

JENNIFER

Lying on a hospital bed with the curtain open between us, I watch the resident physician and a nurse tend to Jayden's wounds. I only see the back of the doctor's white coat, but the nurse is facing me. She has a kind, round face framed by shoulder-length tarnished-gold hair. She looks up at me at times through her clear framed glasses and smiles reassuringly. She gives me the impression that my son is in good hands until the medevac helicopter arrives.

The doctor moves to the right, opening my view to my son's face. His eyes are open, and his lips are quivering. I can't hear his voice, so I assume his lips are trembling from the cold and pain. He's been a trooper during these past few days, getting over every obstacle, swallowing his pain. Now he can finally relax and heal.

He is mad at me and blames me for what happened to our family, I know. No one can escape their fate, but by Jayden's logic, if I hadn't divorced Connor and met Tyler, we would have never been on this mountain and, consequentially, never attacked by a manic. He would never tell me any of this, of course, but his actions toward me speak louder than words. I can only hope he'll be able to forget the things he's seen and once again look at me as a loving son looks at his mother.

My eyes blur with tears as I watch him. He must sense my stare because he turns his head toward me. His face is pale and distorted by pain, yet his lips stretch wide and his eyes shrink. One smile from him was all I needed in the past three days, and he is giving it to me now. I can no longer contain my tears.

His expression is honest and loving. I smile back and reach for his hand, warm teardrops trailing down the side of my face. Jayden extends his arm toward me, but he is too far and our fingers can't touch. But it doesn't matter, because that look on his face says it all. My son doesn't hate me. At last, I can be at peace.

As I look around me in the urgent care's patient room, I'm still in shock at how lucky we were to stumble upon the farm when we did.

If the farmer hadn't been out walking his dog while smoking his cigar, then he'd never have heard the commotion and saw the lights we cast. Him coming to our rescue and firing a warning shot to scare the bear away was the miracle I'd been praying for all day.

He was a strong man with the thickest mustache I've ever seen. The moment he recognized the situation, he picked up

Jayden and carried him across his field to his black truck parked in front of his house. He set my son onto the front seat while Emily, Noah, and I climbed onto the cargo bed. The man tossed us a blanket, and I laid it over my children as they cradled against me.

An overwhelming sensation came over me as I watched the trees race by us underneath the open sky. The air was cold and whipped against my face, but there was no other place I'd have rather been.

"Where are you all from?" our rescuer asked me as I settled into a wheelchair in front of the urgent care.

"California," I told him.

He lifted his cap and scratched his head. "What a coincidence. I met a fellow from California at the police station today."

The words stuck in my chest at the realization that the man who attacked us was still in town. The odds must be low of someone else being here from California besides him and us.

The man's phone rang, and he stepped away to answer it.

I was crossing the automatic sliding doors when he yelled after me. "The police will be here in a couple minutes." Then the doors closed behind me, and I never had a chance to thank him for saving our lives.

* * * * *

The curtain on my right moves to the side with the metal rings scraping against the rod, startling me. Sharp noises still put my nerves on edge. But when I see the faces of my children, I lead my mind away from the discomfort.

Noah pounces on me and lays his body over mine, pressing his warm face against my cheek. I embrace him, holding him tight.

"Do you want a hot cocoa, Mom?"

I look up at my daughter holding two steaming mugs in her hand. It's not the vending machine hot chocolate in a Styrofoam cup I would expect in a place like this, but two porcelain mugs.

"The lady at the front desk made it for us."

Noah raises his head. "It's really good," he gushes, his warm, sweet-smelling breath fanning my face.

I tap his shoulder. "No, thank you, honey, not now." I kiss his hand. I've always loved my children dearly, but the profound feeling in my heart right now is so overwhelming that if I died today, I'd die happy. This is how heaven must feel.

"The helicopter should be here in ten minutes," the nurse who brought my children to me says with a warm smile as she engages in the task of tidying up my bed. She is not much taller than Noah, and fixing the pillow behind my head presents her with some difficulties, but she handles the task with patience and kindness.

"Thank you," I manage to say through pursed lips. I fidget from the discomfort and embarrassment over my smell and appearance. There is nothing I want more than to take a hot bath and wash that animal out and off of me, but it won't happen anytime soon.

Emily hands the mug back to Noah, and she sits down next to me.

"I tried to call Dad on the hospital phone, but there is a police officer here, and she said that Dad is here in Montana.

He came looking for us," Emily says, holding the steaming mug with both hands. She is so beautiful, even now with matted hair and a dirty face. I should tell her more often how beautiful she is.

"Did you hear what I said?" she says louder when my response fails to come.

I shake my head. "Yes, honey. I heard you." There is so much I want to say to my children, but I'm afraid I will break into a crying fit from the relief of being saved. I can't get emotional until all the evidence is collected from my body.

The nurse left the divider curtain open, and I spot a woman in a uniform making her way toward us.

"That's her," Emily whispers to me.

"Hi, I'm Officer Sapp, but you can call me Elaine." She doesn't offer me her hand. She stands by my bed, holding a white pad and a pen. "It seems you've been through quite an ordeal. How are you all feeling?"

The kids look at each other, then at me, expecting an answer.

"Considering the circumstances, I think we're doing okay."

"I've talked to your ex-husband, Connor. He came to the station today. He was worried about you, and he flew here from California this morning. He's on his way here from the yurt, so it will take him a while to get here."

Noah's face lights up, and Emily reacts with an amused expression.

I turn to Jayden. "Dad's here. He came to save us."

Jayden closes his eyes for a moment and sighs. I have a feeling he is fighting against his tears too.

"Ma'am," the officer calls for my attention. "Is there anything you can tell me about what happened to your family?"

I touch my daughter's hand. "Emily, why don't you take your brother to the front desk and see if there's something to eat here."

She looks at the officer and back at me, understanding the nature of my request. When the kids are out of sight, I tell our story to Elaine. The pen never stops in her hand, and she barely even glances at me while I talk.

"The captain will meet you in Bozeman to take your full statement, so this information is enough for now. I'm sorry he couldn't make it here. We are always short-staffed during snow days."

"I understand." My throat is dry, and every word I say seems to scrape its way out of my mouth. I reach for the glass of water on the table. The officer rushes in to hand it to me.

"Do you remember any specifics about your attacker apart from his physical description? Did he tell you his name? What car he was driving?"

I shake my head.

The radio on her hip emits a burst of static. The officer steps away from me to answer it. I watch her beckoning the nurse who tended to me earlier and exchanging words with the doctor by Jayden's side.

"The helicopter is here. Everything will be all right now," the officer tells me, and I feel robbed when I realize that Connor won't be joining us on the flight.

JENNIFER

I must have dozed off during the helicopter flight to the Bozeman hospital because the last thing I remember is watching the medics setting Jayden's stretcher next to mine. The landing must have been smooth if it didn't arouse me from my sleep.

When I awake, I'm in an elevator with Jayden and two paramedics. Guilt plays mind games with me for letting my children out of my sight, and I become emotional. I want to hold them and touch them, but I'm told that Emily and Noah have to wait for the next elevator.

I reach for Jayden's hand, but his eyes are closed.

"Is he okay?" I ask the man standing between us.

"We are taking him into surgery right now. He'll be fine," he tells me with conviction.

"Is he unconscious?"

"No, he's just resting. You have some tough children, ma'am. You must be proud of them."

I am, I want to say, but the words don't leave my mouth as I drown in my emotions.

The elevator door opens, revealing two male nurses dressed in surgical outfits waiting for us. They take Jayden away from me as I continue to ride to another level, feeling as if my limbs have been torn from my body.

"I want to know about everything that happens to my son," I tell the medic in the elevator with me.

He nods at me with a reassuring smile.

The elevator stops on the second floor. There is no welcoming party waiting for me. My escort pushes me through the hallway, past gawking patients, and into an examination room. The news about our kidnapping must have already reached this hospital.

When the door closes, I'm alone in the room. It's cold in here, and I focus on distributing the blanket more efficiently over me.

As quiet settles around me, my senses tune in on the pain flaring up all over my body. My joints ache. My skin is burning in spots where the jagged branches scraped me. My insides are throbbing. But I'm not left to marinate in despair for long. After three knocks on the door, a nurse enters the room with a rectangular paper box in her hand. She is tall and strong-looking—an athlete, perhaps. Her thin hair is pulled back in a tight ponytail, stretching the skin on her face.

She touches my arm with a gloved hand. "I understand that you've gone through a terrible ordeal, but I need you to relax for me for a little bit, okay? I'm here to perform a sexual assault forensic exam on you and collect any evidence I may find."

Sexual assault exam. I never thought I'd hear that expression said to me.

I don't go to the doctor much, only when it's unavoidable. I don't like to be probed and touched and examined. I get a blood test done frequently to make sure my levels are optimal, and I'm taking a sufficient number of supplements, but that's pretty much the extent of my preventive medical care.

Today is the worst day to have every inch of my body examined because I reek and I'm filthy.

"Can you sit up for me, please?" the nurse says, holding out a cotton swab. "I'll take a saliva sample first."

I do as she says, but I can't even look into her eyes when I open my mouth. She rubs the inside of my cheek with the swab, then puts it away in an evidence bag.

"I'll take some pictures of your injuries if that's all right."

I lock eyes with her for a second for confirmation. Then when she opens my hospital gown, I divert my attention to the posters on the wall educating patients about the importance of cancer prevention.

The nurse shoots about twenty pictures of my face, neck, torso, arms, and legs. I shudder every time the flash goes off.

After she puts down her camera, she ties the strings on my pale blue gown.

"I need you to lie back down on the bed. Here, let me help you."

I watch her unroll a sheet of paper. She places it underneath my head. "I'm going to comb your hair for trace evidence," she notifies me.

The paper rustles near my ears, and I clench my jaws, hoping she finds a piece of hair with the skin tag to identify my attacker.

Next, she scrapes out the dirt from underneath my fingernails. I don't remember scratching the man, but some parts of my memory remain hazy.

She uses a piece of tape to collect fibers and forest debris from my skin. I feel like a frog in a middle schooler's science class.

She leans over me to call for my attention. "This next sample will be the most uncomfortable part, but I'll try to make it as smooth as I can."

She grabs my calf and thigh and props up one leg, then another. I hear the legs of a chair scrape against the floor as she sits down between my knees and positions herself.

"This might be a little cold," she warns. I hear her blowing air and rubbing something smooth.

I close my fingers over my chest and look to the side. Just because I haven't been to an ob-gyn for years, it doesn't mean I don't know what's coming next.

When I feel the pressure from the penetration, I press my teeth together hard and take tiny breaths. My skin burns on contact despite the cooling touch of the metal. The pressure is intense, and once again, I feel violated. I have to keep telling myself not to start crying.

The snapping sound of the latex glove marks the end of the examination.

"This might be our only chance to collect DNA from the attacker. I found trace amounts of semen, which is very helpful, but do you remember him leaving a saliva sample as well? Did he kiss you or lick you somewhere?"

The disgust turns my stomach. I touch my lips, straining my brain to remember. "He tried, but I didn't let him kiss me." I know this is a lie, but I can't bring myself to tell her that his tongue was in my mouth. Not yet.

"Okay, no problem. What I've collected should be enough."

She closes the box, seals, and signs it. "Please verify your information here."

Reading my name and birth date written on the line makes this entire dreamlike experience more real.

As she puts the blanket back over me, a memory rushes to my mind. "I think he may have licked my ear."

"That's useful. Do you remember which one?"

I touch both sides of my face and close my eyes. "My right ear."

She swabs both of my ear canals and signs and seals another evidence bag, then tapes it to the box.

Once again, I'm left alone in the room, and I feel so angry and frustrated and helpless that I want to cry.

I'm still lying on the bed, my entire body pulsing, when the door swings open, followed by raised voices.

"You can't go in there, sir," I hear a loud, insistent female voice.

"I want to see my wife. Arrest me if you want!" Connor bursts into the room. From one look at me, his facial muscles droop and his shoulders slump. With a long sigh, he hugs me on the bed.

"Sir!" the nurse sternly calls out to him again.

"It's okay. I'm fine," I tell her.

With a frustrated face, she leaves us and closes the door behind her.

When Connor releases me from his arms and leans over me, his face is a mask of fury. "I'm going to kill that motherfucker!"

"How are the kids? Did you see them?" I ask calmly.

"Not yet. I came straight to you." His rage is noticeable as he bites his lips and rolls his fingers into fists.

"I need you to check on Jayden. I want to know how the operation is going."

"All right, I'm gonna go." He brushes his hair back with his fingers, visibly shaking. "Are you okay?"

"Considering."

He touches my hand for a brief moment. "I was up at the yurt and saw everything. I also heard what happened to Tyler. I'm so sorry."

"I heard. Thank you." I breathe the words.

He starts pacing, seemingly torn between staying with me or doing what I asked and checking on the kids.

"Please go and get Emily and Noah. I want them by my side. And make sure you find out how the surgery is going."

He reaches toward me again but stops himself halfway. "I'll be back in a minute."

When the door closes behind him, I stare at the ceiling, thinking how can we ever move forward from this?

JENNIFER

THREE WEEKS LATER

This beautiful sunny morning, I've decided that it would be healthier for me if I started living in oblivion instead of dwelling on the past. My plan is to forget and pretend that the horrible event on that mountaintop never happened. Until I let go of my fear, I can't return to a somewhat normal life.

The police collected enough evidence from my body and at the crime scene to create a profile for my attacker, but it is worthless until they have a suspect for a DNA comparison.

The last time I heard from the Montana police was four days ago when a detective notified me about a new development. They tracked down the location of the YouTube user called Persian Prince who I suspected to be the man who followed us to Montana. I didn't understand all of the technical jargon, but it is my understanding that he used public Wi-Fi connections at multiple locations in Southern California, including Lake Isabella in Kern County, Long Beach in Los Angeles County, and even in my hometown of Woodland Hills.

I don't know how to feel about this information. I've always considered the idea that I'd met him sometime, somewhere, but receiving confirmation from the police makes it all too real.

Every day I spend hours sitting in my reading chair by the window, trying to recall his face. Did I see him at the market? Or at the gym? But no matter how hard I try to remember, I can't place him, and my paranoia grows by the day from the unknown. I'm at the point where I'm scared to let my children out of my sight when they go to school, and I haven't left the property since we returned.

Connor has been there to support us every step of the way. He's been staying in the guest room to guard us at night. He has taken time off work to drive the kids to school and prepare meals for us. He even supports my decision to hire a therapist for the kids to help them cope.

The days move slowly, especially since Tyler's funeral. His mother wailed throughout the entire service like a woman who had lost everything. She refused to sit with the kids and me in the funeral home but sought me out during the reception. I was rearranging the flowers on the round table at the entrance as an excuse to get away from the crowd when she snuck up on me.

"You barely knew my boy. It's not right that I had to come to your house to say goodbye to him. I protected him for thirty-five years, and you got him killed in one." She grabbed my arm and squeezed it hard.

"You're hurting me," I hissed.

"You should have died, not my Ty. He had nothing to do with your narcissist life."

Shame has been my constant companion since I arrived back home, and you can't fill a cup that is already full. I tried to do a nice thing for her and take on all the responsibilities of organizing Tyler's funeral, but if she can't set aside her hatred for me on an emotional day like this, then we have nothing more to talk about.

So after the incident, I asked Traci to leave my house and never come back.

Based on Jayden's description, the Ennis police found Tyler's ravaged body in the forest two days after my children and I were rescued. We weren't married, so I didn't have to be the one who notified his mother, for which I was grateful, but she did call me a few times in a state of madness.

"The only reason he went to that stupid mountain was to impress you. It's all your fault!" Traci would scream at me from the other end of the line. "I told him not to go, but he didn't listen to me. What am I going to do now?"

Then she would begin to cry, saying random slurred words. I would hold the phone to my ear and give her the time she thought she deserved from me.

"Block her number," Connor would tell me. "Don't let her mess with your head. I mean, how insanely insensitive does she have to be to talk to you like that after what you've been through?"

Connor was right, of course, but I felt for the woman. But she crossed the line at the funeral when her verbal abuse turned physical. She still calls, but I no longer answer the phone. She is calling me now as I'm lying in my bed, reluctant to get up and start my day.

Emily pokes her head into the room. "Mom, you want some breakfast?"

"I'm not hungry, but thank you, honey."

She gives me that sad, pitying look I'm starting to get accustomed to, then pushes the door open, comes to me, and climbs under the covers.

I love this type of morning. It reminds me of the times when as a little girl, she'd come to us in the middle of the night, bringing her favorite pillow and blanket. She would talk in her sleep and flap her arms around, slowly pushing Connor out of our bed. In the morning, I'd find him sleeping in Emily's room surrounded by fluffy pillows and plush animals.

Those were happy times.

I wrap Emily tight in my arms and kiss her head, my love for her expanding in my chest.

My cell phone vibrating on my nightstand breaks up our special moment. I peek at the clock. It's nine thirty.

Before the attack, I never answered a "No Caller ID" call or a phone number I didn't recognize, but I answer it now because I've been getting many of those since I'm part of an open murder investigation.

"Hi, this is Jennifer."

"Jennifer Parker?"

"Yes, speaking?"

"I'm Special Agent Kimberly Young from the Los Angeles office of the Federal Bureau of Investigation. We have a development in your case, and we would like to talk to you. Are you available to come down to our office sometime today?"

My heart rate accelerates, and heat disperses in my stomach like a dozen hot bouncy balls jumping around inside of me. "Did you catch him?"

"I think it's better if we talk in person. What time would work for you?"

"I could be there in an hour."

"Sounds good. Ask for me at the front and I'll come down to escort you. Again, my name is Kimberly Young."

After setting my phone back on the nightstand, I catch Emily standing by my bed and watching me with inquiring eyes. "What's going on?"

"It was the FBI. They got something."

"Did they arrest the bastard?"

"She wouldn't say. I'm going to meet an agent in an hour."

"You want me to go with you?"

"Go with you where?" Connor calls out from the hallway.

"Can you drive me to the FBI office downtown?"

"The FBI? Why? What's going on?"

"I don't know, but I need to get ready."

Despite the comfortable temperature in the bathroom, I'm shivering in the shower. My fingers turn into icicles as I dress. I manage to gulp down a protein shake Emily made for me, but not a bite of solid food goes down my throat.

The sun is blindingly bright outside my home, and I put on my sunglasses as I get into Connor's truck.

It's not even close to rush hour, but the traffic downtown is already insane. I watch Connor swallowing his frustration and not getting into road rage with other drivers like he usually does. Keeping my eyes on him helps me hold my anxiety at bay. As much as I used to love being around people and absorbing the city's energy, now I find the noise and colors attacking my senses.

I'm grateful to roll into the parking lot at the FBI building and find some peace inside the tall structure whose facade looks like a radiator screen.

Special Agent Kimberly Young is a kind-faced woman with big pale blue eyes and naturally curvy brunette hair that sweeps along her shoulders. She looks to be a few years younger than me.

She shakes my hand with a pitying look in her eyes that she tries to offset with a smile.

"You said you had some new information." I cut to the chase because being in the same area with so many agents only agitates me.

"Let's head to my office, where we can speak in private. We'll be joined by another agent."

Agent Young leads me to a room furnished with a desk, a few chairs, and not much else. A gray-haired gentleman in slacks and vest rises from behind the desk and comes to greet us. There is a laptop open on the desk, sitting between picture frames and office essentials.

Nervousness ripples through me, and I close my arms over my chest to stop my body from shaking.

"I think it's better if we discuss this issue in private," Agent Young says, glancing at Connor and back at me.

"Whatever it is, you can say it in front of my ex-husband. He's familiar with the case."

The agents exchange silent glances. "All right," Agent Young agrees and shows us to our chairs. "Please take a seat.

Special Agent Jim Hodges will brief you on a new development in your case."

I lower myself onto the soft cushion of the chair, my stomach in a knot. Agent Hodges props himself on the edge of the desk and clamps his hands over his thighs. "After you mentioned that the offender had used his cell phone to record you and mentioned his plan to share these videos with his fans, we've been surveilling the net for your name and face."

At his statement, my entire body tenses up, and I sit there in front of these strangers, terrified, fearing the next few words that will leave the agent's mouth.

"Okay," I say weakly.

"This morning, we had a hit. Multiple hits, actually, from our facial recognition program."

"Okay." I can't seem to say much more because there is a little bird in my chest, and it's flattering its wings around, panicking, choking the words in me.

"I'll show you part of these clips, and I need you to verify it is indeed you in the video. Can you do that for me?" Agent Young's voice is full of compassion that only makes this whole situation more emotional. I want to fall into a hole in the ground and disappear.

I nod. Connor takes my hand. I've never told him about the videos, and I can't look at him now. Maybe I should have asked him to stay outside the room.

Agent Hodges clicks away on the laptop. A small window pops up on the screen, playing a low-quality video of me showering naked in the shed underneath the yurt.

"Yes, that's me," I confirm through clenched teeth.

"All right," says Agent Young, then she motions her partner to go to the next video.

It's me again, lying unconscious on the futon with my attacker on top of me, but we can't see his face, only his giant hands grasping my breast. His sweat is dripping onto my chest. A feeling of disgust starts coiling inside of me.

"That's me too."

They show me three more videos recorded while I was unconscious and one more that I remember.

"Can you take them down from the internet?" I ask, gripping Connor's hand hard.

"We're working on it, but once a video is uploaded to the internet, people can download it. The distribution of these illegal materials has already begun."

"How many people have watched them?"

"There are about five million views on all six videos combined, but I can't tell at this point how many downloads."

For a few moments, no one says anything.

"What are you saying?" Connor's crisp voice penetrates the silence in the room. "Are you saying that millions of people watched my wife being violated? How is this even possible?"

"I'm afraid yes," Agent Young answers for her partner. "There are hundreds, if not thousands, of websites on the darknet where people trade illicit content undetected. Finding these videos is like looking for a needle in a haystack. We got lucky finding these videos."

"*Lucky?*" Connor scoffs. "So, people are downloading them and watching them as we speak?"

"I'm afraid so, but we are doing everything we can to scrub the internet of these videos."

I place my hand on Connor's thigh. His face is red, and his lips are quivering. He has always been protective of me, and I know he feels helpless and angry now, but I can't have him attack the agents who are here to help me.

"Did you watch these videos?" I ask, swallowing hard.

"Yes, we both did."

There is a moment of silence. The room is filled with an uncomfortable air. How do you talk to strangers about something so intimate and humiliating? I see violence in movies or read about it in books, but it's me on those videos. The mere thought of these agents and millions of other people watching me in such a vulnerable state is too much to bear.

"Did you find anything that could help you identify my attacker?"

"Unfortunately, we did not. He was very careful not to share any part of the videos that could identify him."

"Then I wish you wouldn't have shown me these videos." There is a lump in my throat. I avert my eyes and clench my teeth to keep my emotions at bay.

"We needed you to identify yourself on these videos."

"It's clearly me. What am I supposed to do with this information? How do you expect me to go out in public and move on with my life when anyone I meet could have downloaded these videos?"

Agent Young drags her chair closer to mine. "I can't imagine what you're going through right now, and I know it's very difficult to process the things that have happened to you and it's even more challenging to move on. But you will get through this in time. You won't be a victim forever. You can choose to be a survivor instead."

I get up from my chair and start pacing. "I can't do this," I tell Connor. "I can't—"

He embraces me tight. "We'll get through this. I promise."

At the protective touch of his shoulder and the familiar scent I know all too well, my legs weaken. "How is it even possible to share videos like these online? Don't you guys have some kind of safeguard to protect people? I mean, Twitter can remove people's tweets on a whim, but you can't control the internet? You are the government. You have all the access and tools and money to protect your citizens," Connor says over my shoulder.

"I understand your frustration, Mr. Parker, but every day there are two point five quintillion bytes of data uploaded to the internet, and many sites are not regulated. We simply don't have the human resources and technology to monitor it all."

"So, people can upload and download illicit content all day long without consequences?"

Nobody answers. I don't blame them. What else is there to say?

"Once the perpetrator uploaded these videos, he committed a federal crime, so now the FBI is involved with your case. We are working with the Montana State Police to apprehend your attacker. We'll notify you if there is another development in the case. Thank you so much for coming in."

"I should say the pleasure is mine, but I'd be lying. I wish you'd never called me," I say and step out of the room, leaving my dignity behind.

JENNIFER

I've been sitting in the parking lot for over twenty minutes, yet I still can't bring myself to get out of my car and walk up the stairs. I'm here because I promised my parents and Connor that I'd come and talk about my trauma with this therapist, an acknowledged pioneer in the field of psychotherapy. My kids see him once a week, and I've noticed some progress in their willingness to return to everyday life. But they are children, and I'm an adult. I don't need hand-holding.

I don't understand why my parents think talking about what happened on that mountain with a stranger could help me heal faster. The only thing that may help me return to my old self is the complete removal of my memories of those horrific events. Talking about my pain and humiliation over and over again is like scratching at the same scab. My wound will never heal if I don't leave it alone. My mother counters by saying that I'll have scar tissue if I don't heal my wound correctly. I'd rather have scar tissue than an open wound.

I lean forward and rest my arms on the steering wheel. I wonder how many men and women have sat in front of this office building, contemplating suicide, hoping that one last session with their therapist will take the pain away—make them see the world they are boxed into in a better light. Probably more than I can imagine.

I spot a couple in their mid-twenties crossing the sidewalk, seemingly arguing. Connor and I used to bicker like that during the early stages of our marriage. Then came the period of calm and familiarity, which led to boredom and tiredness. If we hadn't let our marriage rot, if we kept the fire going with fun trips, family game nights, and partying with friends, then Tyler and I may have never happened. Then Tyler would be alive today, my kids would be okay, and I wouldn't be sitting in this parking lot, staring at the two-story plain building that houses the room where I'm supposed to sit on a sofa and pour my heart out. My parents say I shouldn't blame myself for what happened, but how could I not?

The ringtone of my phone makes me jump—Connor's calling.

I answer the phone. "What's up?"

"Did you go?"

"I did. I'm sitting in the parking lot."

"You are going in, right?"

"Right."

"Look, I can leave work and come to you."

I rub my forehead. I feel exhausted, which makes no sense because all I have been doing for weeks since we returned is resting. Maybe I should get back to my exercise routine to pull myself out of this self-destructive state.

"No need. I got this. I still have fifteen minutes. I'm going in now."

"You sure? Because I don't mind meeting up with you." If Connor had been this supportive during our marriage, I'd never have felt so lonely and suffocated. Why only after tragedy strikes do we see what's important to us in life?

"I need to do this alone, but thanks for checking in. See you later?"

"Yeah. I should be home early."

I disconnect the call, slip the phone into my bag, grab my keys, and exit the vehicle.

I take the stairs to the second floor. The air in the atrium is drenched in a flowery scent that rises from the tropical garden below.

With a big breath, I enter the door marked 213 with Ed Garrett's name engraved on a small sign. I could have picked a female therapist, but I don't need any sympathetic pity from a fellow woman who thinks she knows what I went through in that yurt.

The waiting room is small and bright with beige walls. The furnishing is simple: only two single leather armchairs in a color that nearly blends in perfectly with the walls. A few potted green plants and massive works of colorful art mounted on the walls stand out against the uniformity. After a closer examination, I determine they are oil paintings from artists I've never heard of—though that doesn't say much. I'm not an art expert. I've always envied people who could carry on elaborate conversations about a painting or a statue. It's even sexier when a man tries to impress you with his vast knowledge of art. Maybe I should start educating myself about contemporary painters. I need a new hobby to make me feel excited about life again. I'm sick of this constant state of gray and lack of passion my life has descended into these past months. My attacker didn't just vandalize my body and soul; he burned down my entire life.

Without a receptionist to greet me and keep me company, I linger about aimlessly in the waiting room. I stop at a small coffee table holding a variety of magazines, but I can't bring myself to pick up any of them. Thankfully, my story of kidnapping and torture has already disappeared from the headlines. There is no more meat left on the bone of the story that the media hasn't chewed on already. Yet I don't want to risk grabbing a magazine with my face all over it. On second thought, I decide to shuffle through the magazines to ensure none of them mention my family and me. My kids come here too.

The calming music that plays creates a similar atmosphere to a massage parlor, and I begin to feel the embrace of tranquility as I flip through the publications. All the magazines are scientific issues. Not one is gossip trash.

Reassured, I start moving again. I make my way across the room. A sign is pinned to the door asking clients to wait to be escorted into the office and to knock only in case of an emergency. I observe an APA Rollo May Award for "independent and outstanding pursuit of new frontiers in psychology," a diploma from the California School of Professional Psychology, Berkeley campus, and a membership certificate from the American Psychological

Association hanging in neat frames on the wall. It all sounds impressive, but I still don't see the point of me being here.

Coming here too early was a mistake. I start to get agitated, so I pace around some more, examining the room. I used to pass any waiting time by checking my phone, but I don't do that anymore. I fear a few accidental clicks will take me to pages I don't need to see. I should have brought a book. I used to be a reader, but these damn electronics are so much more entertaining, and I've been too weak to resist the temptation. Humans are self-destructive creatures.

I'm about to take a bottled water from a basket when I hear footsteps and a door opening. A man wearing slacks, a button-down shirt, and a gray cardigan and who is about half a head shorter than me appears in the room. He looks much older than his professional profile picture and at least ten pounds lighter. He looks at me through his round glasses and smiles.

"Jennifer Parker?"

I nod.

"I'm glad you could make it. A patient just left, so please allow me a few moments to gather my paperwork, then I'll see you in my office."

"I didn't see anybody leave."

"Oh, I have another exit from my office. It's for patient privacy."

Learning that I don't have to allow the next patient to see my teary eyes and pain-distorted face lifts some weight off my shoulders.

I have time to finish a bottle of water before Dr. Garrett reappears and leads me into his office. With an extended arm, he offers me a place on a love seat. This room is decorated with the same monochrome colors as the waiting room, warm and soft, only here the walls bear only shelves with books and not one colorful painting. Nothing in this dull room could draw my attention away from my therapist—away from my problems.

Dr. Garrett already knows my story and why I am here. I'd written him an email with a summary of the tragic events in Montana. The email was a simple recollection of facts and offered no insight into my personal feelings. Compared to the faceless storytelling on the computer, I feel more vulnerable and exposed now, sitting only a few feet away from this man I don't know.

"It's a terrible thing what you and your children went through. I can only imagine how difficult it must be for you to find your way back to your former life. It's very common. It's expected. But I'd like to know how you feel today, at this moment." The therapist's voice is soothing. His face radiates trust. Not all men are evil.

I cross my legs and scratch my eyebrow. "I don't know. I don't think I can live here in the city much longer. Connor and I've been talking about selling our home and buying a big piece of farmland somewhere. He's always wanted to have an acreage where pigs and goats roam, where sheep and cows graze on grass. Noah would love to have a pet rabbit. Emily could take up horseback riding."

"You said it's what Connor always wanted. Is that what you want, too?"

I look away and scratch my head. I feel itchy everywhere. This place is squeaky clean. My seat is spotless cream leather upholstery. So, it's not the room that's causing it. It's my nerves.

"I think I want that too. I can't be among people anymore. I can't even walk on the street without paranoia taking over me. Before, you know, before what happened, I never considered that people who watch me online might cross paths with me in real life. Now that's all I can think about." I'm not crying, but there is something ticklish underneath my right eye. I rub it with my fingertip. "I notice people now. I see when they stare at me or just look at me. I can't shake the feeling that they saw what that animal did to me. Over fifteen million people watched the videos that pig uploaded to the internet before the FBI managed to scrub them all from the cloud. But who knows how many people downloaded those videos and shared them? It makes me sick to think about how interested people are in watching someone being raped and tortured." The heat spreads over my neck and chest. Every time I talk about those videos, an influx of images floods my mind. I can't bear it.

"Did you watch any of those videos?"

I look up and into his eyes. "No, but I know what's on them."

"I understand that you feel someone is stalking you. How is your sleep?"

I scratch my other eyebrow. This time my nail digs deep into my flesh.

"You know, I'm in and out of sleep most nights. I still have the nightmares."

"Are you taking any medication to help you sleep?"

"No, only melatonin. It helps. It's just my dreams—"

"Do you want to talk about them?"

I shake my head.

"What do you think would be a fair punishment for the man who held you captive?"

I chew on my nail. I'm a nervous wreck. "I don't think that sick man deserves to live after what he did to my family."

"Do you support the death penalty as capital punishment?"

"You know, I never did, but now I understand those who want it. I don't think it's fair that people who murder other people get to eat a well-balanced healthy meal every day, read books in the library, work out in the gym, get an education, earn money, conjugal visits, and have a life. What about the victims' rights? Tyler is gone. My children are traumatized for life, and me…" The words stick in my throat.

"I think your children will be fine. All three of them are very strong emotionally. They love you. I think they worry about you more than they worry about themselves."

My throat is dry. It's hard to swallow. "I don't know. Noah is so young. I pray every day that the things he saw won't affect him in his adult life too much. I tried to protect him. I tried so hard. I asked him to cover his eyes and ears…" I can't continue, my voice is blocked by the ball that sits stubbornly in my throat. I don't want to cry in front of this man.

"I know you did the best you could, considering the circumstances. You are a great mom."

I lean forward, banging on my chest, feeling defensive. "I could have prevented it. If I hadn't agreed to Tyler's plan, we would have never gone to that mountain."

"Your reaction is normal. Victims often blame themselves for what happened to them. But, Jennifer, you did nothing wrong. What happened was not your fault. People go to the mountains all the time, and they have fun. You weren't attacked because you went to Montana with your family or because you decided to rent a yurt. That man, he planned this attack on you for who knows how long. He was obsessed with you. He would have found a way to get to you regardless of where you were. You could have rented a beach house. Or just stayed at home. He would have gotten to you sooner or later. There is nothing you could have done to prevent it from happening."

"No, it is my fault. It's my online presence that brought this on us. Connor was right. I should have kept my personal life private. I remember an article where the Queen of England was said to have warned Princess Diana to stay professional and refrain from expressing her personal opinion in public. She said the more parts of us we reveal, the more we divide the people around us. Our decisions and opinions make people love us or hate us. I should have listened to her advice. Now I know what she meant."

"But you surely can't live your life with walls around you. You need to let people in."

"I had my family. Why wasn't that enough?"

Dr. Garrett pushes his glasses higher up on his nose. "I understand that you haven't returned to your vlog. How does keeping your distance from people you used to communicate with daily make you feel?"

I scratch my ear. "I don't know. I try not to think about it too much. I feel more relaxed in some ways. When you don't share your life online, people can't troll you, but you also don't get the praise. It's a vicious cycle. You can never stop checking your views and likes. I was obsessed with analyzing why one post was more popular than another. There are incredible highs and rock-bottom lows when you have an online presence like I had."

"I looked at your vlog when you first reached out to me about your children's therapy. It seemed to me that the majority of the people who followed you enjoyed your videos and benefited from your online relationship."

"You know how it is. You need a hundred good reviews to stomp down one bad one."

"According to *Harvard Business Review*, the ideal praise to criticism ratio is five to one. It's similar to online reviews. We need to read at least five positive reviews for every negative one to reassure ourselves that our work is important."

"I didn't know that." I catch myself smiling. This guy is good.

"I read a few recent comments on your vlog this morning. People miss you. Many women were relying on your friendship to get through the day. I know you blame your vlog for what happened to you, but predators find their prey in many different settings. What happened to your family was a horrific and unfortunate event, but I don't want you to start thinking that it was you who did something wrong, okay? The man who attacked you is sick. But there are more good people in this world than bad ones."

"You think so? I'm not quite sure about that anymore."

"Look at the outpouring of support you receive from all over the world. Do you think your followers are bad people?"

"Well, that man thought he loved me." I feel antsy again. My butt is hot on the leather seat. I'm not sure if I can sit here and talk about my attacker for a full hour.

Nothing misses Dr. Garrett's attention, because he asks me if I want to talk about the farm instead.

And that's what we do for the remaining time we have together. We talk about planting tomatoes and grapes. We talk about Connor and me and how stable the kids are since the family is back together. We talk about my parents, who can't stop crying whenever they see me. About my sister who never calls because she can't stand that the attention is not on her.

At the end of our session, I make another appointment for the hell of it. I often come here when I bring all three of my children. One more trip won't make a difference.

On my way home, I drive by a frozen yogurt place and think about stopping and grabbing a cup, but there are too many people sitting on the patio. Instead, I go home and eat ice cream out of the freezer.

CONNOR

There is nothing I want more than to go home and be with Jennifer and the kids, but I'm stuck in the yard waiting for the second crew to return from the last job. Something happened to the new kid's truck, he blew a tire or something, and I promised to give him a lift to his place in Sylmar after work. Acting chivalrous came naturally to me when the kid called me and asked for a ride home, but the last thirty minutes of waiting has made me regret my decision. I'm tired and irritated and want to get home, but I'm stuck here waiting.

"Margo, how far out is the second crew?" I yell to the office manager leaning on the railing and smoking a cigarette in front of the trailer.

"I don't know, hon, five minutes? Ten tops?" she yells back in her nicotine-harsh voice.

In this industry, everybody looks rough, even the women. This company racked up thirty million dollars last year, yet the owner could easily be mistaken for a bum. He wears worn jeans, a plain T-shirt, and work boots, even on weekends and holidays. He drinks Busch beer, eats at McDonald's, and can finish a bag of Swedish Fish in one sitting. If I don't pay attention, I might end up like my boss— a crusty old man who never mastered the art of enjoying the fruits of his labor. Or maybe he enjoys the labor?

The layer of sweat and dirt makes my skin itch. Out here, in the desert, without the civilized world's irrigation system, the land is a dull beige and dressed with only a few drought-tolerant shrubs. Even the scent of the air reminds me of desolation. Living things don't thrive out here. They simply survive.

I get into my truck and turn on the cold air.

Sylmar is a half-hour detour from Woodland Hills, and the mere thought of how long it will take me to get home makes me grind my teeth. My mind is already set on a plunge in the pool, a cold beer, and a peaceful dinner with my family. I've been leaving work early these past few weeks, and I even took a few days off to spend more time at home, but if I want to keep my job, I had no choice but to pull a double today.

I take the last bite of my half-eaten sandwich left over from lunch when I spot the first white pickup truck rolling onto the yard's dirt entrance road. I take a Costco water out of the cooler and empty it. I watch the working men pour out of their trucks as I walk to a trash bin and dispose of the ball of crumpled aluminum foil and empty water bottle. The kid acknowledges my presence with a limp wave of his arm, but he stays with his crew. He's running his mouth to the foreman about something, probably complaining again about the heat or the long day. I head back into my truck and impatiently tap the steering wheel.

When the newbie starts slowly walking toward me with a grin on his face, I lose it and yell out the window. "Hey, Fish, hurry up! Let's go! I wanna get out here!"

The image of him running is almost comical. The kid is no athlete, and his physical coordination is less than desirable. The boss's decision to hire him as a groundsman in training surprised most of us. We are not that desperate to find people to work. Rumor has it that the boss took pity on the kid for being an orphan and whatnot. Or he is the boss's kid from an old fling. The jury is still out. You never know with these guys.

"Sorry, boss," the kid says as he opens the door to my truck and gets into the front seat. One look at his puffy little dummy face makes my anger disappear. His mouth always hangs open, hence the nickname "Fish," and there isn't much intelligence behind those small, beady eyes. Yet I can't help but go paternal over him because he follows me everywhere like a stray dog. I feel sorry for him. The poor kid has nobody.

"Put your address in," I say, holding out my cell phone with the navigation app open.

"Thanks for the ride. Sorry for being so much trouble."

I shake my head. "You aren't that much trouble."

He clips my phone back into the holder. I sigh at the ETA. It will be dark by the time we get to Sylmar, and it's not a place where a guy like me should be roaming around at night.

"Throw your bag in the back seat," I suggest when I notice him hugging his sack as if it contained all of his worldly possessions.

He puts his bag in the back, and as he turns, I whiff his sour body odor. I'm used to being around hardworking men who drop a gallon of sweat on an average day, but this kid is ripe. Our job is tough enough for a well-seasoned trained lineman, let alone a twenty-something-year-old teddy bear who carries around an extra thirty pounds.

"Is that your family?" he asks, pointing at the picture on the dash.

"Yep. A little reminder of how lucky I am."

"I heard what happened to your wife. I'm sorry."

I nod to acknowledge his expression of sympathy. I'm used to people saying sorry to me as if I were the one who suffered.

"I heard from one of the guys that you moved back home."

His statement comes out of nowhere, and I stare at him in stunned silence before I can form a response. "I see I work with a bunch of gossiping old women."

"They meant no harm. They're just worried about you."

"I'm fine."

"How is your wife? Is she fine too?"

That's an odd question. "Considering the situation, yes, she is doing well."

"Do you know who did it?"

Despite my budding annoyance over this unwarranted inquisition, I decide to answer because the world can be a lonely place when you're all alone, and if this kid needs someone to talk to, then who am I to deny him? "The police have a few leads, but nothing concrete yet. We may never know."

"It's been a few weeks since you brought your family home, right? How come the police haven't found the perp yet?"

"That's a good question. There are fingerprints and DNA evidence. My wife even gave a detailed description of her attacker to a forensic sketch artist. I don't know why they don't have him in custody yet."

Fish pulls his signature baseball cap down deeper onto his forehead. I'm not sure what style he has going on. His skinny black jeans must be cutting off his blood circulation and are certainly not practical wear in the field. The waist of his pants is so tight his belly spills over his belt. He fidgets a lot in the seat and keeps airing out his sweat-stained T-shirt, releasing more of his putrid scent in my car.

"So, how do you like the work?" I ask him to lead the conversation away from me.

He snorts, pulling on his T-shirt again. "It's hot as balls out here, man. I don't think I can do this for a living."

The boss is pretty good at vetting new hires, but sometimes soft bunnies slip through the cracks. There is already a bet going on how long Fish will last.

A white Tesla cuts in front of me on the I-15 and then slams its brakes, forcing me to stomp on my brakes too. I lay on the horn.

"I hate these idiots driving these electric cars, acting like they're saving the planet. What a joke."

"I think Teslas are cool," says the kid, like he is trying to poke me.

I pass the car on the right and speed up. "Let's see how cool it will be when cities start drowning in decommissioned lithium batteries, old solar panels, and windmills in ten years. It will be a rude awakening when people realize the number of natural resources—including fossil fuels—these fancy companies used to mine and create this so-called renewable energy, all in the name of greed. It has nothing to do with saving the planet." I shouldn't get into geopolitics with someone I work with, but at least we aren't talking about my family.

"Your wife loves Teslas."

I'm taken aback by his comment. "How do you know what my wife loves?"

"I watched a few of her videos on YouTube."

My stomach contracts as if I've swallowed a rock. He may be one of those sick bastards who watched my wife being violated by that disgusting human being.

"Look, kid. I don't want to talk about my family, okay?"

"I understand. I'd feel horrible, too, if I couldn't protect the ones I love."

I feel as if the kid is testing my temper. "I wasn't there."

"Yeah, I read about the case in the papers. But your wife's boyfriend was there. Didn't he get killed?"

"What are you trying to say? I killed him?" I want to drop this kid off and be done with this day.

"No, and even if you had, I'd understand. I'd be mad if some loser was in charge of my family and not me. I'd kill anybody who touched the people I loved."

His transformation from happy-go-lucky to a calculated man filled with rage surprises me. "Do you have a wife? Kids?"

"No, man, but I'd like to get married one day. I only need to find the perfect woman, like you did."

I scoff and offer him a rueful smile to ease the tension in the car. "Perfect woman? No such thing, Fish. Don't kid yourself."

He sucks at the straw of his oversized soft drink and stays quiet for a few miles. I'm leaning away from him, driving with one hand. He is an orphan who must have had a tough life. *Go easy on him*, I keep telling myself.

"So, are you back with the missus?" The kid breaks the silence.

I clench my jaw as I answer. "Jennifer needs a friend right now. I'd be quite the asshole to try and take advantage of her vulnerability right now, don't ya think?"

"But you moved back in, right?"

That's it. I'm done. I'm not discussing my family life with this stranger. "What's with the questions?" I say with a little more edginess than I expected.

"I'm sorry, man, I was just trying to make conversation. I don't have a whole lot of people to talk to, you know, especially about family stuff. It sucks."

His buckling voice gives my heart a twitch. I sigh. "Hey, man, if you ever want to come over for dinner or something sometime…"

"Yeah, thanks, but I don't want to impose."

"Well, yeah, not today, maybe next weekend. I'll have to clear it with Jennifer first, of course."

He stares at me with sharp eyes and a straight face, like someone who's resigned himself to an idea. "It sounds like you are back with your family for good."

"Let me just say that I was an idiot to let her go in the first place. It won't happen again." I nod at him. "Take my advice, Fish, if you find someone you love, hold onto her no matter what."

"Yeah, that's what I'm planning on doing." There is something sinister in his tone, but I don't have much time to mull over this kid's attitude because my phone rings.

It's Jennifer calling, and I put her on speaker. "Hey, are you coming home?"

"As fast as I can, but I won't be home for at least another fifty minutes."

"All right." Her voice sounds disappointed. "I'll leave your dinner in the microwave."

"Are you okay?"

"Yeah, I'm fine. See you when you get home."

Once I disconnect the call, Fish rolls up his sweater into a ball and uses it as a pillow to sleep on as he leans against the door.

I wake him when we arrive at his apartment in Sylmar. He asks me to drive around the back, and as reluctant as I am to spend a second longer than I have to in this sketchy neighborhood, I do it because I worry about the kid's safety.

He gets out of the car and grabs his bag from the back seat. He knocks on the passenger window, and I roll it down. "Thanks for the ride, boss."

"No problem. Be safe, all right?"

"Say hi to your beautiful wife for me."

I only nod because his fascination with Jennifer irritates the crap out of me, and if I open my mouth, I'll say something I'll regret.

"Oh, one more thing," he says as he leans through the open window again. "My name isn't kid or Fish. It's Paul. Paul Hoffman. Got it, loser?"

A blast in my ears and a burning pain in my neck rob me of a chance to respond to his remarks. As I start choking, I press my hand against the side of my neck. What is going on? Where is this pain coming from?

Holding my neck and coughing up blood, I turn to my passenger. The gun still sits in his hand, and a smile spreads wide on his face.

My mind swims with confusion. I need help. Someone needs to call an ambulance, but a hunch tells me it won't be the kid who just shot me. My heart needs to stop racing because it's pumping my blood too fast, and at this rate, I'll bleed out quickly. My hands can't contain all the blood that's pouring down my chest and shoulders. *Why?* I want to ask him, but the words don't form in my mouth. Urine soaks my pants as I realize that this moment will be my last on this earth. As consciousness slowly leaves me, I think of my family. Like a home video on super speed, my entire life plays in front of my eyes, yet I seem to relive every moment of it. Panic leaves me, and I slip into a state of peace. I hear another muffled shot, then the movie in my head cuts off, and after that, there is nothing.

JENNIFER

I've been on the phone with my mother for over an hour, reminiscing over my childhood memories. Before our family's trip to Montana, I could barely squeeze a short courtesy call with her into my busy schedule, but now we are talking every day.

All these years, she had never complained because she understood how my life had to be organized around daily routines that seemed to consume every minute of my day—the same way her life was overwhelming when she was my age. There was always something more important to do than chat on the phone or visit with my parents. As the years passed and I became swept up in the current of a working mom's responsibilities, it seemed nearly impossible to change the course of my life. And the sad thing is that I was a happy hamster in the wheel. I eagerly welcomed the growing popularity of my lifestyle vlog, even when the complexity of creating high-quality content to satisfy the insatiable hunger of the audience consumed my life.

But my chores as a mother never waned. Despite my busy schedule, I made breakfast and packed lunch for the kids because I cared about what they put in their bodies. I put a home-cooked dinner on the table almost every night, and I insisted on eating together as a family despite the kids' desire to eat a slice of pizza in their rooms while playing video games instead. Creating an opportunity to sit down and talk as a family was always important to me.

But there are two sides to every coin, and if you ask my kids, they will tell you how I never had time for them. How I became obsessed with my business. I was always very defensive when they tried to talk to me, but I see their point now. I've reached the level of consciousness to realize that my success was all smoke and mirrors. And my former standpoint that I only did it for the money was a lie. Fanning the flames of my ego and pride was what motivated me to put myself out there as much as I did.

Since Tyler is gone, and I don't go online to connect with my followers, and my crew no longer comes to my house to work with me, I'm truly alone. To my surprise, I find solace in solitude.

I haven't decided if I will continue my vlog or not. The only definite action I took was firing my assistant, Zoe, for building a personal relationship with an obsessed fan in my name that ultimately led to my trauma. The police couldn't file charges against her, and their incompetence makes me angry. I should sue her, but first, I need to talk to my lawyer to see if I have a leg to stand on. But not today. I don't have the energy or the motivation to take on a lawsuit right now.

Bryson, my artistic manager who designs, shoots, edits, and shares my posts, and Adrianna, who hunts down my partners for sponsored content, are still contracted with me. Their earnings are royalty based. The more money I earn a month, the more cheddar they bring home. A few weeks after my return, they both expressed compassion over what happened to my family and me, but their patience with me is wearing thin.

"Your fans need you, and you need them," Adrianna would say. "I'm not a therapist, but people always say that if you fall off a bike, you need to get right back on. I think reaching out to your fans would help you heal faster."

"Maybe next week," I'd promise her.

Bryson is more subtle. He emails me scripts to restaurant promos and sponsored posts with a note: *Look at this when you feel up to it. Hang in there!*

Creating content is easy, but creating exciting content that keeps people engaged is hard. My team and I would spend countless hours brainstorming and designing, and still we missed the mark sometimes.

Now I have a story everybody wants to hear, but I've never been more reluctant to share a part of me as I am now.

Since my world has shrunk to the confines of my home, I've been speaking a lot with my mom. There are things I don't feel comfortable sharing with anybody else except the woman who breastfed me and changed my diaper. She is the only person who has seen me helpless and vulnerable and still loves me. *How could I forget that? How could I have ever given up on our special bond?*

"I don't understand what you're saying, sweetheart. You think there is a ghost in your house?" Mom asks in a tone that's filled with curiosity instead of judgment.

I rub my face and lower myself onto the barstool in the kitchen. "No, Mom, I don't see ghosts, but I hear things, and sometimes I even sense a presence in the house." I prop my elbow on the countertop to support my head as I continue. "And there is this weird noise in the house, like footsteps coming from the ceiling. I think I'm going crazy."

"After what you've been through, nobody could blame you for seeing danger lurking in every shadow."

"I don't only hear him. I can smell him too. It's like his terrible, rotten smell never left my nose. It hits me sometimes out of the blue, and I can't make it go away." My chest tenses up as I speak, and I take deep breaths and hold them in my lungs to relax. My anxiety attacks have never been so frequent as they are now, since I've returned home, but I refuse to take any prescription medications. I promised myself never to allow my brain to lose control ever again.

"Did you talk to Dr. Garrett about this?"

I grab a pen from the notepad and start doodling. "You are the only person I talk to about this."

"Oh, sweetheart, I'm glad that you trust me with your secret, but I think you should talk to a professional about this. Maybe your therapist can prescribe something mild for you."

I start filling in the circle I drew, pressing the pen down hard and moving it fast. "I don't need medication."

"Then what do you need? Tell me, how can I help?"

"I don't know, Mom. Maybe Connor is right, and we should sell the house and move. He's been looking at

Flagstaff, Arizona, and a few places in Colorado. I could open the bakery I always wanted. Or have a bicycle rental shop in a small beach town somewhere, I don't know."

"So, you and Connor are back together?"

I slam the pen on the counter. I don't know what's going on between Connor and me. I enjoy his company, and the kids love to have him back, but Tyler hasn't been buried for two months, and being intimate with someone else, even if that someone was my husband for nearly twenty years, feels wrong.

Last night, Connor came home early from work. After dinner, he asked me if I wanted to sit in the secret garden we built together and have a drink with him. Numbing my brain with a few shots of Jägermeister sounded tempting at first, but as I neared the chair where Tyler sat when we first talked about the yurt vacation, I sank to my knees. I started crying like a schoolgirl whose boyfriend broke up with her before prom night.

"I can't do this, I'm sorry," I told Connor and rushed back into the house, where I changed into my athletic wear and got on the treadmill. I turned up the speed as high as I could go, and I ran so fast, trying to get away from the thoughts in my head, that I nearly tripped. The body heals, but it's our memories that hold us back from recovering completely. I wish there were a device that could extract specific memories from my brain and make me forget. Then I could pretend the yurt and Tyler and the reasons that led me to leave Connor never happened. If I could only go back five years, I would.

"Are you still there?" Mom asks when I hold the phone in silence for too long.

"Yes, I'm here. I'm thinking."

"About what?"

"About your question. About Connor and me."

"You know that your father would want nothing more than to see you two back together. Not only as housemates but seeing you happy together as you used to be."

"That was a long time ago, Mom."

"Your father would do anything to get you guys back together. When you started dating Tyler, he was crestfallen. He thought all hope was lost, but he is hopeful again."

"What do you mean by 'he'd do anything'?" I ask, feeling irritated by the recurring topic that our recent conversations seem to lead to every time. I appreciate Connor's support, but I don't want to use him or make him promises I might not be able to keep.

Before I can ask my mother to elaborate on Dad's plans, the Ring's chiming interrupts my train of thought.

"Someone's at the door. I'll call you back later, okay?" I say, somewhat relieved to have a reason to cut our conversation short.

"I'll stay on the line while you answer the door," Mom says quickly.

I peek at my watch to see the time before I look at the video screen by the door to see who is visiting us at this late hour. A police officer and a woman in a suit stand on my doormat. I recognize the woman. She is a detective at our local police department who interviewed me after I returned from Montana. I assure my mom that I'm safe before I put my phone away.

"I'm sorry for bothering you this late, Mrs. Parker, but may we come in for a minute?" she asks when I greet them at the door. Her face is too somber to bear good news, or maybe her face is always like this, I can't tell.

I lead them both into the sitting room, but they remain standing even after I take my seat.

"To what do I owe this pleasure? Do you have a lead on my case?" I ask, getting back to my feet to be at eye level with my guests.

The officer and the detective look at each other rather obviously, then the woman moves a step closer to me. "I'm afraid we have some terrible news to share with you." Her eyes are dark and serious, and my entire body soaks up her negative aura, sending my heart racing. "About an hour ago, the local police in Sylmar identified a gunshot victim as Connor Parker, your ex-husband."

"I don't understand what you're saying. Sylmar? We don't know anybody in Sylmar."

"I'm so sorry to bring you the bad news, Mrs. Parker. But your ex-husband was shot while sitting in his vehicle. He's undergoing emergency trauma surgery as we speak."

I grab my forehead to remember the details Connor told me on the phone when we spoke last. "No, it can't be him. Connor is driving home from work right now. He had to pull a double shift today. With the increasing demand for more electric lines and cell phone towers to be updated, they get more work than they can handle. He should be home any minute now." I tap at my watch for confirmation, but when I realize that Connor was supposed to be home by now, my heart leaps with panic.

"I understand that you have questions, Mrs. Parker. But we are here to take you to the hospital."

"Look!" I say, putting my hands out to emphasize what I'm saying because these detectives aren't listening to me. "I've recently been through a terrible ordeal. Lightning doesn't strike twice in the same place. You must be mistaken."

"We checked the victim's driver's license for confirmation. He also had his car registration in the glovebox with his name and address on it. We are positive that the man Sylmar PD found in the truck is Connor Parker, but we still need you to identify him and fill in the blanks."

"Mom?" Emily is holding onto Noah's shoulder as they both stand in the entryway by the staircase. "What's going on?"

I look up at them, but my eyes don't seem to perceive the complete picture. It's as if I had scratched-up glasses on, blurring my vision. "I need you to take your brother back to his room. I'll come and see you in a little bit."

She obeys me without pushback, which is never a good sign. I take my phone from my pocket. "Look, let me call him. You must be mistaken. There has to be an explanation. I talked to him a few hours ago, and he was fine. He had no reason to be in Sylmar." I dial Connor's number, and it rings and rings until it goes to voicemail.

"Ma'am, I'm very sorry. I know it's a lot to take in, but please come with us, and I can fill you in on the details in the car. Do you have someone to look after your children?"

I scratch my head and look around, confused. "Yes, my son is in his room. He is seventeen. Let me get him."

Millions of thoughts run through my head as I walk toward the bedroom. I don't tell Jayden why I need to leave, because there is no reason to freak him out when I'm sure this is a mistake that we can clear up as soon as I get to the hospital.

I don my jacket and get in the back of the police cruiser. I'd offered to drive myself, but the detective insisted on giving me a lift. I keep telling myself that this is simply a big mix-up. Even when the trauma center tells us that Connor is still in surgery, I'm convinced that all these people are mistaken because they don't know Connor. They've never met him.

The detective leaves me in the waiting room while she answers a phone call. I grab myself a cup of coffee out of a vending machine. Then I sit down in the corner on a sofa chair. I haven't been out much lately, and the bright lights and conversing voices make me nervous. Two guys in their thirties keep looking at me, and I can't shake the feeling that they've seen the videos of my torture online.

After devouring a Snickers bar and downing my second cup of coffee, I seek out the cops because I don't want to be here a minute longer. Connor must be at home. His phone might have died, and that's why he didn't answer my call.

The elevator door dings, and I spot an unconscious man on a gurney with all sorts of tubes and devices coming off of him. The detective beckons to me, and I join her in a nearby room where the male nurse parks the bed.

"This is not Connor. It's someone else," I say to the detective. "Connor's skin is tan, almost sunburnt. This man looks pale, lifeless."

"Please take a second look, Mrs. Parker."

I shake my head because I don't understand how many times I have to tell this woman that whoever this man on the bed is, he is not my ex-husband. But when I look again, past all the tubes, the tapes, and the bruising on his face, the recognition hits me like an electric shock. "It is Connor. Oh, my God. Oh, my God." I'm not crying. I'm in shock. "I don't understand what's happening. He was supposed to drive straight home from work. What was he doing in Sylmar?"

"Do you need to sit down?" the detective asks, and I feel her fingers folding over my elbow.

"I'm sorry, but I don't understand what is going on. He was fine. He was…" My voice buckles.

"The Sylmar police don't have any leads yet, but what we know is that he was shot twice while sitting in the driver's side of his vehicle. Once in the neck and once in the chest. But I can assure you that we are working closely with the Sylmar PD in their investigation."

"Is he going to be okay?" I aim my question at the surgeon stepping into the room.

"He's in a medically induced coma right now. He lost a lot of blood, but we are hopeful."

I can't breathe. I think I'm going to be sick.

"Does the name Paul Hoffman sound familiar to you?" the detective asks me when the doctor leaves the room.

"Who? No. I've never heard of him. Why?" Staying focused on the conversation is a struggle because I'm staring at the lifeless man underneath the pale sheet, and the image is surreal.

"According to his boss, Mr. Parker was giving a ride home to his coworker, Paul Hoffman, after work. We tried to locate him in Sylmar, but the address he provided on his paperwork is fake. Right now, we have a strong suspicion that Hoffman had something to do with the shooting of Mr. Parker."

The detective is consulting with her cell phone, and then she holds it out to me. "That's him, Paul Hoffman. Have you seen this man before?"

I look at the screen half-heartedly because my mind is taking me to some magical land of oblivion.

I recognize the man on the picture at once and my eyes open wide.

"That's him," I scream, bringing my hand up to my mouth. "Oh, my God, that's him," I repeat as my stomach contracts, sending me rushing to the wastebasket, where I part with the coffee and the Snickers bar I had earlier.

JENNIFER

My ears hear the sweet melody of my cell phone alarm, but my body doesn't respond to its call as it usually does on school mornings. The music plays on and on, louder and louder as if it were losing its patience with me and resorting to yelling at me to get me out of bed.

I reach over Emily, who sleeps on my left in an identical position to mine, to silence my phone on the nightstand.

Noah is in bed with us, too. His body is rolled into a ball, his knees against my lower back. I remember holding my children in my arms all night, but now I'm lying on my side, my face pressed into the pillow, damp from my tears.

My body feels numb and dehydrated. My breathing is shallow and raspy, and simply getting enough air to survive is a task. I can't stop thinking of what I have done to deserve to be struck down with so much tragedy.

"Are we going to school today?" Jayden asks, appearing in the door in a crinkled white tee and boxer shorts. His eyes are small and red, but his pupils are dilated. He has always been a lean kid—an athlete with a fast metabolism—but now he appears as if he lost ten pounds overnight.

"I'll call the school," I whisper, trying not to wake Emily and Noah. I lift my arm to invite my oldest into the bed with the rest of us, but he turns around and leaves the room.

Emily opens her eyes and scootches closer to me. I embrace her so tight I might break her. My arms hold onto her as if she were hanging on the edge of a cliff for dear life and I was her last hope at survival. I kiss her head and inhale her scent deeply. My love for her is as profound and unconditional as it was on the day she was born. Nothing matters now. Not her grades or game scores. Not college applications or internships. Every argument we ever had over chores or money seems irrelevant now. I only care about this moment to hold my children and never let them go—if only Jayden wouldn't push me away.

My heart is too heavy to carry, so I go back to sleep.

* * * * *

The next time my eyes open is when Noah climbs out of my bed to visit the bathroom. All the drapes are drawn in the bedroom, but I feel the heat radiating against the windows. I realize that I forgot to call the school. Oh, well.

There is so much to do today. I need to feed my children, talk to Connor's parents, make an arrangement with the kids' schools, pay bills, go grocery shopping, walk the dog, and visit the hospital. The day's tasks loom overwhelmingly over me, and once Noah returns to the bed and lays his head on my chest, I close my eyes again.

* * * * *

Jayden shakes me awake. "Mom, you need to get up. We should go to the hospital."

I sit up in a panic when I don't feel Emily and Noah beside me.

"They're in the kitchen. I made some ramen," Jayden says as if reading my mind. He holds out a mug for me. The scent of fruit tea rides on the steam.

"Could you sleep last night?" I ask him.

"No, not really."

"I'm so sorry," I say, tears welling up in my eyes.

"Mom, I can't," he says, then sets the mug on the nightstand and leaves me.

I slip my feet onto the floor and drag myself to the bathroom. I can't even look in the mirror because I'm scared of the reflection staring back at me.

Weakness takes hold of me as I shower and dress. Suppressing my urge to cry consumes all my energy, and it takes me some time to make myself presentable and join my kids in the kitchen.

As I enter, Jayden rises from his chair and walks away, stunning the rest of us into silence.

"I'll talk to him," I say.

Emily drops the fork in her bowl. "No, Mom. Let him be."

"I'm sorry, but I can't have him acting like this. I know he blames me for everything, but this behavior must stop."

"He isn't blaming you. He's just angry."

"We all are, but that doesn't give him the right to treat the rest of us, or me, like a stranger. Not now. Not after what we've been through. Not with what we still have to face together."

Jayden doesn't hear me opening his door because the music is blasting in his ears. He lies on his bed on his stomach, screaming into his pillow.

My touch on his shoulder makes him jump. His face is red and wild, like a madman, and I can barely recognize him.

"What are you doing?"

"Leave me alone!" he shouts at me, making me shudder.

"No, I'm not leaving you alone." My throat is so parched that every word I say hurts.

He gets onto his knees and flings his arm at the door. "Get out of my room!"

"What the hell is going on with you?"

"What do you think? I'm angry. I'm fucking angry!" he screams, ripping the AirPods out of his ears and hurtling them against the wall. He is scaring me.

"I need you to calm down."

"I can't calm down. I feel like there's a rope around my neck choking me. I want to fucking die!"

"Don't say things like that. Please." His behavior fills me with worry but also enrages me. I need him to be the man of the house and be a pillar for the younger ones in these difficult times, but I also understand that he is still young and in need of guidance, no matter how mature he considers himself to be.

"Why? What's the point of living? What's the point to anything?" He's battling with his tears.

I reach for him, but he pulls away. "Your whole life is ahead of you. There is so much to live for, Jayden."

He scoffs. "Yeah, like you and Dad? Your lives turned out perfect, right?"

"You need to calm down," I say as collectedly as I can. Violence begets violence. But rage also generates more rage.

"Stop telling me to calm down! I've been calm," he shouts so loud the neighbors might call the cops on us. "I've been keeping all this anger and frustration bottled up inside of me, and I have no way to let it out."

"Then lift some weights or punch a boxing bag at the gym."

"It doesn't help. Nothing does." He pulls his hair and plows his face with his fingers. I don't know what to do. My instinct says to hug him, but my mom used to put me in a cold shower when I raged as a teenager. The cascade of cold water always snapped me out of my mental breakdowns.

"Get in the shower!" I bark at Jayden as I get ahold of his arm and start pulling on him. He resists, but I'm stronger than he thinks I am. "Take a cold shower before your head blows up," I order him firmly, leaving no room for discussion.

"Just let me be!" he begs in a desperate voice, and I know at that moment that he needs me now more than ever.

"Get in the shower to calm down, or I'll call an ambulance to admit you to the hospital before you hurt yourself."

His eyes light up with hatred, but I'm firm in my decision. I pull on his arm until he takes the first step off the bed.

He steps into the shower in his clothes, and I turn on the water. At the first touch of the cold spray, he winces. "Are you happy now? Seeing me like this?" he shouts through quivering lips, spitting water as he talks.

"No, seeing you like this doesn't make me happy. It makes me sad, very sad. Now go back under the water."

"It's freezing."

"Good!"

He closes his eyes and holds his head under the showerhead. His hair is soaked.

I watch his fingers slowly open from his clenched fists. He presses his hands against the tile and looks up into the center of the water cascade. I wait for a few more minutes and then turn off the water.

He looks at me with desperation in his eyes, breaking my heart in two. I lost Tyler. We may lose Connor too. If something happens to Jayden, I'll crack. Then who will take care of Emily and Noah?

Jayden takes the towel from my hands and dries off his hair.

"Feeling better?" I ask, eyeing him carefully.

"Whatever," he growls. Then he grabs another towel off the rack and walks out of the bathroom.

I sit down on the toilet and drop my face into my hands, my heart still racing. I sit for a few minutes to compose myself. We need to get going with this day, yet we move with the speed of a turtle.

Silence and peace return to our home, but my ears are still ringing from Jayden's elevated voice. And when my pulse seems to go back to normal, and I'm about to gather my children to get in the car, the sharp ringing of the home phone rips through the house.

JENNIFER

"Who is this?" I hear Emily talking with suppressed rage in her voice. "Stop calling us, you sick bastard!"

As I round the entryway to the kitchen, I catch my daughter slamming the phone back to its place on the wall.

"We need to tell the police about these phone calls. Maybe they can trace them," I observe.

"The police have fingerprints, DNA, IP addresses, a sketch of our attacker, yet they still can't identify him? But you think a random ten-second phone call will help them find who's been harassing us? I don't think so," Emily says indifferently as she carries her soup bowl to the sink. "We should get a new number and make it private so no one will call."

I sigh. "All right. I'll put it on my to-do list." I always considered technology an advantage in our lives—a practical way to get in touch with people faster and gain knowledge at lightning speed, yet lately, I wish we had chosen a more uncomplicated and straightforward life. I grew up without cell phones and the internet. If I wanted to talk to someone, I had to memorize their number and call them on the home phone or walk over to their house and talk in person. When I got upset with a friend, I didn't have the tools to unleash my feelings on them instantly. I had plenty of time to simmer down before we would meet again. Sparing each other anger-driven theatrics and hateful name-calling must have saved countless relationships. Our world has gotten so small it suffocates us.

"Lay the receiver on the counter for now. Then no one can call us."

Emily looks at me, pondering for a moment, then does as I say.

"Let's get dressed. We'll go to the hospital to visit your father."

* * * * *

I notice Jayden's slight limp as he walks in front of me toward Connor's hospital room. His doctor said that he could expect a full recovery, but it would take three to six months to return to playing sports. I expected him to be devastated by this news, but he accepted the doctor's advice in silent resolve and has shown little interest in getting back onto the field since the bullet was removed from his thigh.

On the other hand, Emily has matured a lot since the yurt incident. She spends less time on her cell phone and more time helping her brother with his homework and school projects. She even started paying more attention to her baking and cooking, resulting in some pretty tasty dessert creations. She also takes Milo on a long walk almost every day on her own, without me nagging her about it.

Noah has become quieter and more withdrawn than usual. Dr. Garrett is hopeful about his mental state. He believes Noah is processing the trauma rather well. He had a couple of issues at school when other students were asking too many questions about what they read in the news. The principal had to set some ground rules for the parents and students regarding our case. I asked Noah if he wanted a fresh start at a new school, and he said there are no schools in this country where people don't know what happened to us. There is no escape from our past. We have become a statistic. A new episode in a true-crime podcast.

I never told my children about the embarrassing videos of me circulating online. Still, I imagine it's a matter of time before they come across someone whose cousin's nephew's neighbor surfs the darknet and has already watched me being violated and feels inclined to share or talk about the video with my children.

Maybe moving to Arizona or Colorado won't be far enough for us.

The nurse is leaving Connor's room as we enter, and she greets us with a warm smile before she diverts her eyes. She must see people on the worst day of their lives: sick, injured, and fighting to stay alive. But this situation is new to us and nearly impossible to process fully.

The beeping of the monitor and the smell of disinfectants drag me back to reality. One glance at my powerful and animated ex-husband lying in bed, now so fragile, brings down an emotional waterfall within me. My children seem to be going through the same emotional journey, and suddenly my decision to allow them to see their father in such a tragic state doesn't seem too smart. But I couldn't keep them away from their father even if I tried.

We spend the next four hours by Connor's side. Noah reads *Star Wars* comic books for his father. He doesn't fully understand the difference between a real coma and the medically induced one that Connor has been put into to help him heal. Noah believes that hearing his voice will make his father come back to us.

Emily talks about the healing power of music, and she plays songs from her playlist on a Bluetooth speaker.

Jayden sits in the corner, his presence barely noticeable, like a ghost; his keen eyes are on his father, unwavering. I stand on the other side of the bed from him, praying silently.

The resident physician enters the room to check on Connor. I pull him to the side to ask for an update.

"As I mentioned yesterday, Mr. Parker was extremely fortunate to have both bullets miss his major organs," the doctor says, standing in front of me with an air of authority and professionalism that puts me at ease. "We removed one bullet from the right posterior cervical region of his neck near C6 and C7. There was no damage to the trachea, esophagus, carotid and vertebral arteries, cervical spine and spinal cord, phrenic nerve, and brachial plexus, but there was significant tissue damage and blood loss. No neurological deficiency was noted during our examination. The torso wound resulted in major internal bleeding. The second bullet lodged underneath the left lung, clipping the top part of the left lobe of the liver. We were able to recover the bullet from the tissue and stop the bleeding. There was also some intracranial hemorrhaging and swelling of his brain from a contusion. But the results are promising, and we will start lowering his medication and bring him back from the coma tonight. If there are any new developments, we'll let you know."

I thank him for the information and for saving Connor's life. He nods with an encouraging smile and leaves the room.

"We need to eat something, and we also need to feed Milo," I say to the children. "Let's go home for a little bit. Then we can be back by the time your father wakes up."

"Can we stay here, and you just bring us some food?" asks Noah, looking at me with his cute begging eyes.

"I can drive home," Jayden offers, but I know that his leg is still too weak and gets stiff sitting in the car.

"It's fine. I'll run home, feed Milo, and bring back some food. Jay, make sure you stay with Noah and Emily," I say as I gather my purse.

He gives a slight nod, indicating that he knows what to do without me telling him.

"All right. I'll be back in an hour. Call me if you need anything."

On my way home, a stone sits heavily in my stomach from leaving my children alone. They are in the hospital with security and cameras watching, but I can't help feeling guilty. I turn off the music in the car and speed as much as the traffic will allow.

Without the porch light on, the house is clothed in darkness. I enter through the garage and close the door behind the car as fast as I can. Before we went to the yurt, I'd leave my car running in the driveway whenever I had to go back to the house to get something I forgot. Now the simple act of walking in the poorly lit garage sends a chill up my spine.

The side door from the garage to the yard is open, and Milo usually runs to greet me before I can get out of my car, but he isn't here now. Sometimes the kids leave the side gate locked by the secret garden and he can't get to the garage, so I don't think much about it.

I turn on the lights one by one as I move through the house. Seeing my surroundings in light should put me at ease, but my nerves tense up in alarm. One should feel the safest in their home, but I no longer like this house. Maybe it's because without having to focus on my work, I spend too much free time here, thinking and observing. I'm not sure why, but I've been getting a sinister vibe from this place lately.

I set my purse and keys on the kitchen counter and pour myself a glass of water.

The sharp ringtone of the home phone slices through the silence, rattling me to my core. I remember Emily setting the receiver on the counter before we left the house, so hearing it ring feels odd.

Injected with a dose of fury, I rush to answer the phone to give a piece of my mind to whoever is playing this sick game with us. "Hello!" I answer the call with aggression.

The line is silent.

"I hope you are enjoying yourself, you sick fuck, for doing this to us!" I scream into the phone.

"Oh, yes, I do," says a male voice I recognize. My fingers lose their grip, and the receiver slams against the wall, where it keeps bouncing up and down on the cord.

As the rhythmical dial tone buzzes in my ears, I move back a few steps, my hand pressing against my racing heart. The light fixtures illuminate the house behind me, but ahead of me is as dark as a cave.

A series of shaking and scratching sounds slice through the air, followed by frantic barking. Milo is attacking the glass patio door, teeth bared, saliva frothing.

Fear paralyzes me, and I don't move to return the phone receiver to its place and stop the unsettling beeping, nor can I bring myself to run to the back door and let Milo inside the house.

I hear a dull sound from the direction of the living room, followed by heavy breathing, but I can't see what's on the other side of the entryway in the dark.

Connor purchased a handgun for me a few weeks back, but it's in my nightstand drawer in my bedroom. I look around for another weapon of self-defense. The set of knives in a hardwood block by the stove are just as far from me as my purse with my cell phone. I've been carrying bear spray since I ventured outside to see the therapist. The liquid can shoot out up to thirty feet, blinding my attacker from a safe distance, which would make it a more effective weapon than a knife.

I'm going to get my purse first.

I round the barstools and yank my bag off the countertop.

"Put it down!" The thundering voice folds around me like chains.

The man of my nightmares steps out of the shadows. "Hello, Jennifer. Did you miss me?" In contrast to his dark clothing, his face is lit, not only with the light from the kitchen but with a sinister grin. He steps into the pool of light, flashing his gun. Before I can react, his scent reaches me, and bile rises in my stomach.

"How did you get in here?" I feel a strange familiarity with this man.

"I've been in here for months. Only you didn't notice." He wrinkles his forehead, trying to look cute.

"What are you talking about?" I breathe the words.

He points at the ceiling. "I've been watching you from up there. I have to tell you that your attic is nicer than my apartment. Life is so unfair." He sounds sincere, which, considering what he just shared with me, is the most insane behavior ever.

My eyes follow the direction he is pointing, but his words make no sense. "Watching me from where?"

He sighs and waves his gun, indicating to me to put my purse down on the table. I do as he says because I already know that he has the guts to shoot.

"You never figured out where you knew me from, did you?"

I shake my head with the slightest movement because I know he is temperamental, and I don't want to do anything that would set him off.

"I was working with your landscaper last winter. You walked by me almost every week, but you looked right through me. I tried to talk to you a few times, telling you that

I was the one chatting with you online, but my boss said if I bothered you again, he'd fire me. And he did. But not before I managed to build a trellis against the house that was strong enough to hold my weight. I've been watching you from your attic for months."

"Months? That's not possible. I would have noticed you."

"You knew I was here. I heard you telling your mother on the phone that you hear voices and footsteps in the house."

"You were up there when I was talking to my mother?"

He smirks. "Obviously. That's how I know about your conversation."

Heat disperses in my body, yet I'm shivering. "Why would you do that?"

"I wanted to meet you in person. But you were never alone in this damn house. There were always people coming and going. Your kids, your boyfriend, your ex-husband, your assistant, or other people who work for you. It's ridiculous how popular you used to be. I was beginning to wonder if I'd ever get a chance to be alone with you." He shakes his head, amused, as if this were only a casual conversation between friends. "I was applauding Tyler when he came up with the idea of a secluded mountain vacation. I knew I'd never get a better chance at spending time with you. So, I followed you to the yurt." He smirks as he scratches his eyebrow while measuring me up with his eyes. "We had our fun there, didn't we? Too bad things didn't turn out as I had planned. When you had that episode, I thought you were going to die. I was very disappointed in myself for stressing you out that much. I never meant to hurt you. I love you, Jennifer. That's why I went to get more supplies and food for your kids. But I shouldn't have trusted you, because you didn't wait for me. You left before I got back. Then I couldn't find you. So here I am again, back in your attic, watching you like a creep."

My chest is tense. My breathing is becoming shallow.

"You are a creep," I say with utter disgust.

"No, I'm not. I only wanted to be in your world. Is that too much to ask? But you wouldn't let me in. What was I supposed to do? You wouldn't even look at me when I worked in your yard. I had to find a way in." He is pacing as he talks, creating a comical illusion of us having a heartfelt discussion.

"Normal people don't invade other people's lives like this. You need to get help. I can help you," I say carefully, but when he halts and fixes his eyes on me, I fear I may have crossed the line.

"What are you saying? That I'm not normal?" He taps his chest with his gun, then points it back at me. "You are not normal. How about we talk about you? What's Connor doing back in your life? Are you really that weak that you can't be without a man to support you for a minute? What would Tyler think?"

"Tyler is dead. You killed him."

He rolls his eyes like a teenager. "I did you a favor."

"Please don't do me any more favors."

"No, no. Stay where you are. I see what you're doing. Stay away from your purse."

"I'm not doing anything. I just need to sit down. It's been a trying few days." I need to come up with a plan, but my mind is paralyzed with fear. I can't go through the same horrors I endured in the yurt. I won't survive it.

"You can sit, but no funny business, understand?"

I pull out a barstool and sit on top of it. "Why are you here? What do you want? Haven't you taken enough from me? Is your plan to completely destroy me?"

His eyes shrink in disbelief. "I don't want to destroy you. I want to be noticed and liked just like you are. Your videos made me famous. I've become a big deal."

I take a deep, ragged breath. I don't know what to say. My mind is blind with the terrifying images of my days in the yurt. The humiliation. The powerlessness. The fear and terror. I don't want to remember the moment when his moist, fat hands were touching me or when his 250 pounds pressed down on my naked body. I prefer not to revisit those memories, but what my mind does is out of my control.

He moves to the refrigerator, takes out a bottle of lemonade, and pours himself a glass. "I love this stuff you make. I could hardly wait for you to go to sleep every night so I could have a glass."

I picture him creeping around the dark house while my children and I are sleeping, and I can't breathe.

"You know, in the past few weeks, I haven't had enough time to spend with you because I was working at the same company your favorite ex-husband works," he says between sips. "First, I had hoped that his presence in the house was temporary, but he kept coming back. I had to get a job at his company to get close to him and learn about his plans. Yesterday, he made it clear to me that he wouldn't let you go this time. I got rid of Tyler, and now I had another man standing in my way. Even on my best days, I could barely get a date, and here you are, men fighting for your attention. See what money does? If I had money, girls would have dropped at my feet too."

"Is that what you want? Money? I can get you money." I sound desperate.

"No," he snaps, offended. "I want everything you have, including you." His eyes are menacing. He isn't joking.

"Look, I'm seeing you now. I hear what you're saying. I can help you."

He sets the glass of lemonade on the counter. "Yes, you can. Come here." He opens his arms, and I know what that means. Like a glass vase, I'm shattered inside, and I suspect that the combination of panic and fear will make me collapse and weep.

"No, please," I beg, though determined not to buckle under his threats.

"Just come here. I've missed you." He makes a sweet face that fills me with more terror. This man is a sociopath, lacking any kind of social normality.

Every sensory nerve is on alert within my body, bringing back painful memories with a warning. I'd rather die than let this disgusting human being touch me again.

Driven by survival instinct, I pretend to slip off the barstool, but I collapse to the floor instead and speed-crawl out of the kitchen and into the living room.

The gun goes off two times. Something has shattered and fallen to the tile in pieces. Milo's barking stifles every other sound in the house. He is desperately trying to get inside the house to help me, but the door has double-paned glass he can't penetrate.

"Shut up, you dumb dog!" Hoffman yells, frustrated.

Both exits from the house are covered by Hoffman, and I have no choice but to run upstairs as fast as my legs can carry me. I burst into my bedroom and lock the door behind me. I kick off my shoes to soften my footsteps.

At my nightstand, I rip open the drawer to get my gun. It's not there. Hoffman must have taken it.

My heart is beating out of control. I ransack the entire place for another possible weapon, but there is nothing here but a curling iron and an electric toothbrush with a pointy metal end.

The door handle rattles, followed by full-fisted banging. "Open the door, Jennifer. I'm done playing games."

I stay silent, pacing around and trying to think of what to do.

I look out the window for a possible escape route, but it sits on a sheer wall with no ledge or windowsill to stand on. If I jump from this height, I'll break a leg at a minimum.

I crouch down and hold my head in desperation. I should have run into Jayden's room. There is a small man cave adjoining his room with a crawl space access to the garage below. I should have thought of that before I trapped myself in my bedroom.

Hoffman kicks at the door and bangs on it harder. "I know you're in there. Open the door. Stop acting so childish."

I'm at the point of tying the bedsheets together and using it as a rope to climb out of the window when a stream of light crosses the ceiling. A car has stopped in our driveway. I watch Jayden get out of a yellow sedan. He must have taken a taxi home. I pull the blinds up with urgency and yank the window open. "Jayden! Run! Get help! Don't come inside. *He's* here!"

He stops and looks up at the house, the taxi disappearing on the street. "What's going on? I've been calling you."

"He is here. Paul Hoffman. The man from the yurt. Run and get help!" I scream, but I already hear Hoffman's footsteps descending on the stairs.

"Jayden, run! He's coming to get you!" I scream again, but he is not listening to me. Instead, he approaches the front door.

I race across the room and pull the bedroom door open. I storm down the stairs, taking two steps at a time. From the lack of traction, I slip and skid down a few steps, banging my back against the sharp corners.

Pushing my pain aside, I collect myself and keep running until I land on the first floor with force. A bullet whizzes by my head and lodges into the wood trim of the arched family room entryway. I drop onto my knees and lean back to get out of Hoffman's firing range. He is leaning against the coffee bar in the kitchen, waiting for Jayden to come through the main door.

I should open the patio door and let Milo in to help us, but I can't do it without exposing myself.

I left another canister of bear spray in the laundry room not so far from the main entry. I have a better chance of getting to that room than trying to go for my purse in the kitchen. If I start running, Hoffman has a choice to make: come after me, or stay put and ready himself for Jayden.

I make a run for it, hunching over and keeping my body low. I swiftly grab hold of the doorframe to pull myself into the laundry room. I hear the click of the door lock, and once again, I'm at a crossroads. The moment I lay eyes on my son, my decision is made. As the door opens, I pounce on Jayden.

Bang! Bang! Bullets are flying around us, and it's a mere miracle we aren't hit when we slam onto the floor.

"Get in the laundry room!" I scream, pulling on my son's sweater.

Jayden's face is flushed with recognition, and he rushes after me into the laundry room while Hoffman is running to catch up to us.

Jayden pushes himself up in a heartbeat and slams his shoulder against the door, but it won't close—Hoffman has wedged his foot in it. Judging by the clicking sounds, he is out of bullets and trying to reload.

"Hold the door," I tell Jayden while I rip open cabinet drawers, looking for the bear spray. My fingers touch everything from keys to pens to flashlights but not the one thing I need. In the third drawer, I see the can with a bear on the label and grab it quickly.

I hear the click of the magazine snapping into place. "Move!" I shout at Jayden.

Once the pressure releases, the door flings open, and Hoffman barges into the room. I squeeze the lever on the bear spray, drenching his face in the deterrent liquid. He screams out as he tries to cover his eyes with his arm, but I don't let go of the trigger.

Soon the air in the small room becomes saturated with the eye-irritating vapor, and I sneeze and cough while my eyes well up with tears.

Holding the neck of his sweater over his nose, Jayden kicks Hoffman square in the chest. He falls backward and to the ground, rolling on his side, the gun dropping from his hand. Jayden lands a second kick—this time across Hoffman's face. I see blood explode from his nose and splatter across the floor.

I stop spraying, and Jayden uses this opportunity to seize the handgun from the floor.

"Don't move!" he shouts at the shrieking man, trying to rub the burning liquid from his eyes.

"Do you have your phone?" I ask my son.

"It's in my pocket."

I take his cell phone and dial 911. The dispatcher asks me to stay on the line until help arrives.

The gun is shaking in Jayden's hands. "I'm gonna kill him," he says through clenched teeth.

I disconnect the call. "Don't do it, Jayden. I know you want to, but please don't pull the trigger. The cops will be here in a minute. We got him. He can't hurt us anymore."

"He needs to die for what he did to you and Dad." Jayden's eyes are tearing up, and he wipes them one by one with the hem of his sweater.

Hoffman moans on the floor. I'm confident he can't clearly see what's going on around him, but he still hears us. "Do it, Jayden! Be a man!"

"Don't listen to him."

"I can do this. I can kill him."

"I know you can, but he isn't worth it. He'll go to jail for the rest of his life. Don't let him make you a murderer. You are better than that."

"No, I'm not. I want this animal to die." Jayden sounds desperate enough to follow through, and a sense of urgency makes me put my hand on the gun.

"Give me the gun. He's done. It's over."

Jayden looks at me. His eyes are red and irritated. I try to hold back a sneeze, but it slips out.

His finger flexes on the trigger. We are all on edge.

"I can't lose you. If you shoot an incapacitated, unarmed man, that's murder. We are in California. The courts will crucify you."

"After what he has done to us?"

"You know how twisted things are here. Don't risk it, please. I'm begging you."

"We can make it look like he attacked us and overpowered us, then we had no choice but to shoot him in self-defense."

"Yeah, do it, Jayden. I know you want to."

"Shut up, you pig! Just shut up!" I scream at Hoffman. My hatred for this individual is so profound it's eating me from the inside like acid.

"What do you say, Mom? I know you want to do it too. Please say yes."

My silence is my answer. Yes, I want this man to die and not have a free roof over his head in prison with three square meals a day, medical care, and access to free education. I'm almost selfish enough to have my son do it for me, but then a little voice of reason whispers inside my head.

"You are better than him. Don't let this pile of shit bring you down to his level. What becomes of you if you kill a man? Please think about it."

Hoffman manages to roll onto his knees, but before he can attack us again, I press the lever on the spray bottle and drench him until he's squealing in pain, begging me to stop.

Red and blue lights flare up through the windows, followed by boots pounding on the pavement. With weapons drawn, four police officers pour into my home, grab Hoffman, and seize the gun from Jayden.

When we both feel safe, Jayden turns to me and wraps me in his arms so tight that it makes me cry. Not from the pain but from the joy of getting my son back. Even his breathing is different. It sounds easier, as if a ton of weight has been lifted off of him.

His arm is still draped over my shoulder as we watch the cops shove Hoffman into the back of the police cruiser, taking him out of our lives forever.

ALEX

Today is my fifth and hopefully final visit to the California State Penitentiary in Lancaster. I haven't seen Paul Hoffman for nearly a month because he was recovering at the infirmary after an attack. The officer wasn't at liberty to tell me on the phone what exactly happened to him. I have been impatiently counting the days until being allowed to revisit Paul.

For a fifth time, I walk these bare corridors to the private meeting room, but it's the first time I find my soul at ease. I think I feel so calm because I have finally succumbed to the idea that Paul Hoffman is a sociopathic murderer who will never change. He deserves no redemption. No amount of mind-altering medication or therapy will make him better. He may have been born defected, or somewhere in his early years he went off the rails, but in the end, it doesn't matter what turned him into a monster. I only consider what he has become and will always be.

My road to recognizing the obvious wasn't long. At my first visit, I held out some hope of forgiveness for Hoffman. His stories of a difficult childhood may have made me feel some empathy for the guy, but once I talked to his brother, Josh, I realized that Paul has been manipulating me. The worst thing is that I can't be sure if he lies on purpose or if he simply can't tell the difference between truth and lies anymore.

Once I reached my conclusion, I committed to my plan. Any hint of doubt in the back of my mind that made me question who I am to judge other people had vaporized. Sociopath killers don't deserve to live while their victims rot in the ground. It's not right. Our justice system has failed us.

I've spent enough time in this prison in the past few months for most correctional officers to recognize me. We've developed a basic routine. They nod at me, and I say hi to them. If a guard feels chatty enough, they even strike up a short conversation with me as they unlock the gate or check my belongings.

I send the burger meal in a paper bag through the scanner like I do every time I arrive.

"That bastard doesn't deserve to eat a meal like this," the correctional officer who checks the bag remarks.

I offer him a drab look as I retrieve my belongings. "No, but that son of a bitch won't talk unless I bribe him."

"Talking to this bastard is really that important to you, huh?"

"If I want to finish my book, yes, I need to talk to him."

"I hope he doesn't get paid for this. I'm gonna lose my shit if I find out that he gets rich on killing innocent people."

"He will receive a percentage of the royalties when the book is published—if the book is published. That was our agreement."

He sucks at his teeth. "That's bullshit."

"Life is rarely fair."

The next guard opens the door and ushers me into the waiting room. He checks over his shoulder, then leans onto me. "Did you hear what happened to Hoffman?"

All too hungry for news, I say, "I heard he had an accident and was at the infirmary for weeks, but nobody would tell me any details."

A smug grin stretches on the guard's round face. "The bastard got jumped in the laundry room by five inmates." He puts his hand up to his mouth. "They did a real number on him. He got torn up so badly that he'll have to shit in a bag for the rest of his life." He chuckles.

"You must be joking," I say, stunned. "They raped him?"

"Oh, yeah." The guard bobs his head. "They also beat his face to a pulp." He makes circular motions with his hand over his face. "Those hardcore guys fucking broke him, man. You won't even recognize the dude. That smug look is gone from his face. He might've thought he was a tough guy outside, terrorizing a family with a gun, but he's a nobody in here."

I don't even have time to respond because Paul steps into the room, his ankles and wrists bound with chains. The guard wasn't joking. This person in front of me is a shadow of his former self—a shell of a man. The bruises are no longer visible on his face, but there is some significant scarring, and the light is gone from his eyes. He was always a hunchback, but now he walks as if every step pains him. His eyes pop wide open at the sight of the food bag.

"Gimme."

"Nah-ah! First, we talk."

"I don't like cold burgers."

"Then you better talk fast."

He gives me a cold stare. "Look at you, Alex. All eager to hear my story. Be careful now, okay? I don't want you to become obsessed with me. Look where I ended up for my obsession." I glimpse his yellow teeth as he smiles, and it takes all my self-control to hide my repulsion. "Did you miss me?" he asks, trying to be clever and in control, but this man across the table from me is not Paul Hoffman—he is a shattered human being.

"As a matter of fact, I did," I tell him because there is some truth in that statement. This past month was a waste of time I didn't foresee. "I heard you were not well."

Paul raises his brows, and his chains rattle. "That's putting it mildly. Some fucking lowlifes cornered me and got the better of me. If it were only two or three of them…" He trails off.

"I hope you gave them hell."

"Yeah, yeah, you know. It wasn't a fair fight, but I did what I could."

I hear a clicking sound followed by a long hiss, like gas escaping from a pipe. A second later, a terrible rotten smell saturates the air.

"Sorry about that. I got this freaking valve on my side now. Those amateurs screwed up my surgery. Idiots! I'm gonna sue the shit out of this place."

"I'm just glad you're okay," I say, and the lies burn on my tongue.

I picture Paul lying on his stomach, face pressed into the dirty floor, big, hairy hands holding him still. I imagine the pain and humiliation he must have felt from being so powerless and struggling at the mercy of others.

Karma is a bitch.

"All right, where did we leave off?" I say, consulting my notebook to keep the smile of satisfaction off my face. "You told me everything that happened in the yurt, how you shot Tyler and wounded Jayden Parker." I flip the page and run my fingers along the lines. "You've told me about your private times with Jennifer Parker in the yurt and about how you tried to save her when you thought she had a heart attack. Then you decided to leave because you didn't want to hurt her. You drove for hours, only to change your mind and drive back to the yurt. But not before you so generously picked up some food for the kids, even milkshakes, right?"

"Yep," Paul says, pointing at my notes. "Make sure you include the part that I picked up milkshakes for the kids. I got them iced teas too. People can get dehydrated spending time at high altitudes, you know. It was a long three days. *I was wiped out.*"

"Yes, I've written it all down here," I say through clenched teeth because hearing Paul talk about what he did to Jennifer Parker has taken everything out of me, but I was glad he didn't touch Emily. "Then we talked about how the Parkers weren't in the yurt when you returned, and you were trying to find them and bring them to safety, right?" I look up at him, my face void of emotion.

318

"Yes, yes. Don't forget that part about how I was going to take Jayden to the hospital. He was bleeding, and I didn't want him to get an infection."

Paul feels very comfortable with me. I've made him believe we are friends. Compared to our first couple of meetings when he made me pry out every bit of information from him, now he talks to me as if we were old college buddies going out for a beer and reminiscing over the good old days. His twisted sense of what's right and wrong still astonishes me.

"But you were the one who shot Jayden and left him chained to the bed for three days. So, it's hard to believe you cared about his leg getting infected."

Paul shakes his head. "You weren't there. You don't know shit. I had to shoot him because he was running away, and I couldn't have him warn Jennifer before I could make it back to that shack. Besides, he seemed fine to me. He was conscious. He wasn't even crying."

"That makes sense." In my hours spent interviewing Paul Hoffman, I've learned that if I pretend that I can rationalize his actions, he will be more inclined to give me details.

"I did what I had to do because it was my time with Jennifer. I knew I'd never get a second chance at us being together," he adds, as if forcing a woman to be with him is the most natural thing in the world.

"So, when you couldn't find Jennifer and her kids in the woods, you drove back to California, where you learned that Connor Parker moved back to the house, right?"

"Yes, I told you about that last time. That motherfucker even took leave so he could spend more time with his family. I really wanted to talk to her, you know, especially after my videos went viral, but she was never alone. That's why I had to get a job at the company where Connor worked, to get a chance to remove him from the chessboard, you know?"

"I remember you telling me all this. You sold the boss a sob story about you being an orphan, left all alone in this cruel world. It's here. I've written it down. Which was all a lie, of course, but it got you a job, right? However, I forgot to ask you—how come you didn't kill Connor Parker? You only wounded him." I gaze at him while suppressing my urge to stab him in the eye with a pencil.

Paul leans back and laughs. "I fucked up, that's why. When I leaned into the car to shoot him, he moved backward, so I accidentally shot him in the neck instead of the head. It was dark, too, man, and I had to hurry. I didn't want someone to see me. That would have been messed up." He shrugs. "I thought the second shot in the chest had finished him, but I guess I was wrong. He also smashed his head into the dashboard, but that didn't kill him either." He shakes his head with a wide smile. "That lucky son of a bitch."

"So, at this time, you were already living in the attic space of the Parkers' home?"

"Yes, I was." He leans forward, wide-eyed, all too proud of himself. "Oh, man, can you believe that I was in the house with them for months, and they didn't even notice?" He snorts with a devilish laugh.

It's nearly impossible for me to comprehend that he still doesn't repent after the suffering he went through a month ago. He has no regret for his actions, the agony *he* caused.

"This is a part that's hard for me to believe. They even had a dog. How come the dog didn't sniff you out either?"

"It wasn't that hard to hide, trust me. That house is freaking huge, and it was always busy. The fan was always running, the music was blaring, people coming and going. Jennifer had her minions working for her all day. Then the kids got home and that idiot Tyler showed up too. And yes, Milo was barking a few times, but they told him to shut up, or they simply put him outside."

"So, the Parkers never went up to the attic? Most families keep stuff in the attic. Not the Parkers?"

"Oh, yeah, they had some Christmas decorations in boxes stacked up there and a few storage bins. Once Jayden climbed up on the ladder to look for some old clothes Jennifer was giving away to a charity. When I saw him coming, I hid in the crawl place above the garage and stayed quiet until he left."

"How come you didn't make contact?"

"Why would I? I had no business with that kid. I was only there for Jennifer, waiting for my perfect moment, which came, of course, when they decided to drive to an isolated mountain. That's why I followed them to Montana. It was easy to overpower Tyler and Jayden and take charge of the family. We had all the time together we wanted."

I don't think the Parkers wanted any time with you, I want to say but bite my tongue instead.

"You do know that you have destroyed that family completely, right?"

Paul tenses up from the sudden change in my tone. "What are you talking about?"

"A lot has changed in the past six years since you have been locked up in this place. The Parkers don't live in Woodland Hills anymore. That little boy, Noah, he was terrified to go to school because the kids wouldn't stop asking him questions and treating him like a victim. He couldn't take it anymore. He wanted to have a normal life, but he couldn't do it here in California. The girl, Emily, she spent years in support groups, not able to move on with her life or have a normal relationship. Jayden did get married. He spent some time overseas and met someone. They have a beautiful little girl, but he is so protective of her that she will never be able to have a normal life because of what you have done to this family."

Paul stares at me suspiciously. "Why are you telling me all this? How do you even know how the Parkers are doing? This is my book, not theirs."

I fold my arms on the table and lean toward to him. "No, this is my book," I say, piercing him with my eyes.

He licks his lips, presses his hands against the edge of the table, and stretches his arms to push himself away from me. "You know, I don't like your attitude today. I feel like you're judging me."

I don't reply, just stare at him. He's looking a little sick. The skin on his face is ashen, and his eyes are yellowish. "How is your health otherwise?" I ask.

"Been better. Why?" He is short with me, snappy, like a kid who had his toy taken away.

"Are you sleeping well?"

"No, not really. I've been having chest pains. I saw a doctor two days ago. He said I need to lose weight because my blood pressure is really high, and my heartbeat is all messed up, or some shit."

I grab the bag of food and pull it closer to me. "Maybe I shouldn't bring you junk food, then."

Paul reaches for the bag with so much force that the guard puts his hand on his baton.

I let go of the bag. "I think it's better if I leave you to rest. I'll check on you tomorrow."

"We still got more time, and I wanted to tell you what I saw through the holes in the ceiling."

"You can tell me next time, big guy," I say and start packing up my stuff.

Paul opens the bag and inhales deeply. "Man, this smells so good."

"Enjoy!" I say as I stand up and walk away from him.

* * * * *

I hit rush hour traffic back to Santa Monica, and it takes me nearly three hours to get home. After I unload my stuff onto my bed, I check my emails out of habit, even though I know she won't write to me. It's dangerous. Emails can be subpoenaed.

I pour myself a glass of whiskey, neat, and take it with me to the bathroom.

I rinse the prison smell off me, dry off, and get dressed.

I pour myself another glass of whiskey and start packing my suitcase. I don't have many belongings, so all my clothes fit in one bag. Tomorrow morning, I'll have time to take my furniture, the few knickknacks and decorations I possess, and my books to the storage unit.

I gather my notes and slip them into my backpack.

I take the photo of my father and me out of the frame and hold it in my hands. This is the last picture we took together. I was only fourteen when a drunk driver killed my father. It still pains me to look at this photo because it reminds me that I'll never be able to hug him, or wrestle with him, or talk to him about anything ever again. I loved my father. We had the best relationship a son could ask for.

The man who hit him also died in the accident. Maybe that's why I've never felt closure or even that I've gotten justice. The drunk bastard who killed my dad had died too fast. I've spent my high school years wishing he had suffered more. A quick death was a punishment that didn't fit the crime.

I close my eyes and take a few controlled breaths to compose myself. Then I open the envelope on my IKEA desk and check the airplane ticket and my passport. Everything is in order. I also shuffle through the thick wad of cash one more time. This money is everything my mother left me.

I eat the leftover pizza from the fridge while sitting on the sofa and watching TV, hoping to fall asleep soon to bring me closer to tomorrow.

* * * * *

My fingers are ice-cold as I hold the phone in my hand. "Today is the day," I keep telling myself as I wait for the operator to connect me to Paul Hoffman's prison block.

"I'd like to make another appointment to see inmate G35450 for an interview," I say as I always do when I call the prison.

"One moment, please," the female voice says.

I hold my fist against my mouth, every muscle in my body flexing. I recall her face and the scent of her skin. It's been so long since I've seen her. I can almost hear the sound of the waves crashing on the shore.

"Hello, Mr. Fox."

"Yes, I'm here."

"There has been a development. Paul Hoffman suffered a cardiac arrest last night, and he won't be able to see any visitors."

All my muscles relax, and I feel as light as a feather. "Is he okay?"

"No. Unfortunately, he didn't survive the heart attack. That's all I'm permitted to disclose."

"Oh, no! There was so much more I wanted to ask him about for my book," I say for good measure.

"I don't know what else to tell you. Sorry for your loss, I guess."

"All right, then."

I double-check to make sure I've hung up the phone, then I leap onto the bed and start jumping up and down, screaming with joy. It worked. I did it.

An overwhelming feeling of accomplishment accompanies me throughout the morning as I transport my stuff to the local storage unit. Finally, I won't have to change my flight again. My work is done.

I take a taxi to the airport, where every minute of waiting by the gate feels like an eternity.

After one stop in Houston, I land at Costa Esmeralda International Airport in Nicaragua. I pick up my rental car and drive a little over an hour to my destination: San Juan del Sur, the city of my dreams.

My heart is in my throat when I turn onto the mile-long driveway flanked by tall palm trees. I roll the window down to hear the birds and the insects creating a beautiful harmony with their songs. The hot, humid air pours into the car, and sweat breaks out on my forehead, but it's a pleasant discomfort I welcome.

Soon my eyes behold the two-story white house with a romantic balcony wrapped around the second floor, and a group of four dogs runs to the car, led by Milo. I can't contain my happiness as I exit the vehicle and step onto the cobblestone.

"Alex!" I hear her voice, which is like sweet heaven to my ears. I open my arms, and she runs to me with her auburn hair flapping in the wind, her sparkling hazel eyes glistening with joy.

She jumps onto me and wraps her legs around my waist. I hold her tight in my arms, the back of her head cupped in my right hand.

"Oh, you've no idea how much I've missed you," I say, kissing the bare skin on her neck.

"I almost called you last week. I was having these weird dreams and wanted to talk to you so badly," she gushes, and the thought of being wanted and missed fills me with love.

"I know it was a difficult five months, but we've made it."

She gets back onto her feet and looks at me with childish eagerness. "Did you do it?"

I bob my head with a reassuring smile.

She starts bouncing in front of me, holding her fingers in fists in front of her face. "Oh, my gosh! I love you so much. I knew it would work. So how much nicotine did you use?"

"The last dose seemed to do the trick, sixty milligrams."

Her shoulders slump, and her eyes go wide. "Are you sure they can't trace it back to us?"

"Even if they test his blood for nicotine, which I doubt they will since he had become a heavy smoker in prison, there is no way they can prove I dosed his burgers. He was a fat pig with very poor health. No one will be suspicious of him having a heart attack. At least I hope they won't waste more tax dollars on some elaborate testing."

The dogs have finished sniffing me, and they lie around us on the cobblestone, panting heavily from the humid air. Milo has more gray hair on his muzzle than the last time I saw him.

I can hear the roar of the ocean in the distance and the swaying of the tall trees as the fronds and leaves rub against each other in the breeze. After years of hating my life, talking to strangers about my feelings in group therapy, and keeping diaries about how fucked up my life was, I finally feel free. I may not have been able to get justice for my father, but I was able to get it for the Parker family.

"Emily?" Mrs. Parker calls as she approaches us from the path that leads to the front garden, carrying a basket of freshly cut birds of paradise flowers.

"Mom, look who's here!"

"Oh, Alex, it's so good to see you. Emily has been dying to have you back."

"I'm sorry I couldn't come earlier. I had a few loose ends to tie up with work before I could move down here with you guys."

Mrs. Parker touches my arm. "All that matters is that you're here now. Let me go and get Connor. He's fishing with Noah on the dock. We're about to eat breakfast. Are you hungry?"

"Like a wolf."

Jennifer Parker is still a beautiful woman. She must be almost fifty now, and she wears her age with grace. Her face glows with a golden-brown shine, and the wrinkles that were carved into her forehead when I first met her have now disappeared.

I remember being devastated to hear that they sold their house in Woodland Hills and bought a new estate on the beach in Nicaragua. Then Emily invited me to move in with her family. My decision to move in with my girlfriend was a turning point for me.

Jayden also lives here with his wife and baby girl.

Feels like a happy ending.

As I carry my luggage into the house, the scent of tropical flowers flows into my nostrils, and my heart is whole.

I remember the first time I saw Emily at the group meeting. My life was going nowhere before I met her. My future was dark. She wasn't as broken as the rest of us in the group. She had her ideas of vengeance that kept her spirits high. It was a powerful idea that I soon adapted for myself. A need for revenge became a strong bond that tied us together.

However, feeding Paul Hoffman nicotine-laced burgers was my idea. It didn't only give me satisfaction; it also bought my ticket into Emily's life forever. My mother died of cancer two years ago. I had nobody left in this world. Now I have a new family I can call my own.

"Alex, it's good to see you, bud," Mr. Parker greets me as he steps into the foyer and relieves himself of the fishing gear.

Noah is nearly a man now, not the little boy Paul Hoffman terrorized. He smiles more than I ever did at his age. Uprooting the entire family and creating a new life for themselves in paradise was a much better way to cope with tragedy than how my mom and I did it. We wallowed in pain and depression, which ultimately made her sick and took her from me.

"Mom! Dad!" Emily calls for everyone's attention. "Alex comes bearing good news."

"Well, let's hear it," Mrs. Parker says excitedly as she pulls a gardening glove off her hand.

"Paul Hoffman is dead. He died in prison from a heart attack," Emily announces with so much pride and joy that she makes me feel like a million bucks.

Everyone in the room lets out a collective sigh. It's like they all simultaneously released a demon that still held them hostage after all these years. The family cuts into each other's words, trying to hear all the details. And in that moment, I know that God will forgive me for what I have done, for destroying one despicable life so that a family might heal. And thrive.

It seems like a good trade-off to me.

ALSO BY A.B. WHELAN

<u>Psychological Thrillers</u>

14 Days to Die

As Sick as Our Secrets

If I Had Two Lives

This Love Kills Me

<u>YA Romantic Fantasy</u>

The Heroes of Arkana Saga

Field of Elysium (Book One)

Valley of Darkness (Book Two)

City of Shame (Book Three)

Return to Innocence (Book Four)

Safe and Sound (Novella)

ABOUT THE AUTHOR

A former IT engineer and marketing director, A.B. Whelan is an Amazon bestselling author of psychological thrillers.

She currently resides in California with her husband and two children. When she isn't writing, editing, marketing, or researching her next book, you can find her walking her two rescue dogs, socializing online, coaching soccer, or doing another DIY project with her husband.

BOOK DISCUSSION QUESTIONS

1. What do you think of online influencers?
2. Is it safe to share our personal moments online with strangers?
3. What do you think why Paul Hoffman was so detached from reality?
4. Have you ever taken an off-the-grid vacation?
5. What would you be capable of doing to protect the ones you love?
6. How far would you go to stay alive?
7. Do you think people can move on from traumatic events?
8. Did the intruder get a fair sentence, in your opinion?
9. What do you think about Jennifer's relationship with Tyler and Connor?
10. What was your favorite part of the book?
11. What was your least favorite?
12. Did you race to the end, or was it more of a slow burn?
13. Which scene has stuck with you the most?
14. What did you think of the writing? Are there any standout sentences?
15. Did you reread any passages? If so, which ones?
16. Would you want to read another book by this author?
17. Did reading the book impact your mood? If yes, how so?
18. What surprised you most about the book?
19. How did your opinion of the book change as you read it?
20. If you could ask the author anything, what would it be?
21. How does the book's title work in relation to the book's contents? If you could give the book a new title, what would it be?

22. Did this book remind you of any other books?
23. How did it impact you? Do you think you'll remember it in a few months or years?
24. Would you ever consider re-reading it? Why or why not?
25. Who do you most want to read this book?
26. Are there lingering questions from the book you're still thinking about?
27. Did the book strike you as original?